P9-CFY-633

FRENZY

ROBERT LETTRICK

Disney • Hyperion Books
New York

Copyright © 2014 by Robert Lettrick

All rights reserved. Published by Disney • Hyperion Books, an imprint of Disney
Book Group. No part of this book may be reproduced or transmitted in any form
or by any means, electronic or mechanical, including photocopying, recording,
or by any information storage and retrieval system, without written permission
from the publisher. For information address Disney • Hyperion Books,
125 West End Avenue, New York, New York 10023-6387.

Printed in the United States of America
First edition
1 3 5 7 9 10 8 6 4 2
G475-5664-5-14015

Library of Congress Cataloging-in-Publication Data
Lettrick, Robert.
Frenzy/Robert Lettrick.—First edition.
pages cm
Summary: Chaos ensues at Camp Harmony when a virus turns the animals
in the surrounding wilderness into raging, foam-spewing predators.
ISBN 978-1-4231-8538-3 (alk. paper)
[1. Camps—Fiction. 2. Survival—Fiction. 3. Virus diseases—Fiction.
4. Horror stories.] I. Title.
PZ7.L56895Fr   2014
[Fic]—dc23   2013025622

Reinforced binding

Visit www.DisneyBooks.com

SUSTAINABLE FORESTRY INITIATIVE   Certified Sourcing
www.sfiprogram.org
SFI-00993

THIS LABEL APPLIES TO TEXT STOCK

For my parents:
My mother, for always encouraging
me to let my imagination run wild, and
my father, through whom I learned
the value of hard work, a writer's
most essential tool after imagination.
—R. L.

We know you'll love Camp Harmony,
We're all so glad you're here!
There are some problems, you will see,
But there's no cause for fear!

It's true the camp bus has no brakes,
And they fired all the nurses!
It doesn't matter anyway,
Since we all go home in hearses.

The craft hut is a sweatshop,
The cook serves grubs for dinner,
The wolves are howling nonstop,
And the pool's filled with thinner.

The outhouse leaks into the lake,
Where many swimmers drown.
It's not their fault, for goodness sake,
The water's thick and brown.

You'll love our dear Camp Harmony,
It's not our intent to scare.
The staff here means no harm, you see,
It's just that they don't care.

And so we write our parents
Because we cannot call.
Before the bears pick up our scents,
Save us, SAVE US ALL!

HEATH LAMBERT'S PARENTS had been bitten and turned into zombies, and now it was up to him to decide the method by which to destroy them—bashing their skulls in with a rock or chopping their heads off with the edge of a shovel. The two other boys stared at him, awaiting his decision.

"I don't know. . . ." he stalled. "Why can't I just lock them in the basement or something? Why do I have to kill them? What if someone finds a cure? It could be in the cards."

"Dude, I'm familiar with the cards. Trust me—it's not going to happen." Dunbar Frye fidgeted, studying Heath's eyes for a clue to which way he was leaning. "Hurry up already. We haven't got all day."

Heath sighed. "It doesn't feel right. I know my parents would do everything they could to keep me alive if the situation were reversed. This was easier when it was just killing zombies I'm not related to."

Dunbar set his playing cards facedown on the picnic table and impatiently thrummed his fingers on their waxy cardboard backs. He had only two left, and Dunbar had an irritating tendency to rush other players when he was on the verge of winning Zombie Buffet, a game he took far too seriously. "First of all," Dunbar lectured, "you can't kill *or* cure a zombie because they're already dead. Second, you'll be doing your parents a favor—putting them out of their misery. Being a zombie isn't a lifestyle choice, like going vegan or moving to Canada. How would *you* like it if you suddenly craved human flesh over pizza? And started walking all funny, like you just messed your shorts? It's not a good look."

"And the flies. Don't forget the flies," added Cricket Simms. Cricket was a short, scrawny kid with both hair and skin so fair that he looked like an albino, except his eyes were green instead of pink. Cricket hailed from Seattle and had never been to a summer camp before. Heath was impressed with how quickly and wholly the city kid had embraced the outdoors. Cricket and Heath had something else in common: Camp Harmony was their escape from some rough times back home.

"Flies! Exactly! Who wants to deal with flies all up in their nostrils and eye sockets?" Dunbar said, as if this were an entirely reasonable conversation. "I bet *you'd* be pretty grateful to the guy who puts a bullet through your head and ends your unquenchable thirst for brains." He stretched out the *A* sound in *brains*, providing Heath with a questionable imitation of the living dead. "So what's it gonna be? Rock or shovel? You have to choose." Dunbar slouched back on the bench, freeing his paunchy belly from the bottom of his extra-large Camp Harmony T-shirt. Confident he'd made his case, he waited for Heath's answer.

Heath didn't have much in common with Dunbar, who wasn't the most athletic boy—with his pear-shaped body and round cantaloupe face he looked like a human fruit basket. And Dunbar liked to sit down a lot, Heath noticed, which wasn't really his thing. Heath was more of an adventurous spirit. Sitting was boring, especially at summer camp, where there were so many other things to do, like swimming, waterskiing, and hiking. There was even a zip line that carried kids over the entire length of the campground, which, sadly, was closed until the staff could figure out how to stop riders from spitting on people below. One of the counselors suggested dog muzzles. Heath didn't think she was joking.

He hadn't known Dunbar very long. In fact, if it weren't for the kid's overly sociable personality, which skirted the line of obnoxious, and because they'd been assigned the same cabin—Grosbeak—they probably wouldn't be friends at all. Despite Dunbar's flaws, Heath liked him and was glad they were friends. Together with Cricket they made a fun trio, even if he *was* forced to play Zombie Buffet now and then.

"Since I *have* to choose," Heath said reluctantly, "I guess I'd cut their heads off with the shovel."

"Wrong!" Dunbar proclaimed, then made a buzzer

sound between his clenched teeth. "Now you've got two decapitated zombies holding you down with their arms while your parents' severed heads bite you in the shins. You lose, Zombie Junior. Now you're part of the herd."

"It's called a mob," Heath corrected him. "Just because they're sick doesn't mean they're cattle. The proper term for a group of zombies is *mob*." Heath knew immediately he'd sounded harsher than he'd meant to, but Dunbar had struck a nerve. People were still people and deserve to be treated with dignity, whether they were dead like zombies or just really sick like—

"Okay, relax!" Dunbar laughed. "Don't give yourself a wedgie over it. Fine, they're a mob. Whatever. Now hit the deck."

Heath sighed and drew two more cards, per the rules. Why he bothered to eat lunch while playing such a gross game was beyond him. He wrapped the uneaten portion of his chicken salad sandwich, which was most of it, into a napkin and slipped it into the pocket of his swim trunks for later. There was something liberating about wearing swim trunks all day, every day. It was one more reason on a long list of reasons why Heath loved summer camp.

"Not hungry, Heath?" Cricket asked.

"Not really."

"You look a little pale. You okay?" asked Dunbar.

"Yeah, sure," Heath replied, but a flash of prickly pain jabbed at the base of his neck, and the reflexive wince gave him away.

Dunbar squinted at him like he was trying to peer through Heath's skin to examine his insides. "You don't look fine."

"It's nothing," Heath lied. "I pulled a muscle waterskiing yesterday." He redirected their focus back to the cards. "I stink at this game. If the human race is ever plagued by a zombie apocalypse, I'll probably end up as people chow in two minutes or less. I'm just not the skull-crushing, head-chopping type. I guess it's lucky for me it'll never happen for real."

Cricket's eyes grew owlishly wide. "Oh, it could definitely happen. In fact, there's a species of carpenter ant in Thailand that—"

Dunbar snorted. "Here we go again."

Cricket's real name was Kevin, but he'd earned his camp nickname for his encyclopedic knowledge of all things bug related. If it skittered on six legs and ruined picnics, Cricket was on a scientific name basis with it. His hobby had earned him a reputation for being the creepy kid at Camp Harmony, but Heath was fond of Cricket and was amused by the way he connected all of life's experiences to the insect world.

"Shut it, Dunbar," Cricket huffed. "Do you want to hear about zombie ants or not?"

"Not really," Dunbar said dryly, "but go ahead."

"Okay, then," Cricket continued. "In the jungles of Thailand there's a species of fungus that invades the bodies of carpenter ants." He scissored two fingers to impersonate ant legs walking across his pickle slice. "The fungus creeps into the ant's brain, overriding control of its central nervous system. Basically, it turns the ant into a tiny zombie." Cricket shuddered in mock horror, then picked up the pickle and took a crunching bite. "The fungus forces the ant to leave its colony, find a nice leaf—the perfect breeding ground for the fungus—and bite down on the underside of it. The ant dies because the fungus won't let it open its jaws again."

Dunbar shivered spastically like he'd just sucked on a lemon. "Ew! Your bug stories get more disgusting every day."

"I don't know," said Heath. "That giant hornet from Japan he told us about yesterday—the one that sprays flesh-melting poison. That was worse, I think."

"And don't forget the bullet ant from Nicaragua that jumps out of trees and shrieks before it bites you." Dunbar tossed a Cheeto at Heath's shoulder. "That one gets my nomination."

"All I'm saying"—Cricket picked the Cheeto off the ground, dusted it off, and popped it into his mouth—"is that maybe someday humans will be plagued by a fungus that turns us into zombies, too, just like it does to those ants."

A caterpillar crawled across the picnic table toward Heath's elbow. He considered flicking it away, but rather than risk upsetting Cricket, he moved his arm off the table instead. While Cricket jabbered on about the zombie ants, Heath turned his attention to the far end of the airy picnic pavilion where two fellow campers were sitting at a table, setting up a chess game. One of the boys, Will Stringer, was Heath's cabinmate, although they'd barely exchanged two words since the camp session started. Will was the same medium height and lean build as Heath, but their coloring was drastically different. Heath was flaxen-haired with a year-round surfer tan while Will's skin was nearly as pale as Cricket's, his hair as black as a crow's feathers. But Will's eyes were his most remarkable feature. They were technically blue, but such a pale shade that on first glance they almost looked white, as if the pigment had been leeched from his irises. They were icy. Maybe that explained why Will's gaze always made him shiver.

Cricket stole a second Cheeto from Dunbar's plate and gnawed on it in a very bug-like fashion before finishing his nauseating story. "Once the ant sinks its jaws into the leaf and dies, the fungus—and this is the best part—sprouts upward, straight out of the ant's head like a tiny stalk of corn, growing spores from the tip of the stalk. Those spores attract even more ants, starting the cycle all over again. It's a beautiful thing, don't you think?"

Dunbar rolled his eyes. "Dude, our ideas of beauty could not be more different. Now Emma Barnes on the other hand . . . *that's* beauty."

"Emily's prettier," Cricket said with authority, as if he were the camp's expert on hotties. He plunked down a card with an image of a zombie getting shot through the side of his head with a nail gun.

"You're stupid," Dunbar snorted. He rolled the dice, chuckled at the outcome, and handed the nail-gun card back to Cricket. "How could Emily be prettier? They're *identical* twins."

"I can tell the difference," Cricket insisted. "Emily's nose leans slightly to the left."

"Not this again," Heath groaned.

"So a crooked beak makes Emily prettier than Emma? Then come closer and I'll make you prettier, too." For the third time that week, Dunbar and Cricket bickered over which of the Em and Em Twins was the more attractive. A debate that Heath thought was pointless, since neither of Camp Harmony's most-prized bachelorettes would ever give him or his socially challenged friends the time of day. Girls just weren't into zombies *or* insects. And they definitely weren't into guys who liked that stuff. This was, in Heath's opinion, a blessing. He thought Cricket's story about the ants was a good analogy for the twins, because, like the zombie fungus, once the Ems got into your head, they pretty much owned you.

Heath quickly lost interest in the argument and gazed out at the beautiful scenery. On the east side of the picnic pavilion he could see the sprawling campground. In the forefront were the main lodge, the mess hall, and the camp director's residence. Past these buildings he could just make out the tail end of the string of cabins (all named for birds found in the state of Washington). On the opposite side of the pavilion, he had a great view of the perpetually green Dray River and the picturesque Cascade Mountains beyond. The Dray was, for the most part, a shallow, peaceful river, snaking its way slowly through the Skagit Valley. Its gurgling waters glistened like an emerald necklace in the summer sun. The river slowed and deepened alongside Camp Harmony, forming a waist-deep pool, and while most campers preferred to swim in Lake Tupso, a mile hike to the east, Heath favored the Dray. He enjoyed the feel of the gentle current tugging at his body. In the river there was more than a feeling of weightlessness. There was a feeling of *lift*.

It reminded him of his favorite book, *The Adventures of Tom Sawyer*, where the author had meant for the river to represent freedom from life's troubles. The very first time Heath submerged in the Dray's soothing waters he felt all his anxieties drain away. Then and there he decided that Mark Twain was a pretty smart guy. The Dray *did* feel like freedom.

"Checkmate!" Heath heard Will declare from the other end of the pavilion. He'd beaten his opponent in less than ten minutes. Impressive. The loser stood up, retrieved something from his pocket, and slapped it angrily into Will's outstretched hand. Then he turned and flounced away. Will inspected his prize. From a distance it looked to Heath like an extra-large pocket watch. Will turned it over in his hand admiringly before setting it down on the table next to the chessboard.

Chess wasn't a game Heath played often, but he liked it way more than Zombie Buffet. "I'll see you guys later," he told his friends, sliding his remaining cards into the bottom of the deck, but they were too busy arguing about the Ems to notice he'd left. He strolled over to Will and sat down on the opposite side of the chessboard. "How about a game?"

"Sure. What have you got?" Will asked. "I don't teach chess for free."

"I didn't realize this would be a lesson."

"You will." Will held up a compass—the thing Heath had assumed was a pocket watch. "If you beat me, you can have this."

Heath shrugged one shoulder. "I don't have anything on me. Except half a chicken salad sandwich."

"Pass."

"I've got a few things back at our cabin. A pair of sunglasses . . . a can of tennis balls . . . a book—"

"What's it about?" Will's interest piqued.

"Genghis Khan," Heath replied. "He was the leader of the Mongols. He and his army tried to breach the Great Wall of China back in—"

"I know who Genghis Khan is. The book is acceptable."

Will set up the board. Once the game started he wasted no time. He began collecting Heath's pieces almost immediately. Eight moves in and Heath was forced to sacrifice his queen to avoid being put into check. He attempted to initiate small talk, but Will ignored him, so he quickly stopped trying. Heath was looking for a way to save his knight when Will finally broke the silence.

"You're losing because you're not thinking ahead."

"Believe me, I'm trying," Heath said with a laugh.

"If you play more often, you won't have to try," Will told him, his tone dripping with arrogance.

Heath considered himself to be a fairly smart kid—he got mostly As in school. But he could tell Will was a genius. The type to make sure that everyone knew it.

"Your brain is a computer," Will told him, "but you're responsible for programming it. It's powerful though. If you play enough chess, you'll train it to see several moves in advance. It'll just happen. You'll find patterns—options."

"How long have you been playing?"

"Every day since I was four years old," Will told him. He moved his bishop diagonally into battle. "The game seeps into all areas of your life. You start to see the world as your opponent and to not only anticipate the attacks it throws against you, but to counter and beat them as well."

"Huh," was all Heath said in reply. He wasn't sure he agreed. He knew firsthand there were some things life throws at you that you just can't prepare for.

The game wasn't totally lopsided. At one point Heath caught Will's bishop napping and for a moment he unbalanced him, almost putting him in check. He had the feeling that it wasn't something that happened to Will often. But in the end, Heath never had a chance.

"Checkmate in three moves," Will declared. "Do you want to keep playing?"

Heath studied the board but couldn't foresee the series of moves that would lead to his defeat. Still, he was fairly sure Will was telling the truth. "No, I believe you. Good game."

"You too," Will said. Then, shutting the door on a rematch, he added, "See ya."

Heath started to get up from the table but was shoved back down roughly by two heavy hands on his shoulders.

He craned his neck around and found an enormous teenager looking down at him. The kid dug his fingers into the cluster of nerves above Heath's collarbone to show he meant business.

An even bigger camper shimmied onto the bench alongside Will and introduced himself. "Hey, boys. We haven't met yet. I'm Thumper. I'm just goin' 'round gettin' to know the newbies." He sounded pleasant, but there was a look in his eyes that promised this wasn't a social visit. Thumper, a hulking brute with long, greasy hair and the shadow of a goatee that framed a smirking mouth, probably weighed as much as Heath and Will combined. Heath thought that with the addition of a whistle around his neck it'd be easy to confuse Thumper for a camp counselor.

"I know who you are, Thumper," Will said, calmly transferring his chess pieces into the wooden case. "Your real name is Renny Thomas. You and your friend stay in the Oriole Cabin."

"That's right. But call me Thumper. Or just Yes, Sir. Here's the deal, Snow White—"

"Snow White." Will grinned. "That's clever."

"Shut your cake hole," Thumper ordered, but Will continued to smile. "This summer you and Goldilocks there"—he nodded at Heath—"are gonna be our runners. That means if one of us tells you to go get something, you get it. If you don't, I'll thump you, and *then* you'll get it. We understand each other?"

"Sure," Will said without a trace of stress in his voice. "We understand what you're saying, right, Heath?"

Heath scowled. Inside he was furious. This was not the way he wanted to spend his summer, playing fetch for Neanderthals, but he couldn't see any way out that didn't end with a visit to the hospital. If it was one-on-one, he could fight back, but that's not how bullies worked. They were cowardly. Cowardly, but effective. "Sure. . . ." he muttered.

Thumper said, "Great," and started to rise from the table.

Will, however, had more to discuss. "Hey, Renny, your dad is Carl Thomas, right?"

Thumper's smirk vanished. "You—you know my father?" He sunk back down to the bench.

"Not personally," Will replied. "But when I first arrived at camp, some of the kids told me all about you, Renny. They said some unflattering things, especially the ones who've been coming to Camp Harmony for a while. They really don't like you *at all*. No surprise there—you've been 'thumping' on them since your ridiculous growth spurt three years ago." Will was still packing his chess pieces as he spoke.

Heath wanted to tell him to shut up before he got them both killed, but Will's superhuman gall had rendered him speechless.

His cabinmate continued. "I wanted to give you the benefit of the doubt, Thumper, so I did a little research on you. It's amazing what you can find out about a person on the Internet. Did you know if you ask the camp director nicely, he'll let you use his office computer? Great guy, that Uncle Bill. Not like your dad, who, from what I read about him online, doesn't seem very nice at all. Your mom dropped you off at camp, didn't she? I saw her in the parking lot helping you with your bags. I guess your dad was . . . detained."

Thumper slammed a fist down onto the picnic table, and a few of the unboxed chess pieces jumped, then clattered over onto their sides. "You're going to keep your mouth shut about my dad, you understand me?" he roared. "You're not going to say a word about him to anyone or I'll—"

"Here's the thing, Renny," Will interrupted, the temperature of his voice dropping abruptly from confident cool to ruthless subzero. The change was startling. "My friend Heath and I expect to enjoy a Thumper-free summer. You're going to pick someone else to be your runners. I don't care who, although I reserve the right to veto your choice. So you and your pal Floaties are going to leave us alone or the entire camp will know exactly what your father did. Do you understand me?"

The kid behind Heath—Floaties, presumably—let go of his shoulders and lunged across the picnic table toward Will, but Thumper intervened and pushed his crony back. Floaties had a murderous look in his eyes, but he didn't try for Will again.

"Yeah, I get you." Thumper's fists were clenched and trembling on the tabletop. His knuckles were grinding against the weathered wood.

"And see those two losers over there?" Will asked, pointing at—

"Cricket and Dunbar," Heath identified his friends. They were still arguing about the Ems, oblivious to his plight.

"Yeah. I see the dweebs." Thumper eyeballed the boys. "What about them?"

"You're going to leave them alone, too."

Thumper snarled like a dog that'd been teased just enough. "Fine." He slapped the black knight off the table. "Just—just stay away from me."

Heath was dumbstruck at how easily Will had taken control from Thumper.

"You got it, Renny," Will said amicably. "Do what I said, and you and Floaties can expect a Will-free summer." He smiled sweetly, but Heath caught a flash of something wicked flickering in Will's pale eyes. It gave him the creeps, and for a moment he was more afraid of his cabinmate than he was of Thumper.

The tamed teenagers left the pavilion quickly. Heath was fairly certain Thumper would leave them alone, but he could tell by the dark glare Floaties shot them as he glanced back from the trail that he might be trouble down the road.

"That was something," Heath said, exhaling in relief.

"*That* . . . was chess."

"Why'd you call Thumper's friend Floaties?"

Will smirked. "Didn't you notice the pale stripes on his biceps? Those are tan lines. The big idiot can't swim, so he wears children's water wings—inflatable floaties—on his arms whenever he goes to the lake. He'll get in the water, but only up to his knees, even with them on. That's how he earned the nickname."

"I've never heard the other campers call him Floaties," Heath said.

"Not to his face. Did you see the size of that gorilla? He'd kill them if they did."

"But *you* called him Floaties," Heath pointed out.

"That's different." Will grinned. His smugness was grating.

"Please tell me you dug up some dirt on him, too?"

"No, but Thumper will keep him in check. Renny won't risk the other campers finding out his little family secret. He's the alpha male of his cabin. Floaties won't cross him."

Heath didn't think that was necessarily true, but he was in a grateful mood, so he dropped the subject. "I know Dunbar and Cricket will appreciate what you did, so thanks for that. I bet they'll—"

"Let them know they owe me a favor." Will stood abruptly, picked the knight off the ground, flicked off a bit of dirt, and placed it in the box. He gathered up the rest of the set, then slipped the compass into his pocket. "I'll collect the book you owe me when I see you back at the cabin."

"Yeah, sure. No problem." Heath watched Will stride away.

After a moment Heath rejoined Dunbar and Cricket who'd come to a mutual consensus on which of the Ems had the cuter smile—Emily. Finally, there was peace in the Land of the Lovesick.

Out of the corner of his eye Heath saw something move. A bushy-tailed Douglas squirrel was inching its way across the ground toward an acorn that had fallen from a nearby tree. Heath took the sandwich out of his pocket, broke off a bit of crust, and tossed it in front of the squirrel. The squirrel considered it for a moment, its eyes shining wetly like little bits of black glass set into its sweet face. It crouched low to the ground, stretched out as far as it could, and grasped at the bread with one tiny paw. In the end it was too afraid to take it. The squirrel scampered empty-handed from the pavilion and raced up a tree, disappearing into the high branches. Heath put the rest of the sandwich in his pocket and forgot about it.

Heath realized there was a small, metal plaque that had been screwed to one of the pavilion's rafters. It was old and corroded to such a condition that it appeared camouflaged against the wood. On the plaque was a quote from Dr. Seuss: *Sometimes you will never know the value of a moment until it becomes a memory.* Maybe that was true for most kids, but Heath was different. The things he'd been through in his short life had taught him that every second was a gift of priceless value. He thought of Will and wondered what kind of life he'd had. The boy was so observably different, and not in any way he'd seen before. What happened in Will's past to turn him into such a cold, calculated thinker? Then again, maybe he didn't want to know. Will's mysterious threat against Thumper had worked, but it made Heath feel germy. Like he'd gotten too close to someone with an infectious disease. He'd keep an eye on Will. The thing that made him uneasy was he knew without a doubt that Will would be looking back.

A faint, mournful howl split the air far off in the distance. It went on and on. At first Heath tensed—it sounded like a wolf—but then he decided it was probably just a dog. Hikers were always bringing their dogs on the trails, and if one became separated from its owner, that'd be a scary thing for a pet. Heath thought if he got lost in hundreds of acres of forest, he'd probably howl, too. There were wolves in the mountains, he knew that. Washington had a small population of twenty to thirty gray wolves, divided into five packs, and the Cascades were home to at least three of those packs. But wolves usually howled at dawn or dusk, rarely during the day.

It wasn't their nature to howl nonstop at the bright noon sun.

Unless there was something horribly wrong.

We are the Cootie Patrol!
Avoiding all girls is our goal!
If they get in your head,
then eggs will they lay.
As soon as they hatch,
you just better pray . . .
We are the Cootie Patrol!
Avoiding all girls is our goal!

AFTER LUNCH, Heath, Dunbar, and Cricket cooled off with a quick dip in the Dray River. They were in the middle of a record hot summer, and the water was warmer than a river stemming from the Canadian mountains had a right to be. But the Dray was shallow and slow, heated at a gradual pace each summer, like an earthworm basking on a sunlit sidewalk. When Heath and his friends were sufficiently cooled off, they started on the short hike to the horse stables, letting the sun dry them on the way. It was Tuesday, so, according to the schedule, activities at Camp Harmony were limited to riding lessons, archery, baseball, or making bleach-bottle pigs and dream catchers in the craft hut. Heath would have preferred archery, but he was outvoted two-to-one for a simple reason: where there were horses, there were Ems. The twins, Emma and Emily Barnes, were budding equestrians who spent most of their time riding or grooming the camp's six horses. Dunbar and Cricket were practically skipping as the trio followed the dirt path that wound through the camp's center and ended at the gate to the riding arena where they were sure to find the twins.

Heath took a deep breath of clean, pine-scented air and admired the majestic fir trees that rose mast-like toward the cerulean blue sky. It was a beautiful day, not a cloud to be spied, not even at the summit of the Cascades where they tended to flock like woolly sheep against the peaks. They'd had a run of great weather since the session started—mornings cooled by the mist coming off the mountains; hot, sunny days, perfect for swimming; and chilly campfire evenings where on more nights than not, a fleeting rain shower would snuff the glowing embers long after the last overcooked marshmallow had slid off its stick and sizzled in the flames.

The boys passed by the main lodge. The residents of the Blue Jay Cabin were practicing a play on the building's wraparound porch. Judging from the cardboard whale and the boy with the fake beard and the umbrella harpoon, it was *Moby-Dick*. The campers were required to meet at the lodge every morning for the daily affirmation and announcements. It was also where they gathered for sing-alongs, talent shows, and cover during rainstorms. It was the heart of the camp and the only building that could fit all one hundred and thirty campers and twelve staff members comfortably inside. The other buildings on the grounds, including the resident cabins, spiraled in the clearing like a giant question mark, with the lodge in the center of the hook and the tail of the question mark pointing toward the Dray River. Farther out, fanning around the buildings, were the ball field, the teepees, an obstacle course, the health center, and the bonfire pit. The camp's trails were well-maintained, and the layout was easy to navigate, designed to keep new campers from straying into the surrounding woods, where it was ridiculously easy to get lost. If there were two points the counselors liked to drill into the campers' heads, it was *stay on the trails* and *don't go into the woods.*

"I don't see what the big deal is," Cricket said, staring off at the green blanket of trees that covered the valley and mountain range except where the barren peaks poked through like great gray spearheads. "The woods don't scare me a bit."

"They should," Dunbar said, his tone foreboding. "This is Bigfoot country."

"Don't listen to Dunbar. Bigfoot is just a myth." Heath was worried Cricket might just be citified enough to believe Dunbar's nonsense. Unfortunately, all he managed to do was set Dunbar loose on the topic.

"A myth, huh? I bet neither of you has a clue that Washington is famous for having the highest rate of reported

Bigfoot sightings in the country. Five hundred and thirty-four to date. That's a hundred more than the runner-up, California. And that doesn't include the people who've seen Bigfoot but are afraid they'll look stupid if they go public."

"Now why would they be afraid of looking stupid, Dunbar?" Heath said mockingly. "Could it be because the whole idea is crazy? A ten foot tall half-man, half-ape strolling through the forest, carelessly allowing himself to be seen by hundreds of people. Yet isn't it strange that not one of those so-called eyewitnesses can produce a single shred of concrete evidence? No video? No photos? I could see that being the case maybe ten years ago, but not now when everybody's got a camera on their phone."

"I don't get it," said Cricket, who seemed officially weirded out. "If there's no such thing as Bigfoot, then what exactly *are* all those people seeing? Has to be *something*, right?"

"I don't know," said Heath. "Some goofball in a Bigfoot costume, maybe? But it's more likely they're crossing paths with bears. Bears are big and shaggy—they fit the profile."

"Watch the news sometime, Heath," Dunbar shot back. "Remember that hiker who got mauled last year? He was killed not too far north of here."

"I do watch the news," Heath rebutted. "The reporter said it was a grizzly bear."

Cricket interrupted the discussion to point out a flash of red and yellow up in the boughs of a hemlock tree. It was a western tanager. A male, judging from the brilliance of his plumage. Heath thought it was ironic that something so luminous and delicate could flit so fearlessly through the big, bad forest. Then he remembered that even the songbirds had to be constantly vigilant or risk being shredded apart by an owl or hawk. Just because they made forest survival look easy didn't mean that it was.

"Grizzly, huh?" Dunbar scoffed as if the idea were preposterous. "So if it was a bear, then how come they found the hiker's guts spread out around the forest, his intestines decorating high branches like Christmas garland? Does that sound like something a bear would do?"

Heath found the conversation more tiring than the walk. "Maybe the sparkly vampires did it. I've read Washington is crawling with them. Then they framed Bigfoot and let him take the bad press."

"Sure, make jokes, Heath. But think about this. Those woods run all the way to Canada," Dunbar said. "That's a lot of wilderness for a creature to hide in, even a big, murderous hominoid like Sasquatch. If you want to traipse around in there, go ahead. Be my guest."

Their conversation reminded Heath of the drama that had occurred back at the pavilion. "Speaking of aggressive man-monkeys . . ."

Along the way, Heath let his friends in on what happened between Will and Thumper. "Good for him," Cricket said. "It's about time someone put that gorilla back into his cage." Heath didn't go into too much detail about the disturbing way in which Will dominated Thumper or that he suspected Floaties would be trouble down the line. There was no point in ruining such a perfect day.

The trio cut through the tight alley between the boys' bathhouses, brushing aside a spiderweb in their way (only after Cricket checked to make sure its architect had safely abandoned the web beforehand). They took a short march through a copse of Douglas fir trees and funneled out onto the archery range. Two dozen kids were trying their best to hit round targets mounted on bales of hay at the far end of the clearing. Another dozen campers had gathered around a tall, athletically built black boy named Sylvester, whose target was so loaded with feather fletchings that it looked like the rump of a turkey.

Sylvester was one of those kids that had it all. His dad was the CEO of a major company, and Sylvester was being groomed to follow in his footsteps. Besides being rich and good looking, he was also an incredible archer with a slot in the Junior Olympics next year. He was putting on quite a performance; every bull's-eye brought on a shower of praise and back pats.

"He's a show-off," Dunbar grumbled, clearly envious of Sylvester's popularity.

"I don't know," Heath disagreed. "Looks to me like he's just really good. You can't hold that against him."

Dunbar pouted. "I guess."

"I like him. He's a cool guy," said Cricket, which Heath understood to mean that Sylvester was one of the few older boys who didn't pick on him for his diminutive size or his obsession with bugs.

If any of the targets had been free, Heath would have opted to join Sylvester, but since they were all occupied, he continued on with his friends to the stables, where they found Mr. Soucandi, the camp's horse trainer, in an especially irritable mood.

"It's about time you three arrived!" the old man growled over the white corral fence, yanking off his rawhide riding gloves and stuffing them into his vest. "I called you over an hour ago!"

Heath, Cricket, and Dunbar exchanged looks of confusion.

Mr. Soucandi was the stable manager's real name, but the kids called him Soup Can behind his back because he had a noticeable dent in the side of his head like those banged-up cans of soup you find in the bargain bin of any supermarket. Rumor was that Mr. Soucandi had been kicked in the head three times, twice by horses and once by a mule during a pack trip into the Grand Canyon. The mule had been the one to put the dent in Mr. Soucandi's noggin, but the other two kicks had no doubt softened the spot and contributed to the man's occasional delusions.

"Don't just stand there gawking at me," Soup Can said. "Tell me what you plan to do about *those!*" He pointed at a cluster of chickens that had settled into roost-mode on top of a stack of tractor tires leaning against the side of the stable.

"Um," said Heath. "What do you think those *are,* exactly?"

"What do I think—?" Mr. Soucandi threw his hands up in the air. "Are you pulling my leg or are you just stupid? Now quit fumfering and get those dang *dragons* out of my corral! They're spooking the horses!"

"Ohhhhh, the dragons." Heath played along. He tried to determine which of the chickens' features might seem dragonesque to Mr. Soucandi's dented brain. Strangely, Soup Can's delusions were always temporary, as if his mind had a reset button that would go off every few minutes. The old man was the previous camp owner's father. He'd been tending the stables since the seventies and loved his job and the horses. His feelings for the campers, however, were debatable. He wasn't that great with kids. When Uncle Bill bought the camp a decade ago, letting the old man stay on had been part of the deal. He was harmless enough, even if he was a bit of a loon.

Dunbar leaned in and whispered to Heath, "Since it wasn't us, who do you think Soup Can *did* call about the dragon-chickens?"

Heath shook his head. "I dunno. The humane society? Pest control? Gandalf the Gray?"

The boys forgot all about Mr. Soucandi's problem when the Ems galloped up to the fence on their horses, Sweet Pea and Rusty. Heath had to admit the twins looked pretty great in their tan riding breeches and knee-high leather boots. He especially liked their acorn-shaped helmets with the chin strap and the cute bow on the front. He wondered how they managed to tuck all of their long brown hair up under them without getting a headache.

"Hey, losers," Emma said, although her friendly smile put everyone at ease. "Back again, Cricket and Dunbar? You two are here almost as often as Em and me. Think you might actually get on a horse this time?"

Dunbar's face turned an interesting strawberry color. Cricket, on the other hand, smiled widely like one of those toy cymbal-banging monkeys Heath had seen in toy stores and horror movies. "Horses are cool," Cricket said dreamily.

Emma looked over at her twin, and they both giggled.

Dunbar elbowed Cricket in the ribs to snap him out of his moony trance.

"Hey, Heath!" Emily said, brushing Sweet Pea's mane with her fingers. Her smile was just as warm and disarming as her sister's.

"Hey, Emily." Heath tried to sound casual, but he was annoyed at how pleased he was that she knew his name.

"Looks like those chickens chased the dragons off," Mr. Soucandi said, scanning the arena to be sure. His brain had come back online. He also seemed to recognize them as campers now that the "dragons" had vanished. "You three ready to ride?"

"Who, us? N-n-now?" Dunbar stuttered.

"Don't be a lily liver, son, of course now. We'll start with the little one." Mr. Soucandi waved Cricket over. "You ever ride before, Short Pants?"

"Not once," Cricket admitted. "The only horses we have in the city are the ones the cops ride in the parks."

"All righty, we'll start you off easy. You can ride with Emma here."

Cricket shot Heath and Dunbar a cheesy grin as Mr. Soucandi hoisted all seventy-five pounds of the boy into the saddle behind Emma. Cricket wrapped his arms tightly around her waist. He pressed himself against her back like a turtle shell and flashed one more impossibly obnoxious smile, which quickly vanished when Emma elbowed him in the gut. "Not so tight, Squid Boy," she warned as they took off into an easy trot around the arena.

Turning to Dunbar, Mr. Soucandi weighed him with his eyes. "Big one, aren't ya? How about it, Lead Bottom? You a rider?"

"I've ridden a few times," Dunbar admitted, then cringed when he realized that telling the truth meant he'd probably just ruined his chances of sharing a saddle with Emily. "Wait, what I mean is—"

"Good! You can ride ole Onyx over there." Mr. Soucandi pointed at the huge black stallion drinking at the water trough near the fence. He fished inside his pocket, pulled out a set of car keys, then handed them to Dunbar. "Here, you'll need these to start 'er up." Clearly his mind had hit the reset button again.

"Um . . . okay," Dunbar said, but as soon as Mr. Soucandi wasn't looking, he stealthily slipped the keys back into the old man's pocket.

"Now let's see about you, Sunny Jim. . . ." The trainer looked around for a free horse for Heath, but they were all occupied. He shrugged. "Looks like you're out of luck, son."

"You can ride with me," Emily offered. She held her hand out to him.

Heath felt the zombie-ant fungus creeping into his brain. The last thing he wanted this summer was a girlfriend. In his opinion, there was no greater time-waster than romance. Heath felt sorry for the camp's couples. They spent all of their time bickering over the stupidest things, writing mushy cabin-mail, breaking up and making up, and worst of all, staring dreamily into each others' sweaty faces as the summer slipped unnoticeably by them. And in the end, they'd just get their hearts stomped on anyway. That's why it's called a crush.

"No, thanks anyway." He pushed aside the urge to climb into the saddle behind Emily. "I have some things I need to do back at my cabin."

Emily continued to smile, but Heath thought he saw a glint of something in her eye that might be . . . what? Disappointment? He decided he was playing tricks on himself, treading on dangerous ground.

"It's probably for the best," she told him. "Sweet Pea is a little fidgety today. She's not her usual self."

Heath pondered this. "Soup Can . . . uh . . . I mean, Mr. Soucandi said those dragons . . . er . . . chickens by the stable were spooking the horses."

"Those stupid hens? Sweet Pea isn't afraid of them. I'm not really sure what's wrong. It's not just her, though—the other horses are acting up, too. It gets worse the closer we get to the north end of the arena."

Closer to the mountains. Heath thought about it, and then he remembered the howling earlier. He wondered if maybe it had come from a wolf after all. Had Sweet Pea heard the howling, too? Heath observed the other horses and noticed they were glancing up at the mountains every few seconds. They fought against their reins like cars with bad alignment whenever they neared the north end of the arena. They definitely sensed something out there, Heath was sure of it.

He wasn't too worried though. Wolves preferred to stay away from human settlements. Once upon a time, there were over two million wolves in the world. Then humans killed off ninety percent of them, because that's what humans do. We're bad news, Heath thought. The worst kind.

"She'll be okay," Emily said, lovingly stroking the side of Sweet Pea's neck. "I just have to keep her attention on me and let her self-soothe. She'll calm herself eventually. She's a great horse. You sure you don't want to ride with me?"

"No, I really do have some things I need to do," he fibbed again. Telling her the truth—that she made his head swim—was unthinkable. His summer policy was firm: no shoes, no shirt, no girlfriend.

"Suit yourself. See you later, then." She turned her horse and cantered after Emma.

Heath was proud of himself; he'd stuck to his guns. He stayed at the fence just long enough to watch Dunbar struggle comically up into Onyx's saddle. Onyx didn't look any happier about their pairing than Dunbar did.

As Heath was walking away from the arena, he heard Emma shout, "Watch where you put your hands, Cricket!" and Mr. Soucandi scolded after them, "No fighting on the bus!"

Heath found the Grosbeak Cabin empty, except for Will, who was lying on his cot, writing in a journal. He remembered he owed Will the book about Genghis Khan. He reached under his bed and dragged his duffel bag out across the plank floor, then hefted it up onto his mattress.

"Hey, man," Heath said, rifling through the bag. "Chess was fun. Anytime you need someone to play against—" A translucent orange vial of pills fell from the duffel bag, hit the floor, and rolled across the aisle to Will. Heath chased after it. It came to a stop beneath Will's toes.

"Give me that," Heath demanded, holding his hand out.

Will picked it up and read the label on the side of the vial. "OxyContin?"

Heath eyed him warily. "Yeah . . . it's—"

"I know what it is," Will said quickly. "It's to relieve serious pain."

There was a long pause as the boys studied each others' faces. The air inside the cabin was stiflingly hot. The three ceiling fans rotating slowly above them did little more then churn the humid air inside the cabin like a spoon in a pot of soup. Heath could feel beads of sweat forming on his brow. Will, on the other hand, may have been carved from a block of ice.

"Look . . ." Heath started. "Don't say anything to Uncle Bill, okay?"

"Why not?" Will asked.

"Seriously?" Anger flooded Heath's face. "Fine! I'll see what else I have in my bag besides the book. Did you want my sunglasses or not?"

Will frowned. "I'm not trying to blackmail you, stupid.

I just want to know why Uncle Bill isn't aware that you have OxyContin. I thought all medications were supposed to be administered by the camp nurse." This was true. With seemingly half the kids on the planet diagnosed with ADHD, gathering up behavior modifying medications like Ritalin was Nurse Winston's first duty at the start of each year. "Why didn't your parents give—?"

"Because I asked them not to," Heath said firmly. The idea of talking about his situation with Will was unbearable. The kid was not someone Heath felt he could trust to safeguard a secret, especially one so personal. He imagined Will would probably use it to control him, like he did to Thumper. "I don't want anyone to know. Okay? Not even the camp staff. I don't want anyone to treat me differently. That's all."

Will held the vial up to the sunlight streaming through the window and examined the pile of little pills inside. Heath wanted to snatch it back. He decided he was willing to fight Will for the medication if it came to that. He clenched his teeth and fists, ready to pounce, but he waited to see what his cabinmate would do.

Surprisingly Will just handed the vial back to Heath, returned to his cot, and resumed writing. Probably adding Heath's OxyContin to a long list of ways to manipulate his fellow campers.

Heath, still furious, carefully rolled the vial up in a sock, stuffed it inside another sock, and then stuffed the whole ball into his duffel bag.

"That sucks," he heard Will mumble in a tone that sounded almost compassionate.

Heath took a deep breath. "Yeah . . . it does."

Then, as if the discussion had never happened, Will said, "Don't forget the book you owe me."

It's time to get nuts! (snap fingers twice)
It's time to get nuts! (snap fingers twice)
Like a squirrel in the fall,
Let's gather them all.
Let's go, 'cause it's time to get nuts!
  (snap fingers twice)

A HALF HOUR LATER, despite the oppressive heat, or maybe because of it, Heath had drifted off to sleep. He'd been taking short naps to recharge his batteries, usually in the early afternoons. After Will had collected the book about Genghis Khan, he'd left the cabin without saying a word, which was fine by Heath. There was something unsettling about the kid. Whenever Heath interacted with Will, he felt like he was being analyzed. It was the same uneasy feeling he got at airports when the guards scanned him with their security wands. Heath was relieved to have the cabin to himself.

He dreamed he was floating on his back in the Dray. A welcomed tranquility seeped into his body as the river quietly stole him away from camp. The green waters widened out until the banks became floss-thin lines and vanished. There was nothing else, just Heath and the river. And blessed peace. He was a leaf, content to let the Dray carry him toward the sea on the back of its meandering current.

He stared up at the sky and was instantly startled by how cold it looked. It was near white, with just a hint of pale blue that seemed so familiar. It took him a moment to match it up with the hue of Will's eyes. Then, absurdly, the sky blinked at him. In the next moment Heath felt a set of hands clamp tightly around his throat, throttling him, plunging him downward beneath the surface. He thrashed hard, desperate to free himself, but there was nothing to grab hold of. A head formed above him, disembodied and out of Heath's reach. Through the watery window between them he could make out Will's visage grinning widely, his cold eyes sparking with mad glee. He tried to fight back, but Will was impossibly strong. Heath struggled to hold what little breath he'd managed to inhale before submerging, but it was no use. He gasped for oxygen, but instead chilled water rushed into his mouth, pouring copiously into his starving lungs. *"You shouldn't have followed me here,"* his cabinmate hissed from above.

Heath awoke gasping for air but found that he was still unable to draw a breath. Because Cricket was sitting on his chest.

Heath shoved him off and sat upright. "Seriously, what's wrong with you?"

"I was trying to wake you up!" Cricket explained. "How about some gratitude?"

"Gratitude?" Heath was confused.

"You were mumbling in your sleep, dude," explained Dunbar. "Mumbling about drowning. Must have been a doozy of a nightmare. You okay?"

"Yeah. . . ." Heath tried to shake off a lingering feeling of dread. "I'm fine." He noticed that his friends were soaked to the bone, holding plastic water guns in their hands. "What's going on?"

"Get up!" Cricket held out a spare gun to Heath. "We need you. Uncle Bill and the counselors started the annual water fight. Our cabin is getting its tail kicked. C'mon, get up and let's go, soldier."

Heath glanced at his watch. It was only one thirty. He'd hoped to sleep at least another hour, but was grateful to have been rescued from Dream Will's clutches. "Why aren't you guys at the stables? I can't believe you left Em and Em for a stupid water fight. Especially you, Cricket. You looked pretty comfy in the saddle behind Emma."

Cricket pouted. "She kicked me off her horse right after you left. She said I was too *clingy*. I told her I was just afraid of falling off."

"Sure, you were," Dunbar snorted. "You're just lucky horses don't have eject buttons. Anyway, that's not why we left. Soup Can canceled the rest of riding today."

"That's weird," Heath said. "How come?"

"The horses were acting . . . jumpy. Soup Can decided to bring them all back into the stable."

"Emily's horse, Sweet Pea, was the worst," Cricket added. "Mr. Soucandi had to blindfold her to calm her down, not that it helped much. When we left, he was still trying to get her into the stable."

"Sweet Pea wasn't going easily," Dunbar said. "The Ems stayed to help."

"It's ancient history." Cricket smacked Heath on the sole of his foot. "Get up, lazy bum! We're missing all of the fun!"

Heath slid his legs over the side of his cot and shimmied his feet into a pair of rubber aqua-shoes, the kind with a pocket for each toe. He wore them everywhere. They were the first thing that had entered his mind when Will asked for his wager, and the last thing he'd be willing to part with besides the orange vial of pain pills.

"Here, you have to wear this," Dunbar said, draping a necklace over Heath's head. It was made of light green sugar candies strung together on a thread. Dunbar and Cricket were wearing necklaces, too, but their candies were smaller, misshapen, and some were missing, like a mouthful of hobo teeth.

"What's this for?" Heath asked.

"Every cabin gets different colored candy," Dunbar explained. "Water melts sugar. When there's no more candy on your string you're officially dead." He did air-quotes around the word *dead*.

"The last kid standing wins the fight for their cabin," said Cricket.

"Cool. What does the winning cabin get?" Heath asked.

"Respect," Dunbar answered, heading for the door. "Let's do this."

The three boys stepped out of the cabin and into a war zone. Campers were whooping, hollering, and laughing as they chased one another with water guns, buckets, and water balloons. The ground was littered with colorful bits of exploded rubber. It seemed that everyone had abandoned the scheduled activities, and now the campground was overrun with lunatics.

"Cover me!" Cricket assumed the role of field commander. He stroked the pump of his water rifle three times. "I'm going after Thumper!" He tore across the dirt ground in the direction of the Oriole Cabin, roaring a war cry as he went.

Heath was reminded of the old expression, *It's not the size of the dog in the fight, but the size of the fight in the dog.* He and Dunbar looked at each other, rolled their eyes, and chased after him. It had suddenly turned into a rescue mission to bring Cricket back alive.

"That was fun on a bun!" Cricket proclaimed as the trio of friends marched back toward the boys' bathhouses, which was the nearest place to reload. "I swear, Dunbar, for a split second, you looked exactly like the house from the movie *Up!*"

"Shut up, Cricket," Dunbar said, flicking a shred of green rubber at his head. Although they never found Thumper, they did manage to get themselves ambushed by a pack of ten-year-old girls from the Chickadee Cabin. They hit Dunbar with so many water balloons that they actually knocked him flat on his back, and of course Cricket had been laughing hysterically ever since. Dunbar was in a pretty sour mood for someone coated in melted candy. He ripped the empty string off his neck. "You just can't trust girls," he muttered as he headed back to their cabin to dry off, leaving Cricket and Heath as the sole survivors of Grosbeak. Heath kept an eye out for Will, but he doubted water fights were his thing.

"Heath, look over there." Cricket pointed. "In the woods. Is that . . . Bigfoot?"

Heath saw it, too, a flash of brown scruffy hair just past the tree line. "Don't get your underwear twisted in a knot," he whispered. "I think it's just a camper hiding in the forest. Trying to wait out the battle till the end."

"Lame. Whoever it is"—Cricket cocked the pump of his squirt gun for dramatic effect—"let's go melt his candy."

They split up. The plan was simple. Cricket would charge from the front while Heath would circle around and flank their target from the far right, in the hope of catching him off guard.

Cricket stayed hidden behind the trunk of a large pine tree, awaiting Heath's signal (they forgot to discuss what the signal should be, but Cricket was sure he'd recognize it when it was given). Heath crouched low, moving quickly, careful to stay hidden behind shrubs and tree trunks as he closed in on his quarry. His route skirted the edge of the forest, but he didn't stray too far from the dirt path. He was hoping to find an opening in the tree line that would allow him to get behind the boy, close enough to ambush without giving himself away beforehand.

Heath froze abruptly. Again he thought about the howling he'd heard that morning. He wondered if he wasn't foolishly serving himself up as dinner for a wolf. But then, through the brush, he caught a glimpse of blue plastic. It was a water wing wrapped snuggly around a massive, muscular arm. Floaties's arm. Heath wasn't stalking an animal or Bigfoot. But something just as dangerous.

Attacking Floaties would be a pretty dumb idea. Heath remembered how agitated the kid had been at the picnic pavilion. And Floaties was *huge*, almost as big as Thumper. Not quite as tall, but definitely broader and more muscular. He wisely decided it would be best to call off Operation Floaties's Revenge.

Heath heard a rattling sound, like reeds rustling against one another, followed by a low grunting noise. The grunts grew louder, interspersed with whistles and whines. If Cricket was trying to signal him, he was going about it in an odd way.

Suddenly, up ahead, Floaties roared. "Get away from me! I'll kill you! I'll kill you!"

Heath assumed he was yelling at Cricket. He bolted out of the forest, sprinting down the dirt path as fast as he could toward the tree where he'd left his friend, expecting to have a fight on his hands. But Cricket was still there, intently watching the forest. When he saw Heath, he pointed at the rustling bushes. "There's an animal in there!"

"An anim—?"

Floaties came crashing out of the woods in a wild panic. Something resembling a long stalk of hay was poking out of his right water wing, deflating it rapidly. His eyes were wide and buggy, and he had leaves and bits of twig in his hair. He came rushing at them like an escapee from a mental hospital. Cricket was right. A creature rocketed out of the forest after him.

"What *is* that?" Heath instinctively jogged backward as Floaties and the strange animal came bounding toward him. At first Heath thought it was a dog or maybe a small bear; it was black, had a high arching back and stubby legs, and it swayed from side to side as it ran. When it was clear of the obscuring grass in front of the tree line, he realized what it was. "That's a porcupine!"

Heath had seen one before at the Woodland Park Zoo in Seattle, but that one was smaller, and its fur and quills were light brown. This one was almost black, except around its muzzle, which was bearded and pure white. When they used their quills it was usually to defend themselves from predators. Normally porcupines were timid, preferring to escape encounters with humans by climbing trees. The one chasing Floaties, on the other hand, had murder in its eyes.

"Out of my way!" Floaties reached the boys and plowed through them, knocking Cricket onto his back. The porcupine, sensing an easier target, changed direction, charging toward Cricket.

The source of the rattling was apparent. The long quills on the porcupine's back were rustling against one another as the creature moved. The guide at the Woodland Park Zoo had described how painful it was to get stuck with porcupine quills, especially because of the little backward-facing barbs at the tip that made it hard to extract the quill from the skin. With thirty thousand quills protruding from its body, the porcupine could turn Cricket into a pincushion.

It kept pouncing at Cricket, its jaws snapping, its eyeballs nearly popping out of its skull. It was possessed by rage. Cricket kicked at it, fending off the creature with his foot as he tried to scurry to safety. The porcupine latched on to the sole of his sandal with its teeth, but Cricket slipped his foot free of the strap and yanked it clear. "Get it off me!" he cried shrilly.

"Hang on, man!" Heath knew he couldn't touch the porcupine, so he did the only thing he could think of. He aimed his squirt gun and sprayed the animal in the face, hoping to at least startle it enough to give his friend a chance to escape. As soon as the jet of water hit the side of the porcupine's head, the animal let out a horrible, prolonged yowl and flopped to its side, inches from Cricket's leg. It lay in the dirt, motionless.

Cricket scrambled to his feet. Heath kept the squirt gun trained on the porcupine's head for a long time. They watched the creature for any sign of movement, ready to spring into action at the first twitch. A full minute passed before the boys agreed it was dead. Heath lowered his pistol and remembered to breathe.

"You killed it," Cricket panted. He placed his dirty hands

on his knees and doubled over. His whole body trembled.

"I didn't mean to," Heath said apologetically. He'd never killed anything before, besides mosquitoes and horseflies, and he'd even curbed back on that since becoming friends with Cricket.

"No, I mean, *Thanks! You killed it!*"

"Oh. You're welcome, I guess." He couldn't take his eyes off the creature. "I don't get it though. All I did was spray it with water."

"Maybe Floaties hurt it in the forest."

Heath knew that wasn't right. "With what? His fists? His arms would have been covered with quills."

"What if he threw a rock at it?"

"I don't think so. The porcupine was fast. It didn't seem injured."

"It's filthy." Cricket crinkled his nose. "And it smells bad . . . like it died a week ago."

Heath broke a branch off of a nearby tree and used it to lift the porcupine's head so they could get a good look at its face.

"What is that stuff?" Cricket asked, pointing to the animal's mouth.

During the confusion of the attack, Heath had assumed the white on the porcupine's muzzle was a tuft of beard extending down from its lower lip. Up close he saw that the black fur of its chin was actually caked with foamy saliva.

"Well?" Cricket repeated. "What is it?"

Heath lowered the porcupine's head back to the dirt

carefully and slowly so that no spit would flick loose and land on his skin. He tossed the stick far into the woods as if it were on fire, then wiped his hands on his pants several times for good measure.

He turned to Cricket and grimaced. "I think it has rabies."

Timmy was my cabinmate,
He liked to water-ski.
Then one day he broke his neck,
And they did an autopsy.

Poor Timmy was a goner,
So they gave him to Chef Moe.
He ground up Timmy's body.
Enjoy your sloppy joe!

"WHAT A STINK!" Cricket complained, his voice muffled beneath his cupped hand. "Break a window, someone."

"Heath, please open the window above the sink. Breaking it won't be necessary." Uncle Bill, an obese man in a Hawaiian shirt, directed the flow of traffic in the health center, a small, one-room building with a single examining table, a desk, a sink, and several tall white medicine cabinets lining the wall. Physically, Camp Harmony's owner was hardly the type you'd expect to be outdoorsy, but he loved his camp and everyone in it. He liked to wear loud, colorful shirts, which always had dark stains in the armpits, even in the morning when it was cool out. He was joined by Marshall Cooper, the assistant director and a college junior who spent the rest of the year at the University of Washington in Seattle earning his degree in forestry. The men were standing over the examining table, opening the tarp they'd used to conceal the porcupine's carcass as they'd walked it nonchalantly through the middle of the water fight. The animal's quills had poked through it in places, making it a challenge to separate the tarp from the porcupine's body.

"Cricket, see if you can find some rubber gloves," Uncle Bill said. "There should be a pair or two around here someplace."

"Sure thing," Cricket replied.

As Heath struggled to open the window—it hadn't been opened in years and the latch was crusted with rust and flecks of rubbery paint—he heard Uncle Bill and Marshall heatedly whispering. He couldn't pick up every word, but he got the gist: Marshall said they should call the health department in Granite Falls. Uncle Bill was upset and said that if they called, the camp might be shut down by someone named Dee Heck. They couldn't afford that. Marshall bookended the discussion by repeating his opinion that not calling was a bad idea, but that was the end of the disagreement—Uncle Bill won. The window latch finally turned on its screw, and Heath hoisted the window open.

"Open the wall while you're at it!" Cricket said, adding

an exaggerated cough. "I know dead animals smell bad, but this is beyond gross! It's worse than our cabin on taco night!"

"Let's agree to disagree," said Marshall.

"What is that?" Heath asked. He was feeling slightly nauseated from the odor.

"That stench is coming from a patch of skin on the porcupine's back called a rosette," Marshall explained. "They're kind of like skunks in that way. When they're scared they emit a pungent odor from the rosette that rises up and escapes through the hollow quills above it." Marshall was studying to be a park ranger, so he knew a bit about the local wildlife.

"*It* was scared?" Cricket was indignant. "When I saw that *thing* coming for me I nearly peed myself!"

"That would have only made matters worse," Marshall told him. "Porcupines are attracted to urine."

"Serious?" Cricket's eyes opened wide. "That's just . . . sick!"

"Not just urine," Marshall elaborated. "They like pretty much anything with salt in it. They crave it. In the wild they get their fix from salty plants like liverwort and lilies, but they'll also gnaw on fresh animal bones, mud, and tree bark. Sometimes they wander into human habitats looking for salt, too. They'll take it any way they can get it—cured plywood, tool handles, doors, paint, rock salt used to melt ice on roads . . . you name it."

Heath spoke up. "That's not why it attacked Cricket." He was annoyed. Everyone seemed to be ignoring the real problem; the animal was clearly sick with—

"Rabies," Uncle Bill said, shaking his head woefully. "The porcupine must have rabies."

Cricket held out a carton of disposable rubber gloves that he'd found in a medicine cabinet. Both Uncle Bill and Marshall plucked a pair from the box and pulled them over their hands with a snap.

"Let's just be sure though, okay?" Uncle Bill insisted. "Marshall?"

Marshall used his gloved fingers to lift the skin covering the porcupine's gums. Heath was surprised. He'd expected to see rows of jagged teeth, like in a dog. Instead the porcupine had four enormous chisels in the front and receding behind them were flat, crowned teeth resembling human molars.

"Porcupines are rodents," Marshall said. "The third largest in the world."

"So they're basically giant rats?" Cricket scrunched his face in disgust. Coming from the city, he was all too familiar with rats.

"They're in the same family, Rodentia, yes, but they're different in many ways, the quills being the most obvious example. Whenever a porcupine feels cornered, it'll lower its head, raise its quills and lash out with its tail. In fact, the word *porcupine* means *one who rises in anger.*"

"What are quills made of?" Cricket asked. "Bone?"

Marshall plucked one free from the body and held it out for the boys to examine. "Nope. They're actually modified hairs coated in thick plates of keratin, the same stuff that makes up human fingernails and hair. Quills are light and spongy in the middle. That's why porcupines can float in water like a Ping-Pong ball. The rosette quills, however, are hollow." He paused. "Hmm. Looks like it lost a few of those."

Marshall checked the animal's eyes, then rolled the body as far as it would go onto its back. He had to press on its belly to crunch the quills flat. The creature had claws like curly fries. Its underbelly was covered in wiry hair, but no quills.

"Well?" Uncle Bill asked when Marshall had finished examining the carcass.

"I think so." Marshall nodded. He pulled his gloves off and tossed them into the garbage can. "It has many of the symptoms of rabies—foamy saliva, paralysis of the jaw and throat. Its pupils are dilated—"

"I knew it!" Uncle Bill said. He was furious. "It's them! Those . . . those . . . Something fishy is going on, I'm telling you! They're mucking around in the forest, stirring up trouble."

Heath wondered who "them" was, but he knew that asking wouldn't get him any answers. This was what Uncle Bill called "grown-up talk," which just meant he didn't think enough of the campers to tell them the truth.

"Calm down, Bill," said Marshall. "You're being paranoid. I've talked to people at the Forestry Service about them. They assured me there's nothing going on. I'm certain they had nothing to do with our porcupine's death. To be honest, I can't guarantee it even has rabies."

"What exactly *is* rabies?" Cricket asked.

Marshall said, "Rabies is a viral disease that attacks the brain and central nervous system in almost all warm-blooded mammals, including humans. The word *rabies* is derived from the Latin word for madness, which is one of the final and most notorious symptoms of the disease."

Heath remembered how vicious the porcupine had been when it attacked Cricket. It sure seemed crazy.

Marshall continued. "But that's not all. There are other symptoms, too: paranoia, hallucinations, fear of water, violent movements, excessive amounts of saliva and tears. This all leads to paralysis, followed by coma, and then finally death."

"Every time?" Heath asked.

Marshall said, "It's almost always fatal if not treated quickly enough."

"How does an animal get rabies?" Cricket sounded funny so everyone stopped and looked over at him. He'd found a set of giant plastic teeth, the kind used to demonstrate good brushing habits to little kids, and had shoved it into his mouth. He looked a bit like the Joker.

"Put those back in the drawer, please," Uncle Bill scolded. Cricket spit out the chompers and when Uncle Bill looked away, he stuck them back into the drawer still wet.

"Usually rabies is transmitted through the bite of another animal," said Marshall. "That's what's got me so baffled—I can't find teeth marks on this porcupine's body. No wound at all. Granted it takes weeks, and even months, for the rabies virus to take hold in an animal, so it might not be a fresh scar, but there should be a mark at least. If it has rabies, then *something* bit it."

"That *is* odd," Uncle Bill said in such a way that Heath suspected the man didn't know the first thing about the disease. The camp director was a nice guy, but he was lucky he had a pretty smart staff to help him, or Camp Harmony would be in trouble.

"But that's not all that's weird," Marshall said. "Porcupines almost *never* get rabies. Even a rabid dog will break off an attack once it gets a nose full of quills. That's why it's so rare, because it's almost impossible for another animal to bite one."

"Why do you think it died?" Heath couldn't help feeling responsible.

"Honestly? I don't know," Marshall replied. "It skipped the paralysis and coma symptoms. You said it just fell over, Heath?"

"Yep, that's right. I sprayed it and it just dropped dead. You mentioned that one of the symptoms of rabies is fear of water. Do you think it died of fright?"

Marshall rubbed his temple as if he was smoothing out a headache. "I don't know, Heath. . . ."

"Is it possible?" Uncle Bill asked.

"Like I mentioned, hydrophobia—fear of water—is a symptom, that's true. The virus makes it incredibly painful for the animal to swallow, and its diseased brain amplifies that fear to irrational levels. Even still, getting squirted with a water gun shouldn't have killed it. Animals don't just die from fear. This was likely just a freak occurrence. The porcupine was probably sicker than it seemed. You got lucky, Cricket. Rabies treatment involves a series of shots. You wouldn't enjoy that."

"Ya think?" Cricket snorted.

As Marshall and Uncle Bill folded the tarp over the porcupine's body, Heath caught one last glimpse of those impressive chisel-like front teeth. If the porcupine had sunk them into Cricket's leg, they would have gouged out a huge chunk of flesh. The thought of it made him shudder.

"We need to burn it," Marshall said as the two men considered what to do with the corpse.

"No, the campers are everywhere," Uncle Bill replied, dismissing the notion. Outside they could hear the water fight raging in force. "They'll see smoke and come running. Cricket and Heath, you boys head back to your cabin and dry off. Please don't say anything about the porcupine for now. Marshall, you and I will take it to the kitchen midden and bury it." Heath learned through his occasional duties in the cafeteria that a midden is a dumping hole for debris, like animal bones and shells. The midden behind the dining hall was the camp's oldest feature, dug by a prospector who first settled the camp during the gold rush in the early 1900s.

Heath thought burying the diseased animal was a terrible idea, but he kept quiet until after the four of them had left the health center and split in opposite directions.

"Uncle Bill is making a mistake," Heath said as he and

Cricket followed the winding path back to the Grosbeak Cabin. "What if another animal comes along and digs the porcupine up? Then eats it? It'd probably get the virus, too, right?"

"I dunno" was all the discussion Cricket offered on the matter. He seemed in shock, like it was finally dawning on him how lucky he was to have escaped the porcupine attack without injury. Cricket was so out of sorts that he didn't even notice the grasshopper he'd stepped on, and Heath wasn't about to tell him and make his mood even worse.

"Heath! Cricket! Over here!" someone called to them from the gazebo beside the craft hut. There were several campers inside, leaning against the railing or sitting on benches. Heath used his hand as a visor to shade his eyes from the sun so he could see who was there. He was surprised to find Will beckoning them over, and even more surprised to see Dunbar and Floaties sitting on a bench next to him. Floaties was still wearing his water wings, although the deflated left one sagged flat against his arm. He'd extracted the quill and was twirling it in his fingers like a drummer's stick. There were others in the gazebo, too. The gathering included Sylvester (who'd come straight from the archery range and still had his equipment with him) and three older boys—Rich, Quinn, and Saul—who were counselors in training, or C.I.T.s, as most of the campers called them. Heath didn't know any of them that well, and even though he'd talked to Will a few times now, he had a gut feeling he knew him least of all.

"See!" Dunbar said. "I told you they'd be fine."

"You guys okay?" Sylvester asked to be sure. He was restringing the bow resting across his lap. "Floaties told us what happened."

Floaties shot Sylvester a dark look but didn't voice objection to the nickname. Thumper may have been the alpha dog of the Oriole Cabin, but Sylvester was something even more important—popular.

"Yeah, we're okay," Heath told them. "Cricket almost got bit." He glared at Floaties. "Thanks for sticking around to help out. You're a real hero."

Floaties was unapologetic. "If you and Cockroach there—"

"His name is Cricket," Sylvester corrected him.

"Whatever. If you and Bug Juice were too stupid to follow me, then that's your problem."

Will stood up and folded his arms across his chest. "The porcupine had rabies, didn't it?"

Heath and Cricket glanced over at each other, then back at Will.

"How'd you know?" Cricket asked.

"Floaties told us it was foaming at the mouth. Where is it now? Did anyone catch it, or did it escape into the woods?"

"It's dead," Heath announced. "I killed it."

"No way!" Floaties blasted him. "That thing was a monster!"

"It's true!" Cricket snapped. "While you were running away with your tail between your legs, Heath saved me. He squirted it with a water gun, and it just died. That's the truth."

Floaties stood up and loomed over Cricket. "Look, Dung Beetle, if you expect us to buy this garbage—"

"I believe you," Will said, and that was that. Floaties let it go. "Where's the carcass? Did they burn it?"

"They took it to the midden to bury it," Heath told him.

Will shook his head disapprovingly. "Dumb."

"So it *was* rabies?" Quinn asked.

"Yeah." Heath nodded. "Marshall said he couldn't be sure, because there was no bite mark on the body, but I'm almost positive it had rabies."

"Of course it was rabies," Will said. "Animals don't just attack people like that."

"I saw a rabid possum once," Saul said.

"No you didn't," Will informed him. "Possums don't get rabies."

"Sure they do," Saul insisted. "It was acting crazy, puking up . . . then it just fell over dead."

Will snorted. "Possums are great actors. I bet it got up and scampered away the second you left. They don't get rabies because their body temperature is too low. You fell for the oldest con in history."

"And you'd know all this because . . . ?" asked Quinn.

"My grandfather's dog was bitten by a rabid raccoon," Will answered. "He went insane, too, lunging and snapping at anything that came close to his cage. I got to watch my grandfather put him down with a bullet."

Heath thought it was odd the way he'd said, *got to watch,* as if it was something he'd enjoyed. He decided he was probably just reading into it.

"At least my grandfather had the good sense to cremate Bandit's body instead of putting it in the ground where animals could smell it rotting and dig it up." Will turned to Heath. "You squirted it with water and it died? Just like that?"

"Just like that," Heath replied. "Marshall said that when animals are infected with the rabies virus they fear water."

"Yes, that's right," Will said.

"Well . . . water can be terrifying. You know, people even drown in kiddie pools," said Floaties, adding his two cents, and several of the boys laughed at the absurdity of the idea. Heath sensed that Floaties understood better than anyone how a creature could fear H_2O.

"Marshall said animals can't die of fright," Cricket said.

"Marshall is a goof," Will said flatly. "The guy failed his Parks and Recreation Management course. He skipped class half the time so he could hang out with his girlfriend on her lunch break. The only reason he's working here at Camp Harmony is for the extra credit he needs to pull his GPA out of the toilet. I wouldn't exactly call him an authority on animal psychology."

Heath made a mental note. Apparently campers weren't the only ones Will was digging up dirt on. "Marshall seems pretty smart to me."

"Not about this. Animals *can* die from fear," Will insisted. "Happens all the time. In China, three dogs snuck into a rabbit farm. The next day the owner found six hundred dead bunnies still locked in their cages, not a single scratch on them."

"So it is possible," Heath said in a somber tone.

Two young girls came bounding out from behind a tree and aimed their squirt guns at the boys. Saul leapt from the gazebo and roared at them. The girls dropped their guns and ran off crying.

"What's wrong with you, dude?" Cricket asked on behalf of the group. "That was mean."

"What?" Saul said innocently. "I was just testing Will's theory."

"I thought it was hilarious." Quinn laughed. "Guess they're not quite as gutless as rabbits."

Will cocked his head in the direction of the horse stables and held up his hand. "Shut up, you guys."

"I heard it, too," Heath said, tensing.

They listened together. It was unusually quiet except for the muted clapping and cheering of the winning cabin off in the distance: "Woodpecker! Woodpecker! Woodpecker!"

"Our cabin won the water fight," Saul said to Rich, and the boys high-fived.

"Be quiet," Will hissed. "Listen."

Heath glanced down and noticed there was something protruding from Cricket's right heel above the rubber sole of his sandal. It looked like a splinter of straw impaled in the thick, calloused skin directly above his friend's sandal. No, not a splinter of straw—it was a quill, just like the one that had punctured Floaties's water wing. It had detached from the porcupine and embedded itself in Cricket's foot, probably when Cricket tried to kick it away as it charged. "Cricket . . ." Heath said. "You've got—"

The boys heard the sound again. This time it was easily identifiable as the high-pitched whinnying of horses. The whinnies were followed closely by a chorus of howls.

The boys were still, gazing together in the direction of the animal noises, side by side and rigid like a gang of meerkats.

"Are there dogs on the campgrounds?" Floaties asked.

"Just Uncle Bill's beagle, Barkly," Dunbar said.

Will identified the sound. "Those are wolves."

"Are you sure?" Sylvester asked.

"It's wolves," Heath agreed.

"They sound nuts," Saul said nervously. "Is it mating season?"

Will shook his head. "They mate in the spring. This is something else."

"How do you know so much?" Saul asked as if knowledge were a crime.

"How do you know so little?" Will tossed back.

"You've got a smart mouth for a new kid." Saul advanced on Will, his fist in the air. "How about I teach you something you *don't* know?"

Floaties was enjoying himself. "You really know how to make friends, Stringer."

Quinn stepped in and grabbed Saul by the arm. "Easy, man."

"Guys, stop," Heath pleaded. "There's something really wrong about this. Just listen."

The wolves paused for air then began another round of howls. It was slightly louder this time. The howls were long and smooth, like the cry of the horned owl, which Heath knew was a very bad thing. It meant the wolves were calling pack mates to a kill.

"They sound so close," Sylvester noted.

"That's because they are," Will said.

Heath suddenly felt uncomfortably confined, encircled by railing. He led the boys out of the gazebo, but they stayed in a tight group. A light breeze sifted through them.

Far off, two girls came around the path's bend, running toward them at full sprint ahead of the howling. Their equestrian outfits were unmistakable.

"It's Em and Em!" Cricket said.

The twins were yelling in unison; it was hard to understand them that way. Then, when they neared the gazebo, the girls took turns.

"They're coming!" Emily warned.

"Run!" Emma yelled.

The gray wolves broke into view.

They were still a good ways off, but they were coming fast. So fast.

It was a large pack for grays, seven or eight in total. Even though they were still hundreds of yards off, Heath could see that the one in the lead had old scars across its nose, like it had been raked with knives or maybe the claws of a larger animal, probably a bear. The scars separated the wolf's face into different sections, like the stitching on a quilt.

Heath saw the trees around the gazebo starting to jerk

and sway. Something was ricocheting across the branches, obscured by leaves.

In the distance the screams of campers pierced the oppressively hot air in all directions.

It was chaos.

The boys did as Emma told them. They ran.

Like the wolves, they ran as a pack.

The zookeeper had a bad day.
His boss shorted his pay.
Upset with his wages, he unlocked the cages.
And the animals all got away.

The zookeeper wasn't that smart.
The escapees tore him apart.
And now all the beasts
get to run through the streets.
Let's watch the festivities start!

WHEN HEATH WAS NINE, he was confined to a hospital bed for almost two months. He watched a lot of TV, mostly shows about nature. It was his way of escaping the boredom of his bland, tiny room on the pediatrics wing at Providence Sacred Heart Medical Center. Heath was raised to love nature, never imagining a time would come when he'd be forced to experience it through a television.

He remembered a few things he'd watched about the hunting strategy of wolves. First, when attacking deer or other herd prey, the pack will usually try to isolate and pick off one or two stragglers. Second, they usually give up the chase after a mile or so, not that Heath and the others would be able to outrun the wolves for that long. But maybe they didn't have to. They just had to make it inside one of the cabins. Even so, Heath feared the wolves would overtake them well before that. He thought maybe, if he fell to the rear of the group, he could be the straggler the wolves were looking for. He could give the others a chance to make it to safety.

Before he could decide, Emily grabbed Heath by the arm and he was forced to keep his pace up or he'd get her killed, too. "Go!" she screamed, so he did.

Heath glanced back just in time to see the scarred pack leader, Quilt Face, leap through the air at them. He cringed, expecting to feel fangs embed in his Achilles tendon— wolves liked to cripple their prey before killing it—but just then Saul accidentally ran into the wolf's path and it landed on the boy's back. The C.I.T. let out a shriek and fell to the ground where his head bounced hard in the dirt. Unable to look away, Heath saw a weird purple pattern, like vines, spread across the surface of Saul's skin, covering his entire body in seconds. He'd never witnessed anything like it before. What is that? Heath wondered. Saul gasped, then fell still, lying there, unmoving, even when another wolf started tugging at his sneaker. The beast growled and shook its head back and forth in furious jerks. A third wolf, the biggest by far, muscled in and dragged Saul sideways across the ground with the first two wolves in tow, making dirt angels on the trail with the boy's body. Saul was like a rag doll being fought over by selfish children. Heath wanted to help, but in his heart he knew Saul was already dead.

The rest of the pack kept coming. It was like being trapped in a nightmare. The wolves were so close that Heath thought he felt flecks of spittle land on the back of his legs. They were snarling and snapping and producing low, throaty growls, just like he'd seen on TV. Again he looked back. He thought for sure he was next, but instead the wolves snagged Rich. The purple vines bloomed over every inch of the boy's skin. Rich screamed once, then died, just like Saul. Immediately the wolves ceased their pursuit. The pack leader sprinted back and forth between the two bodies, sniffing them to make sure they were finished. Heath and his friends kept moving.

This can't be happening, Heath insisted over and over in his mind. He tried to process his thoughts, but they came in choppy waves as his brain flipped the switch to autopilot, tuned to his survival. The ear-piercing screams around him didn't help his concentration. He forced himself to reason. He knew that wolves didn't raid summer camps. You never saw that on the news. Sure, sometimes you'd hear something about a hiker in the remote Alaskan wilderness getting killed by a wolf, but it was rare, and usually happened because the human had wandered too close to the pack's den. What was happening now was completely unnatural behavior for wolves. It was almost as if they were deranged. And then there were the purplish viney patterns on the bodies of Saul and Rich. It had to be an infection, but what kind of infection resembled an invisible hand scrawling quickly across skin?

Heath put it all together. The wolves were sick. Sick, like the porcupine. There was no other explanation. Marshall never mentioned the purple vines, but maybe that was one of the symptoms of rabies, too. What else could it be?

"This way!" Will shouted. He veered off the path.

Taking a shortcut, they sprinted through Laundry Lane, a growth of pines that supported a cat's cradle of clotheslines. They charged through, brushing aside sopping wet bathing suits and towels, until, finally, they reached the trail again and the cabins and main lodge came into view. They were still a good deal away from the clearing, but at least the buildings were in sight.

"Yes! We're gonna make it!" Quinn laughed in nervous relief, then sprinted ahead of the group.

No one saw the horse coming.

It exploded from the woods on their left, a black blur, and hit Quinn so hard that one of his sneakers came off his feet and cartwheeled through the dirt while Quinn's body sailed into the woods on the right.

Em and Em screamed like victims in a horror movie.

Sylvester yelled, "Whoa!" and collided with Dunbar hard, but somehow they both stayed on their feet.

The world froze, except for the horse, which followed Quinn into the woods, trampling him under its hooves, chomping at him, tearing a scrap of his shirt off in its teeth. Heath thought the animal was the most muscular thing he'd ever seen, and every one of those muscles was working in unison to attack Quinn. The horse was pure power covered in skin and hair.

The stallion was snorting and bucking, smashing the barrel of its body against thin tree trunks as it tried to round on Quinn inside a section of tightly grouped saplings. Its bridle snagged on a branch. It whinnied and jerked its head from side to side, twisting the branch like a corkscrew, but the bridle stayed fast. The horse was stuck. The attack stalled, but the damage had been done. Quinn's body was bent in a weird position on the ground beneath the beast.

"It killed him!" Dunbar wailed. "Oh, man! It killed him!"

"Is that one of the camp's?" Sylvester asked, slightly crouched, staring in disbelief.

"It's Onyx," Emily choked as she identified the stallion. "He was still in the arena when we left. He was fine. It was Sweet Pea that was acting weird."

"I just rode him," Dunbar said numbly.

The group was transfixed, barely there, their bodies heavy and leaden like statues. All except for Will, who was always moving forward. "You guys can stand here and wait for that thing to free itself," he said. "I'm gone." Will continued on down the trail toward the buildings.

Most of the others soon followed, but Emily was rooted in place and Heath couldn't leave her. Horses were her world. He knew there was a part of her that could only ever see Onyx as the camp's pet, but that version of the horse was gone now and Heath needed to get her away from him quickly.

"We have to go, Em," he said softly.

"Heath . . ."

"Em . . . the wolves. We have to go."

Her eyes met his. He hated to see her crying. He hated to see anyone crying as a rule, but especially Emily. He didn't know her well, but from casual observation—okay, maybe more than casual—she seemed very mature. Maybe that had something to do with her equestrian training. Controlling a half-ton animal probably took a level of self-discipline that other girls Emily's age didn't need to develop so soon. Seeing her cry affected him. It made him feel like crying, too, and that made him uncomfortable. After his last doctor visit, he'd promised himself he'd never cry again. Besides, with three campers dead, likely more, he figured there'd be a monsoon of tears in the camp before the day was over.

"Okay?" he said.

She nodded and wiped her eyes with the back of her velvet riding glove. "Okay."

They ran to catch up to the others.

Emily looked back twice.

The others were too far ahead to catch, except for Emma, who had doubled back to find her sister. She scolded Emily as they ran.

Farther up the trail, things went from bad to worse.

The camp was under siege. Animals were everywhere, streaking across the grass, up and down trees, across the plank porches of the buildings. Some were ramming their heads against the windows or clawing madly at the glass. They were all going berserk. The horrific scale of their situation became apparent.

"It's not just *some* of the animals," Heath said, chills running down his spine. "It's *all of them*. They're coming from the forest in droves."

"Look out!" Emma shrieked.

Above them, a raccoon rappelled headfirst down a spruce, sending a shower of bark bits down onto their heads. The creature hissed, then, hanging on to the tree trunk with its back paws, reached out at them. Each paw had five twiggy fingers that looked eerily human. The raccoon's mouth gaped wide, revealing two rows of pointed teeth dripping with saliva. Its fur was filthy, covered in burrs and bits of leaves. Perfectly round eyeballs, fit to burst from the animal's black bandit mask, were wild with rage.

The raccoon clawed at the top of Emily's equestrian helmet, scratching the felt as she ducked under the animal. It jumped to the ground and chased them, but they were too fast, and it quickly gave up and rocketed up another tree.

As they came to the edge of the lawn in front of the main lodge they finally caught up to the others.

"Look!" Cricket pointed. "It's not just the wolves! Everything in the forest is trying to kill us!"

"We know!" said Heath. "They're everywhere!"

Kids were running in all directions, screaming and

clutching one another, pushing, pulling, and tripping as they were chased by dozens of small animals, mostly squirrels, but Heath also spied a woodchuck and possibly a chipmunk or a rat.

Even more horrifying were the ten or more bodies sprawled prostrate across the lawn. They were all covered with the same purple pattern of infection Heath had seen on Rich and Saul. Heath spied the only dead adult among the slaughter, a young woman slumped in a protectoral position over the body of a little girl.

"That's Katey." Heath pointed out the assistant camp director. Every morning it was Katey who led the kids in prayer and the Pledge of Allegiance. She was the closest thing to a chaplain the camp had, and the only staff member Heath had willfully trusted with his secret. She was so easy to talk to and had a way of getting you to spill your guts. And now hers were—

"Oh God," Emily whimpered. "Poor Katey."

"There's Billy from our cabin," Cricket nodded toward a boy not much taller than himself who was wearing a *Ben 10* T-shirt and yellow swim trunks. He was on his back, staring up at the sky with empty eyes.

"And Javier . . . Jenny . . . Levi . . ."

"Ugh, the flies are already—"

"Where's Levi? I don't see—"

"He's there . . . and over there."

Dunbar dry heaved, but mercifully held down his lunch. They didn't need half-digested pizza added to the carnage.

"Thumper!" Floaties shouted.

The group scanned the lawn for Thumper's body, and when they couldn't find it, they followed Floaties's line of sight and saw that Thumper was alive and running toward them farther down the trail. He was still a ways off, waving his arms frantically in front of his face. They couldn't hear what he was yelling, but they didn't need to. They could see why he was running for his life. Barkly was chasing Thumper and quickly closing the gap. Any negative feelings Heath may have had toward the kid were gone; they were all in this together—whatever *this* was.

"Run, man!" Heath yelled to Thumper. "Don't stop! Just run!"

"Run!" the twins added their warnings.

Heath and Floaties picked up rocks and charged down the path with the intent of stoning the rabid dog before he could kill Thumper. They threw and both rocks narrowly missed. There was no time for another try. Barkly caught up to Thumper and the small dog bit into the flesh of his calf. Thumper's face hardened into a squinched mask of pain as purple tendrils crisscrossed his skin, snaked up his neck, and filled his contorted face so completely that only his eyes and teeth remained untinted. He fell backward, landing on top of Barkly, pinning the dog under his weight. Barkly was growling and pawing at the ground, trying desperately to crawl out from under Thumper's body.

Heath was positive that Thumper was dead, but for Floaties this fact wouldn't register. "Get away from him!" he roared, picking up a huge rock and hurling it like a shot put at Barkly. Floaties missed a second time. The rock thudded in the dirt next to Barkly, drawing the dog's attention and fury to their group. He dug his claws into the ground and struggled even harder to free himself. Barkly snapped his jaws at Floaties, exposing black-spotted gums and two rows of sharp teeth, reminding Heath that even a dog as typically friendly as a beagle could rip a man's throat out if it wanted to.

Heath threw an arm around Floaties' neck, which took a jump to accomplish, as the boys were so mismatched in height. Floaties barely noticed the added weight. He carried Heath toward Barkly. The dog had managed to free one shoulder blade. If he escaped, Heath knew he would attack them next.

"Help me!" Heath called out desperately to the others. "I can't hold him!"

Sylvester, Dunbar, Cricket, and the Ems ran to him and swarmed Floaties, grabbing his arms and legs. Everyone was yelling, ordering him to stop. Still, he continued to inch on toward the dog, dragging them forward, too.

"Help us, Will!" Heath cried to his cabinmate, but Will didn't move. He seemed paralyzed, staring at them with no emotion on his face whatsoever.

Finally Floaties dropped to one knee. Their combined weight was wearing him down. "Get off me, you idiots!"

"He's dead, man!" Heath tightened his choke hold. "Thumper's dead, I promise. Please. . . ."

With a yelp of pain, Barkly squeezed his rear half out from under Thumper. The group, including Floaties, froze as the beagle approached them, crouching low, his back and tail raised. A hateful, guttural growl came from somewhere deep inside the dog. He fixed his gaze on Floaties's right thigh. Heath knew these were behavior signs that the dog was about to attack.

"You guys get ready to run," Heath whispered. "I'll hold him off."

Before Barkly could lunge, Uncle Bill, Marshall, and twenty or more campers charged from the far side of the lodge with water guns, shouting loudly like an army of Vikings. They surrounded Barkly and shot him with streams of water. The dog lifted his head high, bayed in agony, then flopped sideways to the ground and died.

Uncle Bill turned away from his beloved pet, dropped his squirt gun to the grass, placed his hands on his knees, and puked baked beans and hot dog chunks onto the lawn.

The kids released Floaties. While the others tried to comfort him, Heath knelt down beside Marshall, who was checking Thumper for a pulse.

"Well?" Heath asked, already certain of the answer.

Marshall shook his head in frustration. "He's dead. The bites are lethal every time."

"You killed Barkly with water, just like I killed the porcupine. I thought you said—"

"I was wrong," Marshall admitted.

It's the rabbit in the cage effect, Heath thought. Fear was the killer. "If it worked on Barkly, maybe it'll do the same with the wolves—"

"Wait—you saw wolves?" Marshall glanced around nervously.

"Yeah, we were attacked by a pack of grays. They killed two campers. They're here somewhere."

"Maybe Uncle Bill was right," Marshall said. "Maybe those people are responsible for this."

"Who, Marshall? Who are you talking about?" Heath asked.

"Them. Downriver. The virus kills so quickly. There's nothing natural about it."

Heath was frustrated by the vagueness of the response, but there was no time to press him.

Uncle Bill had picked himself up and was ready to take charge again. "Okay, everyone," the camp director said shakily, "let's get inside the lodge. It's not safe out here. Are we ready?"

"Bill, I don't think the lodge is safe either," Marshall objected. "The windows are old, held in place mostly by caulk. There's a crawl space under the floorboards. The roof hasn't been inspected in—"

"Nonsense," Uncle Bill said with a dismissive wave. "It's sturdy enough, and it's the only building that will fit everyone inside. We'll be fine. Let's go."

Heath would have preferred for Marshall to lead them. Running a summer camp was one thing; surviving a bloodthirsty assault by rabid animals was another. Marshall seemed more collected and he knew a lot about the disease. But there was an order to things at the camp, and even in this unprecedented situation, Marshall fell back and allowed Uncle Bill to take charge.

The campers, including Heath and his group, followed

the two men toward the main lodge, firing their squirt guns at squirrels that attempted to ambush them as they marched across the grass. They'd made it to the steps when they heard the thudding of hooves hitting the ground. A herd of deer thundered down the trail, across the lawn, and directly into the line of campers. Their leader, an enormous buck, lowered his head, aiming at one of the kids. Marshall jumped between them and the buck caught him square in his wicked antler rack, skewering the man upon the points and carrying him away from the group. The flocking doe knocked several campers down, but continued running, staying close behind the buck that had fixated his attack on Marshall. It happened in an instant and all the kids could do was watch.

Uncle Bill stood there, his mouth agape, stunned into useless rigidity. The screaming campers ran past him, up the stairs, and through the double doors of the lodge.

On the porch, Heath looked around for Will. He saw him racing down a dirt path toward the small, shoe box–shaped building between the main lodge and the Dray River.

"Will!" Heath called after him.

"Where's he going?" Dunbar asked.

"The canoe livery," Heath replied. "He has to be. There's nothing else in that direction."

"What's Will after?" Cricket asked. "Wait—do they keep guns there?"

"Of course not," Emma snapped. She and Emily were holding hands, waiting for their turn to squeeze into the lodge. "This is a summer camp for kids! How *unsafe* would that be?"

Heath, the Ems, Cricket, Sylvester, and Floaties watched Will as he disappeared down the bank where the lawn sloped sharply away.

"Something's up," Heath said. "He's not the type to risk his life needlessly. If he's after anything, I'd say it's probably his own survival."

"Good riddance," Floaties growled. "Useless."

The group was being jostled along toward the doors by a sea of panicked campers. Heath knew he'd be swept inside in seconds, and once inside there'd be no leaving the lodge, on Uncle Bill's orders.

"No! We have to follow him," Heath said, pushing back against the crowd. "Will must know something we don't. If it was safe inside the lodge, he would've been the first inside."

"Maybe he's right," Emily said, and Emma nodded in agreement.

"Will's smart," Dunbar pointed out. "He knows things,"

"You're all nuts," Floaties snorted. "I'm going in."

"I can't stop you," Heath said, "but I'm going to the livery."

"Me too!" Cricket weighed in.

"Okay, let's go." Heath began to weave his way back through the crowd and thumped down the steps, followed by Emma, Emily, Dunbar, Sylvester, and Cricket.

The lawn was a blanket of corpses, but the animals had scattered to attack other areas of the camp. The coast was clear. The group ran down the trail toward the canoe livery as fast as their legs would carry them. Their route was an obstacle course of bodies.

"There's so many . . ." Emily choked, slowing, scanning for foot placement as if she were tiptoeing through a mine-field. "I—I can't help stepping on them."

"Don't think about it, Em. They can't feel it," Heath said, coaxing her back into a sprint. "Just keep moving, everyone!"

They noticed the trees lining the path were swaying despite the lack of a breeze.

"The pines!" Cricket warned. "They're full of squirrels!"

Heath realized too late they should have scavenged the lawn for squirt guns. Without them they were defenseless.

The branches above them started bouncing up and down. Green needles and pinecones showered down on their heads.

"Keep running!" Heath ordered. "We're almost there!"

When they reached the canoe livery the door was shut. Two girls were pounding on it, begging whoever was inside to let them in. Heath stepped in front of them and banged hard. "Will! It's Heath! Open up right this—"

The door swung open wide. Heath ushered the two girls in, then stood back and allowed the rest of his group to enter before him. Will stuck his head out. "Is that it?"

"Yeah, that's it," Heath replied, slipping in past him.

Will tried to yank the door shut, but a huge paw caught the side and forced it back open.

Floaties was standing in the entranceway, his face red and sweaty. He did not look happy. "You ask me to follow, then you try to shut me out?"

"Hurry up," Will said, grabbing him by the arm. He

pulled Floaties over the threshold and slammed the door shut behind them, plunging the room into near darkness.

Something hit the door with such force that it shook the frame and a screw popped free from one of the hinges. They heard a loud snorting sound on the other side.

BANG!

Heath jumped.

BANG!

Someone tried to muffle a scream.

BANG!

And then finally, mercifully, whatever it was went away.

I had a dozen eggs, all
tucked snug in their crate.
I had intent to cook them—
that should have been their fate.
But to my surprise they hatched,
and my cat can hear them shout.
Sadly all my birds are doomed,
inside their box or out.

THE CANOE LIVERY was dark except for a small square of light, a porthole that framed the main lodge perfectly through its dirty glass, as if it were a painting of the nature-besieged cabin. Most of the group stood far back from the window. It was clearly the brick structure's Achilles' heel. Heath and Will, however, took positions on either side of it and peered out, careful not to make any sudden moves that would attract the attention of the rabid animals running pell-mell across the lawn outside. It was fairly quiet

inside except for some panting, muffled crying, and someone with asthma wheezing and puffing on an inhaler. In
the gloomy darkness it was impossible for Heath to tell how
many people were in the building with him.

"What the heck hit the door?" Heath whispered to Will's
silhouette.

"A deer, probably."

"A deer?" Heath found that hard to believe. "It sounded
like a rhinoceros."

"Have you ever seen a car after it hits a deer?" Will asked.
"They're heavy animals and can do some major damage.
Marshall would tell you, if he hadn't just been steamrolled
by one."

"That was a heartless thing to say," one of the Ems
scolded from the darkness.

Will ignored her.

"Can someone turn on the light?" Sylvester asked. His
request was followed by the sound of several feet shuffling
against the concrete floor as campers began groping their
way along the walls, hunting for the switch.

"No, don't!" a girl panicked. "The animals will see the
lights come on and know we're in here!"

Several kids murmured in agreement.

"Everyone needs to relax. We're safe for now," Will
assured them. "We need light so we can see what we have in
here to work with."

Heath assumed Will meant food and other supplies in
case they were holed up in the livery for any stretch of time.
They wouldn't be going outside in the foreseeable future,

that was for sure, and the livery, with its cinder block walls, was undoubtedly the safest place on the campgrounds to hunker down during the attack. He and the others had been right to follow Will. Heath felt a surge of gratefulness toward his abrasive cabinmate, even if he still didn't trust him completely.

Someone found the switch and dusty fluorescent bulbs above hummed to life, filling the livery with a pallid yellow glow. Two dozen canoes and kayaks rested on racks bolted to the concrete floor on the west side of the building. The livery housed more than just watercraft. It acted as the supply depot, too. The north half was full of camping supplies and maintenance equipment organized on several aisles of shelving.

Heath was surprised to see more kids than he expected—maybe double his guess in the dark.

"Shouldn't we do a head count?" Dunbar asked, attempting to be productive.

"Dumb idea," Will scoffed. "What's the point?"

Dunbar was taken aback. "What's the point? We're all in this together, right?"

"We're all in *this building* together," Will replied icily. He turned his back on Dunbar.

"And what's *that* supposed to mean?" Dunbar asked Heath.

Heath shrugged. He agreed with Dunbar, a head count couldn't hurt. He took a mental tally: twenty-three campers, give or take. He might have counted a few kids twice; it was hard to be sure as everyone was either breaking into loose groups, hugging, huddling, or milling around the room. The only one who seemed to be moving with any purpose was Will, who was obviously more interested in *what* was in the building than *who* was in the building. Heath tagged along.

"What are you doing?" he asked quietly so as not to attract attention.

"Taking inventory. Most of this stuff is junk. And there doesn't seem to be any food. Not even marshmallows. That's bad."

"Do you really think it'll matter? I'm sure help will arrive soon."

Will gave Heath a considering look. "Who do you suppose is coming for us?"

"I don't know. People from the Forest Service? The army?"

"Doubtful," Will replied, then he busied himself with a bin of old generator parts. Heath felt like Will was keeping something to himself but decided not to press him. He didn't need another dose of attitude.

They continued taking inventory together, moving about the building, Heath following behind Will when the aisles narrowed. Occasionally Heath held up something he thought might be of value, and Will would either nod or ignore him. They found tents, tire pumps, coolers, deflated basketballs, bags of charcoal, checkered tablecloths, hammocks, cans of bug repellant, lanterns, a big box of party supplies, and a lot more stuff that Heath didn't see as very useful to their predicament. Will was right—there was nothing that could be used as food. Nothing at all.

"Here," Will said, tearing open a box of drinking straws, the wide, bendy type that someone could easily suck a shake through. He drew one out and handed it to Heath. "Hang on to it."

"Gee, thanks," Heath said. "What am I supposed to do with—?"

"Remember what I said about chess? About predicting moves?"

"Yeah."

"When the situation comes, if you need it, you'll understand then."

Will grabbed a handful more from the box and slipped them into his pocket. Heath did the same with his.

After they'd carefully searched the room they rejoined the others. Most of the kids had since clustered around the tiny window to watch the sick animals outside. A red fox stopped in front of them, shook its head spastically as if trying to shake off a blow, then fell on the ground and twitched violently. After several seconds of this bizarre behavior, the fox regained control of its body and took off, unfazed, trotting in the direction of the main lodge.

They're in terrible pain, Heath thought, feeling empathy toward the fox and all of the rabid mammals. They hadn't asked to be invaded by the virus. Who'd ask for something like that? The disease was the villain. He decided then to hate the disease and only the disease.

"Check this out," Dunbar said, holding up a dusty, laminated placard. "It was hanging on the wall behind one of the shelves." He wiped it clean with the blade-edge of his hand. Printed at the top right corner was a block of text that said the placard had been created by the NATIONAL PARK SERVICE: THE DEPARTMENT OF THE INTERIOR. It was a list of every mammal known to live in the Cascade Mountain region. The group looked it over.

Heath felt the sun-bleached hairs on the nape of his neck rise. There were so many mammals, some large, like deer and wolves, others much smaller like weasels, squirrels, and voles. All of them, potential killers. He'd seen maybe eight or nine of them personally, but that was all. Two of those were roadkill, a groundhog and a possum, that he'd passed during the drive to camp. There were at least a hundred species on the list.

"I didn't know there were mountain lions here," Cricket said with a worried frown.

"And bears," noted Emma with dread.

"Black bears *and* grizzlies." Sylvester tapped the word *Ursidae* on the placard. "*Big* bears."

"But they're all up in the mountains, right?" Dunbar said. "I've never seen a bear this close to the valley before. Why would they come down into camp?"

"The wolves did," Will reminded them.

He was right, of course. The wolves had descended into Camp Harmony, killing at least two kids. Heath knew they would have killed him, too, if Emily hadn't inadvertently spoiled his suicidal attempt at heroism.

"The horses smelled the wolves coming," Emily said sadly, her eyes pink and watery. She was still mourning Onyx and the other camp horses. "That's what spooked them. Mr. Soucandi made us dismount and sent us away from the arena. If they hadn't smelled the wolves, Emma and I would have been there when they arrived. We'd be dead now. The horses gave us a head start."

"Huh," Floaties grunted. "I didn't think horses had a good sense of smell."

"Are you kidding?" Emma shot back, offended on behalf of horses everywhere. "Have you seen the size of their nostrils? They have the keenest noses in the world!"

"That's not true," Will interjected. "There are several animals with a stronger sense of smell: sharks, moths, snakes, the albatross. . . ."

And bears, Heath thought, but he kept that fact to himself. There was a joke he'd always found amusing up until now. How does a bear smell? The punch line was: really bad and really well. Bears could smell the carcass of a dead deer twenty miles away. Their noses were seven times more powerful than a bloodhound's, and two thousand times more powerful than a human's—more tidbits he learned by watching nature shows in the hospital. He thought it was entirely possible that somewhere up in the mountains the bears could smell them, even through the locked livery door. He tried to put it out of his mind.

"Whatever," Emma huffed. "The horse has always been a prey animal, so it had to evolve a keen sense of smell to keep ahead of predators, especially wolves."

"The camp's horses aren't prey anymore," Sylvester noted somberly.

"Yeah," Cricket agreed. "*We* are."

There it was, Heath thought, a blunt summation of the crisis. The campers were prey now, and everything outside the livery's door had become the predator. Even the tiniest mouse could kill them, and worse, *wanted* to kill them.

Over by a rack of lanterns, two girls started fighting. Heath didn't know them, or he probably would have told them to shut up. Apparently they'd both had a crush on the same boy, a Brad from the Barn Owl Cabin. They were arguing over who'd miss him more if he was dead. You really couldn't call it fighting. They were just tugging on each other's clothing and pulling each other around in an awkward waltz. He thought they looked silly. The added tension was annoying, but the skirmish was short-lived as the girls were quickly wrenched apart by the closest campers. Heath didn't have to be a psychologist to understand why they were acting out. They were terrified. Fear made people react in all kinds of dumb, petty ways. The longer they were stuck in the livery without food, the more tension there would be, and that meant more fights and more stupidity. It was natural to be scared. Heath was scared, too, but he was trying not to show it. Will was the only one in the room who, on the surface at least, seemed genuinely calm and in control, and that made Heath even more nervous for reasons he couldn't explain.

"Let's talk about what's happening out there and what we

can do to stay alive," Sylvester said. Because it was Sylvester, everyone listened up. "First, we should ask ourselves the possible reasons behind the attacks. Hundreds of animals just came out of the woods, killed dozens of campers for no good reason. It's like they're working together to exterminate us."

"If this is rabies, then how'd it spread so fast?" Dunbar wondered. "Are they out there in the woods biting one another, passing the virus from animal to animal? It's freakin' weird, right?"

"They're not biting one another," Will stated matter-of-factly.

"What are you talking about? They *have* to be!" Sylvester asserted. "That's how animals get rabies!"

Will thrust his chin out, gesturing toward the window. "Do you *see* them biting one another? You said it yourself, Sylvester, they're working together."

"All right, genius," Sylvester put it to Will. "Then why don't you enlighten us?"

"The squirrels are the key," Will said. "The squirrels and the chipmunks—all of the little mammals."

"They're everywhere," Emma noted, and as if on cue, a dirty, wild-eyed squirrel scampered across the outside sill of the building's small window causing some of the younger girls to start crying again.

"And more will come," Will assured them. "The camp is bordered by thousand acres of forest. I doubt it'll be long before there's an army of squirrels outside this door."

"You said the squirrels are the key," Emma said. "What did you mean by that?"

Will explained. "They almost never get rabies. I mean, they *can* get rabies, practically every mammal can, but it rarely happens to the really small ones, like squirrels and chipmunks."

"How come?" Heath asked.

"Think about it," Will said.

Heath mulled it over. He tried to imagine a squirrel being attacked by a rabid fox or a dog, and the same gruesome end came to mind in every scenario. "They're too small! My pet cat, Sammy, used to bring home mice as presents for our family. They were barely recognizable lying on the carpet by his cat flap, all bloody and mangled from being carried in Sammy's mouth. If a squirrel was bitten by anything bigger than another squirrel, it'd probably have broken bones, crushed organs, missing limbs—"

"Exactly," Will said. "The squirrels on the lawn don't have a mark on them."

"Neither did the porcupine," Cricket piped up. "So if the squirrels out there weren't bitten, then how'd they get—"

"It's in the air!" Heath said excitedly. "The rabies virus is airborne!"

The room filled with murmuring.

"That's right. It's airborne," Will confirmed. "This has to be a new kind of rabies. A mutated version of the virus."

"No way," Emma said. "If it was in the air, we'd have it, too, then, right? We're mammals."

"Yeah," Will said. "I'm still trying to figure that one out."

It was the first time Heath had witnessed Will looking frustrated, pained almost by his inability to see every angle of the situation.

"No way," said Sylvester. "Rabies has been around forever, and it's always been transmitted one way, through the bite of an animal. That's it."

"True," Heath said. "But I think Will has a point, too. It's gotta be some new form of rabies."

"Maybe that's why people are dying after one bite," Dunbar added.

"Or why the animals aren't going nutso on one another, just us," said Cricket.

"It's our smell," Will theorized. "It's gotta be what's drawing them to us, like it's irresistible."

"Great," said Cricket. "So there's a virus in the air that makes animals go crazier than Justin Bieber fans. What do we do now?" He looked to Sylvester. "Well?"

Sylvester stiffened and hopped back from the group like a threatened bird, hugging his bow to his chest. "What? Why are you asking me?"

"I don't know," said Cricket. "You *are* the oldest. Plus your dad runs a big company, right? You're probably gonna take his place some day. I just thought you'd be the best choice for leader here."

"That's right, Sylvester," said a girl Heath recognized from the Thrush Cabin. "Just yesterday you were bragging about how your dad lets you sit in on board meetings. Didn't you learn anything? Or was that all just a bunch of garbage?"

Sylvester panicked. "Look, my dad's company manufactures prosthetic limbs. Yeah, I sat in on a few meetings, but they were pretty boring, and not once were we ever attacked by rabid animals. I'm just as freaked out as the rest of you. How should *I* know what to do?"

A glum silence fell over the group. They needed leadership and the natural born leader had declined. Heath was glad. Although he wasn't sure how he felt about it, he suspected there was only one person in the livery calculating enough to outsmart nature. "Will?" he said hopefully.

Will looked around the room for objections but found none. "Fine," he said, accepting Heath's nomination. "Here's our first and only order of business. We have to leave the livery. As soon as possible."

"What!? You're out of your mind!" Floaties railed. "There's no way I'm walking out that door. You're crazy!"

Almost everyone sided with Floaties.

"Why would we leave the livery?" Emma asked. "It's probably the only place for miles that *is* safe!"

Will shook his head. "It's not. See those drainage pipes?" He pointed up at a highway of gray tubes running across the ceiling and up through to the roof. "They're made of lead. Squirrels chew through lead. They can tear off chunks at a time with their teeth. I've seen it. If they want in here, which we know they do, they'll get in eventually. Same with those louvers." Will pointed to rectangle grates imbedded in the walls. "They'll chew through those, too. And that door may have stopped the deer from following us in, but anything bigger or more determined—like that buck that killed Marshall—might be able to break it down. They can smell us in here, and the longer we stay, the riper we'll get. You know that delicious aroma when your neighbor is having a barbecue, and it makes you want to hop the fence? Well, someone pass the A.1. Steak Sauce, because that's how good we must smell to them. Plus there's no food or water. If we don't leave today, we're only going to grow weaker and weaker. We need to escape while we're strong enough to run fast."

"Escape to where?" Emma said, pointing at the window. "Look at the lodge. It's crawling with animals. I bet some have already gotten inside. Look at the lawn! If you think—"

"We're not going to the lodge," Will said. "We're going to the river."

(Sung to the tune of "Home on the Range")

Camp, camp on the Dray,
Where the deer and the porcupine prey.
They run in a herd, all sick, fanged, and furred.
We're inside, and that's where we'll stay.

THE RIVER. As soon as he heard Will's plan, Heath knew he was right. It was the only logical course of action. But going to the Dray River meant leaving the livery, and the animals were out there, waiting for them to emerge. Waiting to kill every last one of them. And yet he knew there was no other choice if they wanted to survive.

"Will's right," Heath said. "We have to get into the water."

Floaties snorted. "Are you sure you and Will don't have rabies, too? Because that's the craziest thing I've ever heard."

"Forget it," Emma said. "We're staying inside this building until help comes. Right, Emily?"

Emily stayed quiet. Heath watched her shift uneasily in her equestrian boots. She looked conflicted. He wondered if she'd choose to stay with Emma in the livery, or follow Will and him down the sloping lawn, across the sliver of stony beach, and into the Dray River. He doubted she would leave her twin, so his task would be to convince Emma and the others that while leaving the livery would be incredibly dangerous, staying meant certain death.

"We know the animals are literally scared to death of water—big time hydrophobia. I don't think they'll follow us into the river," Heath campaigned.

"It's a hundred yards or more to the Dray," Sylvester said. "Even with a head start, do you really think you can outrun"—he jabbed a thumb toward the window—"*them?*" Two deer ran past, bounding on powerful legs.

"We'll wait for the deer to shove off," said Will. "In a hard sprint humans can outrun squirrels, rats, raccoons . . . most of what's out there."

"Most? You're not really selling your plan here, dude," said Dunbar.

Floaties had a good question: "How can you be sure all of the animals have hyrdo—hydra—?"

"Hydrophobia," Heath repeated. "Think about it. Water killed Barkly."

"*And* the porcupine that attacked Heath and me," Cricket added. Heath thought Cricket looked extra pink and sweaty, but it was stiflingly hot inside the livery, so he chalked it up to the heat. He was feeling peaked himself, but there was no mystery there. He thought briefly about his vial of Oxy-Contin back in his cabin, rolled up in his socks and tucked away under his cot. It may as well have been on the moon.

"What porcupine?" Emily asked.

"It doesn't matter," Will said, his patience wearing paper-thin. "To be honest, I don't care what any of you do. You can stay here like flies in a spiderweb, or you can make a break for the river. I'm going."

"Right now? This minute?" Dunbar asked. "Shouldn't you wait? The animals—"

"Are focused on the main lodge for now," Will said.

"Not all of them," Emma said, raising her face to the ceiling. "Not them." Since entering the building they'd heard a faint but steady scraping noise on the roof above. Heath noticed that it seemed more concentrated directly above the vent pipes, and he knew Will was right about the squirrels chewing away at the lead. They were gnawing their way inside. Squirrels were fast and agile. If even one got into the livery, it would be hard to prevent it from biting someone. And once one got through, a lot more would follow. They'd *die* here.

"Let's say we *do* make it to the river," Sylvester said. "Then what?"

Will had thought this through. "The river runs toward town, roughly five miles south. We'll stay in the water and make our way there."

"Oh, that's all, huh?" Floaties sneered. "A leisurely five-mile swim to Granite Falls?"

"The Dray isn't like the Skagit," Will said, referring to the wide, deep river that cut through the Cascades and drained out in Puget Sound. "It's shallow except in a few spots—barely more than a stream. I think we'll be able to wade most of the way."

Floaties swung his head from side to side. His fear of drowning had earned him his nickname. He'd be the toughest one to convince. "The virus will kill them all off eventually, right? A couple days, tops? We'll just wait them out. I can go a couple days without water. Besides, even if the squirrels do get through, I'd rather take my chances with them than the wolves out there."

"You seriously don't get it." Will ran his hand through his thick hair, tugging it at the top. "It doesn't matter if you're bitten by a chipmunk or a grizzly bear. Either way you're dead. Size means nothing."

"A pip-squeak like you *would* say that!" Floaties still held a grudge against Will from the incident at the picnic pavilion and wasn't happy about being challenged. Like most bullies, he immediately flaunted his size, thinking this would shut Will up.

Will wasn't the least bit intimidated by his puffing. "Aren't you listening? The squirrels will get inside the livery. Then what will you do, tough guy?"

"Let him stay in the livery if he wants," muttered an unassuming Asian kid named Theo. Heath knew the boy's name because they'd shared a model rocket kit at the craft hut. Theo was a quiet one. The only time he'd said a word was to ask Heath to pass the glue. The kid sure picked a fine time to speak up.

Floaties was growing more agitated with Will by the second. "What are you getting all up in my face for? Back off, Snow White, or I'll—"

"I'll tell you what you'll do, you stupid lump!" Will cut him off. "*You'll die.* Just like anyone else left in this building when the squirrels finish chewing through the pipes!"

Heath stepped between them and defused what would have been the second fight since they'd arrived ten minutes ago. "Look, we can't wait the animals out. Maybe if this was regular rabies, they would go away and die, but we don't know enough about this new strain to say. This is . . . I don't know . . . Rabies X."

"That's a stupid name," said Elliot Knowles from the Cardinal Cabin. "Let's call it the Grim Reaper, since it instantly kills anyone it touches."

"That's too long," said Dunbar. "I say we call it the Flash. It takes you out in a flash, right?"

"That's not bad," said Floaties. "My dad works at a tattoo parlor. That's what they call tattoo art—flash. And the virus kinda looks like tattoos on the skin. It'd almost be pretty if it wasn't, ya know, deadly."

"Anyone got something better?" asked Dunbar.

"We're not naming a baby here!" Will looked as if his head might explode from their nonsense. "We'll call it the Flash and that's that. Executive decision."

No one objected.

"Like I was saying," Heath carried on, "it may take longer for the Flash to kill off the animals. Or never. The livery may feel safe now, but it won't be for long. I'm going with Will." And then he added, "I hope the rest of you will follow."

From the looks on their faces, Heath figured his plea would go unheeded. He would have to try again—

"I'm going, too," Emily whispered. She gently took hold of Emma's elbow, a gesture that was meant as a sisterly shock absorber.

Emma yanked her arm free and faced her twin. Her expression was a blend of fear and fury. "What? No! You are NOT leaving this building, Em!"

Calmly, Emily said, "Let's talk."

The twins left the window and disappeared behind the canoe racks. It reminded Heath of when a jury retires to their chambers to decide a verdict on a court case. He knew that the Ems' decision would be influential, one way or the other, especially weighty with the boys. He was familiar enough with Cricket and Dunbar to know that if the Ems decided to head for the river, they'd probably be shamed into going, too, and that was what he was desperately hoping for. Convincing a group to do something crazy was a bit like a house of cards. If enough cards fell, the rest of the house would fall, too. This time saving lives wasn't going to be as simple as straggling behind and letting the wolves take him in place of the others. That would have been a passive solution. This was different. Getting everyone to the river would require more effort on his part. If he had to get tough, then he would. Their lives depended on it.

There was no further discussion until Em and Em returned. Emma looked livid, but she stood close to Emily in a show of unity. "We're going to the river," she announced bitterly.

The house of cards fell. Dunbar, Cricket, Sylvester, and a few others agreed to go, and once there was a majority, most of the holdouts surrendered to Will's plan, too. Even Floaties caved to peer pressure, but only after he'd found a life jacket left behind in one of the canoes that fit him comfortably.

"Okay, let's get prepared." Will asked Theo to help him with something and Theo followed him.

Heath heard sniffling and motioned to Dunbar. They tracked the crying to a little girl who was standing alone, half-hiding behind one of the storage racks. She was wearing a pink strappy shirt with a smiling rainbow on the front. The scratch on her cheek and grass stains on her knees and shorts suggested she'd already survived a close call.

"What's your name?" Heath asked, bending to her height and smiling bravely.

"Molly," she said so quietly he thought she'd called him *mommy* until he'd processed it for a second.

"Hi, Molly. I'm Heath, and this is Dunbar."

"I can't go out there," she sniffled. "Don't make me go out there."

"You have to come, too, Molly," Heath insisted, trying to sound as grown-up as possible. "We won't let anything bad happen."

Dunbar frowned. "Hey, weren't you one of the Chickadees who soaked me with the water balloons?"

"Not now, Dunbar," Heath said, elbowing him in the ribs. "Molly, everything is going to be fine. Do you believe me?"

She shook her head.

Heath tried again, this time with a story. "Last year I had to take a home economics class at school. It was okay, but I had to learn how to do stuff I didn't like that much, like sewing and baking cakes. Girly stuff, you know? Can you imagine me in an apron?"

She smiled a little, so Heath guessed she could.

"Yeah, it was kinda funny, I suppose. Anyway, my teacher, Mrs. Faygen, gave my class this really weird assignment on the first day. She paired us all up, one boy and one girl. Then she brought out a tray of egg cartons and handed each couple an egg. It was supposed to represent a baby, I guess. She said it was our job to keep the egg from cracking or breaking the whole semester and if we failed—if our egg broke—then we'd drop a whole letter grade. I really didn't like the girl I was paired up with. She was awful. Do you know what happened to our egg?"

"You dropped it?" Molly sniffed then wiped the tears from her eyes.

"You mixed it into a cake and didn't tell her until after she ate it?" Dunbar guessed. "That's what I would have done."

"Nope and nope," Heath replied. "That girl and I put our differences aside and worked together. At the end of the semester our egg was one of the only ones without a single scratch on it."

"Oh," she said.

"So guess what, Molly. I'm pairing up with Dunbar here, who I don't always like that much—"

"Hey!" Dunbar huffed.

"—and you're gonna be our little egg. Our little project. No matter what happens, we will *not* let anything hurt you. We will get you to the river without a single crack in your shell. Okay?"

This time Molly nodded. Heath took her by the hand and led her back to the others with Dunbar in tow. Dunbar whispered in his ear, "Good job, dude."

They found Will and Theo dragging a huge box labeled PARTY SUPPLIES into the midst of the group. When Will opened it, they saw it was stuffed with clear plastic bags of colorful items: red, white, and blue balloons; rolls of streamers; paper plates with pictures of fireworks on them; boxes of sparklers; and several cartons of noisemakers—mostly stuff for the big Fourth of July picnic, although there was some Happy Birthday favors, too. Will passed out noisemakers, one at a time, to everyone. "Don't use them until we're outside and running."

"What are we supposed to do with these?" Sylvester asked, studying the metal toy in his palm with a doubtful eye.

"Use them," said Will. "Rabid animals are terrified of loud noises. They'll be startled—afraid to approach at first. These will increase our chances of making it to the river."

Heath had never heard that before, but it made sense.

Will rummaged through the bag for a few seconds, then handed Heath a triangle-shaped noisemaker with the words *Star-Spangled Banger* embossed on the side. "Looks like a good one," he said, then moved on down the line. Others got cone-shaped horns, metal poppers, or air-horn whistles.

Will took the last metal popper and scanned the group. "We'll go in pairs—the doorway is too narrow for anything more. That's ten pairs, and I'll take the rear spot alone. As soon as you get out the door, start making noise and don't let up until you're safely in the river. And don't hesitate in the doorway. You'll block the others behind you and give the squirrels on the roof an opportunity. Just get out the door, and don't stop running until you reach the river. Is everyone ready?"

They were ready as they'd ever be.

Em and Em stepped to the door, starting the line.

Heath found Molly an athletic-looking partner close to the head of the line. "Dunbar and I will be watching you," he promised. "Not a crack." She seemed fairly calm when he left her.

A bolt of pain shot up Heath's back, and he thought again about the vial of pills he was leaving behind. One problem at a time, he decided, then shuffled into the middle of the line beside Dunbar, directly behind Sylvester and Cricket. Heath glanced at his partner. Dunbar covered his mouth with his hand as if he was going to throw up.

"You better not," Heath warned. "I don't think Sylvester would appreciate a quiver full of puke."

"I'm not a good runner," Dunbar moaned, as if Heath couldn't tell at a glance.

"Stay close to me. We'll stick together."

Dunbar smiled weakly. "Thanks."

Three kids refused to leave the livery—two girls and a boy that Heath didn't know well—and even when Heath pointed out the tinny scratching sound of tiny teeth against metal, they still wouldn't budge. They were huddled together off to the side, looking shell-shocked by the others' decision to leave. Heath had never felt so guilty in his life. He'd failed them. But he had Molly to think about now. His little egg. And Dunbar, his big egg. Twenty-one campers would leave the livery together with the hope of reaching the river before the animals reached them.

Will slid the dead bolt back on the livery door and wrapped his hand around the knob.

He turned to the group and slowly counted.

"One . . .

"Two . . ."

He flung the door open wide.

"THREE!"

We're running down to the river, whee!
We left behind the livery!
The grass is all a-quivery!
We'll run real fast and live 'r be . . .
Killed! We'll live 'r be killed!

ALTHOUGH THEY'D BEEN in the dim livery for less than half an hour, the comparative brightness of the sun's light was jarring. Heath forced himself into a careful trot until his eyes adjusted. When they did, the first things he saw were the wolves.

No one had spied them through the window as they were over by the cabins, obscured by bushes. But Heath saw the pack now, charging down the hill, heading straight toward them, an avalanche of fur and fangs.

Heath realized they'd made a terrible mistake. He gripped Dunbar by the arm, spurring his friend forward into a sprint. "Run!" he ordered. He heard the door of the livery slam shut behind them.

The group of twenty-one campers stampeded across the sloping lawn toward the Dray River, blaring their noise-makers like a hopelessly bad marching band that had been swept out of a parade and dropped into a marathon. They hooted, hollered, and made as much noise as possible in the hope that the racket would deter the wolves and other animals from giving close chase.

Heath went as fast as his promise to Dunbar would allow him to. When two pairs of campers overtook them from behind, he pleaded, "Run faster, Dunbar." Not that it helped. With his fruit-shaped body parts, Dunbar wasn't built for speed. But being last meant being the choice target of the wolves, and Heath couldn't allow that to happen. If it was the last thing he was meant to do in life, he was determined to escort Dunbar safely to the river.

He looked for Molly, too. She was up ahead, doing fine, faster than he'd thought she'd be. She was staying tight to her partner, which was a relief. In the sunlight her hair was fiery red, which made her easy to keep track of.

The Dray was in Heath's sights the entire time, but it seemed farther away than he'd expected, a thin green ribbon sandwiched between two gray strips of pebbled shore. Focus on the ribbon, he told himself, the same as he would during a track race at school. The ribbon was waiting at the finish line. The ribbon was the prize.

There was movement all around, brown, gray, black, and ruddy shapes in the grass, traveling rapidly in the same direction as the runners. Rushing alongside of them, but also closing in on them, at an angle. Heath knew what those shapes were but refused to take his focus off the ribbon.

Sylvester was firing arrows on the run and amazingly finding his marks, even the little targets, like squirrels. But there were so many animals and only one Sylvester.

The first creature to reach the campers was a mangy raccoon, but it came at them head on, not from the side. It had been hiding downhill between the runners and the river, obscured by a thicket of grass that was too close to a big rock to be mowed. It jumped out, its mouth dripping with a lather of saliva, its fur so grimy with dirt that its whole face looked black, not just the mask around its eyes. It scurried up the hill like a cruise missile on a course toward the twins, who were still in the lead, running so closely together they looked conjoined. Their twin connection worked against them—they seemed unwilling to separate and go around the animal, even though they stood a better chance of getting past it by confusing it with two distinct targets. Heath remembered from a nature show about raccoons that they were great at climbing but terrible jumpers, barely able to get their fat bodies more than a foot off the ground.

"Jump over it!" Heath yelled to Em and Em as loud as he could, but he could hardly hear his own voice over the clamor.

They heard him. The twins leapt high, hurdling over the raccoon. It made a feeble swipe at them but never left the ground. The closest runners behind them were the girls who'd been fighting in the livery. In less than thirty minutes they'd made up and declared themselves BFFs, choosing to run as a pair. They didn't see the raccoon until they were right on top of it. The girl on the right hammered it with her shin, knocking the raccoon onto its back. Still, it managed to clamp its teeth firmly into her ankle. The Flash exploded up her leg, disappeared beneath her one-piece swimsuit, then reappeared again, snaking its way across her back. She collapsed in a heap onto the lawn. Her noisemaker slipped away from the girl, both of them silenced for good. The BFF stopped and ran back to help. She paid for her compassion with a bite from a rat that was lurking unseen in the grass. The Flash claimed her, too.

Heath's brain was on overload, firing off commands to his limbs, driving him on through the death and chaos around him. More runners passed by, and he realized he and Dunbar were quickly falling to the back of the line. The ribbon is the prize—he repeated the mantra over in his mind. It helped that the ribbon was growing wider with every passing second. Heath's heart was pounding so fast he could feel it reverberating inside of his rib cage. Beside him, Dunbar was barreling along; swinging his arms in an awkward windmill style that Heath feared would unbalance the boy and send him toppling forward.

The last pair of runners behind them rocketed by. That's it, then, Heath thought. We're the stragglers.

Suddenly there was movement to his right. Something running silently at his heels. He braced himself, waiting to feel the sharp sting of canine teeth sinking into his flesh.

But it wasn't a wolf. It was Will. Heath had forgotten that Will was bringing up the rear alone.

Will nodded toward Dunbar and said something, but

even though Heath was less than three feet away he couldn't hear him. He remembered that hearing loss can occur when an animal is chased by a predator. It's a physical response that actually helps it to focus better. Everything gets tuned out, except for the escape route. None of that mattered though; Heath didn't need to hear Will's words. They were easy enough to read in his eyes.

Leave him behind.

Will's expression said even more. *The wolves are coming. They're going to kill you. Dunbar is out of shape. That's his fault, not yours. Save yourself.*

It was all true. Dunbar had no one to blame but himself for being fifty pounds heavy. *Who puts butter on Pop-Tarts?* But Heath had promised.

"I'm his friend," Heath mouthed slowly so Will could read his lips.

Will shot Heath a pitying look that said, *It's your funeral,* then he picked up speed and an instant later, Heath was staring at the back of Will's head. Heath's instinct told him to catch up. To leave Dunbar behind. But he couldn't. His promise tethered him to the slowest runner in the group, which meant he was tethered to the wolves.

Heath looked down at the ground. Down at the blurring lawn. Down at his chugging feet chewing away at the lime green grass. They almost seemed separate from him, like they belonged to someone else. He recognized his aqua-shoes—the black ones with the mesh across the top and the blue metallic stripe on the sides. He couldn't run in them as fast as he could in his tennis shoes, but he was still fast enough to outrun Dunbar, not that he would. If he made it to the water, his shoes would give him traction on the slippery rocks paving the riverbed.

If.

He allowed himself a glance over his shoulders. The wolves were closer, but there was still a sizable gap between them. By their choice, Heath knew. Wolves didn't run at full speed until they got as close to their prey as they could. Then, in the last few seconds, they'd hit the gas. It's how they tested their prey. Or how they played with their food, depending on how you looked at it.

A squirrel bit one of the last kids to pass them. The boy's body speared the ground, then kept tobogganing on down the hill. The lawn began to slope sharply the closer they got to the river. They'd have to be careful or risk slipping in the grass and wiping out.

Another person fell. Kids were dying all around them. Animals were cutting them off, racing in from the sides. Three big deer barreled into a pair of runners and carried them out of Heath's line of sight. He tried to shout a warning, but at that moment pain like electricity shot up his spine, then drilled into the base of his neck. It was horrible—the worst since he'd arrived at camp. The worst ever, which was saying something, because Heath was no stranger to pain.

He stumbled. His fingertips grazed blades of grass, but he didn't fall. He straightened a bit but stumbled again. This time his momentum shifted beyond his feet, and he lost his balance completely. But he *still* didn't fall. Dunbar caught him and leveraged Heath back into control of his body. He'd somehow kept them running. Kept them moving forward to the river. His friend, Dunbar, whom Will had tempted him to abandon.

But Heath was still in agony. The pain felt like a blade slicing up through his back, chewing nerve endings and twisting flesh. His vision blurred. The muscles in his neck tightened like wire. Why now? he asked the universe.

His mother's voice echoed in response, a faded memory from years ago. *Don't give up, Heath. You're almost there. Be strong.*

He heard his father, too. *You can beat this, son. But you have to give everything you have. Don't quit on yourself.*

It was working. Recalling his parents' encouraging words was like squirting drops of oil over his pain-rusted joints.

But then he heard another voice, as fresh as wet paint, overheard and unintended for his ears. *I won't mislead you. Heath's chances this time are slim.*

SHUT UP! he thundered in his head. *Shut up and let me try!*

He pushed himself harder, running as if the devil was chasing him instead of just rabid wolves.

As quickly as the pain had arrived, it passed. Heath gasped in relief. He could focus again. His first thought was of his noisemaker. He'd been so shaken by the sight of the wolves that he totally forgot he had it. He flicked the metal tab that should have started it up, but no sound came out. He tried again, but nothing. It was busted! He flung it away. Maybe that was for the best—he didn't think the noisemakers were keeping the animals at bay. In fact, it almost seemed as if they were targeting the loudest runners, but that wasn't right. Could Will have been wrong about that?

Heath spied Will somewhere toward the head of the group. His lean, wiry frame had carried him past most of the others. He was running silently, his hands empty. He wasn't making a sound.

Not a sound.

"Dunbar!" he hollered. "Drop the noisemaker! Toss it right now!"

"What? But Will said—!"

"He tricked us! Get rid of it!"

Dunbar flung his noisemaker away. It smashed to bits against the side of a rock, emitting a final brassy note in dying protest.

In the next breath Heath heard low, throaty growls behind them. The wolves had reached them.

He saw a shaggy gray body pull up beside him. A flash of orange—a lupine eye. Yellow, jagged teeth jutting from hot-pink gums. Foamy saliva spilling from snapping jaws. Fur the color of thunderclouds. The wolf was right there. Heath could have reached out and touched it.

He made a decision. He would make a grab for the leader. The mother. Quilt Face. He'd try to get his arms around her neck and take her to the ground. Maybe the fallen wolf, entwined with his dead body, would draw the rest of the pack, if only for a few seconds. He could give Dunbar a chance to get away. He reasoned it out. Even if he survived . . . made it home to Port Townsend . . . how long did he have, anyway? Five or six months at the most? What were his six months compared to the sixty years he could give Dunbar if he made this sacrifice? This is it then, he thought. At least it would be quick. A better death than—

Quilt Face passed them.

Then another wolf—the big one that won the tug-of-war over Rich's body—ran by on Dunbar's side. Then another. The two boys were running in the center of the pack, but were safe, like being in the eye of a hurricane. When the last wolf raced by, Heath and Dunbar glanced over at each other, a shared moment of relief and disbelief.

The next pair of runners up the line wasn't so lucky. Quilt Face tore into one of the girls' arms. The one swinging her noisemaker. Two more wolves dragged her partner to the grass, quickly silencing his shrill screams.

Dunbar and Heath ran a wide arc around them. The wolves didn't follow. Even sick, the pack was hunting in their established method. They'd taken their kill for now.

Heath glanced back over his shoulder, which is why he didn't see—

"Onyx!" Dunbar screamed. "Look out, Heath!"

There was a flash of black. Heath had a fraction of an instant to recognize Onyx's massive body. The horse had slipped out of his bridle, freeing himself from the sapling, and was now on top of Heath, stomping the ground about his head and feet, gouging up thick divots of grass with his metal shoes. Heath tucked his knees up to present a smaller target as he rolled between Onyx's legs and down the sharply steepening hill. Onyx chased him, rearing up, then slamming his front hooves down, narrowly missing each chance to crush Heath's skull like an egg. When the horse caught Heath's shirt in his teeth, Heath got a good look at those powerful nostrils Emma had bragged about. He thumped the horse's snout with his fist and Onyx jerked away, ripping the shirt off Heath's body as if it were paper.

Heath kept rolling. Everything was happening so fast; the world was a kaleidoscope of images. He thought he saw Dunbar reaching out for him, but his friend was quickly replaced by a bubble—Onyx's glassy black eye. The eye became a horseshoe. Then Heath was looking at his own feet. Then a swatch of offensively blue sky.

Heath rolled to a stop and his view resolved into layers of gray rocks. Rocks that had been smoothed and scrubbed over thousands of years by flowing water. He was lying facedown on the pebbled shore of the ribbon.

No, not the ribbon. *The river.* He'd made it to the shore of the river.

He could hear the water lapping at the rocks just a few yards away.

He began to crawl toward the sound. Off to his right, a squirrel came at him, but an arrow tore through its side and cleared it away. Sylvester.

Keep going. Just a few more yards to the safety of the water.

The rocks had been baking in the summer heat all morning. They burned his bare chest and belly.

Just a few more feet.

A shadow fell over him. Something was looming directly above him, eclipsing the sun. Something big.

Just a few more inches.

He reached out to the water.

Just a few more . . .

There is a sly spider,
  who knows how to weave,
The stickiest strings that he has
  up his sleeve.
His web is stretched taut,
  and coated with lies,
But who will get caught?
  The spider or the flies?

"GET UP!" a voice boomed, then muscular arms hooked under Heath from above and lifted him off the rocks. It wasn't an animal that had him. It was Floaties.

"Easy, dude!" Cricket's scrappy tone was unmistakable. "You're gonna tear his arms off!"

Heath was relieved to hear he still had both arms, because at the moment he couldn't feel them. He was totally numb from head to toe, in complete shock. Onyx hadn't killed him, but the camp's horse had knocked him loopy. His vision was messed up. He could hear the others and knew they were trying to help him, but everything was a blur.

"Get back! Leave him alone! Shoo! Get out of here!" Several voices overlapped. He heard splashing and caught a glimpse of Sylvester and Cricket. Theo too. They were shin-deep in the river, shoveling water onto the shore with cupped hands. It registered with Heath that they were trying to keep the animals at bay while Floaties dragged his limp body into the Dray.

"Hurry! Get him in the water." Emily sounded distraught over him. That's nice, he thought dizzily.

Emma said, "I've got his legs," and now Heath was being carried facedown across the shore. He felt like he was floating through air. There was a ringing noise in his ears, and he couldn't lift his head.

"Easy, easy . . ." Good old Dunbar. Heath's hero. Still by his side.

The sun-bleached rocks got darker, wetter. Then they disappeared beneath the water. He was in the river.

"Keep coming." Emily's voice directed them away from the danger.

"Okay, this is deep enough. Set his legs down," ordered Floaties.

Water flooded Heath's bathing suit. It felt cool against his hot, sweaty skin. The river was up to his waist. He saw a smatter of silver bullets darting away. Trout fry, his mind processed. At least fish are still afraid of us.

"We've got him," Cricket said, and Heath felt more hands land on his body.

". . . can't believe he survived that."

". . . luckier than Quinn."

". . . right under the horse."

Heath tried to lift his head again, and this time he was somewhat successful. His vision was still poor but improving by the second. He could make out the survivors in the water, fanned out around him, all of them except for Will, who was observing the rescue from the center of the river. They'd left the livery as twenty-one. Less than half made it to the Dray: Will, Dunbar, Cricket, Floaties, Em and Em, Sylvester, Theo—and, there she was, his little egg, Molly.

Ten kids alive out of twenty-one. It had been a massacre.

But Will was right; the water was a safety zone. The animals hadn't followed them into the river, although several were tepidly stepping out onto the rocks, spreading out to make room for more. They kept their distance from the river, judging the reach of danger by the location of the dead animals that had been splashed during Heath's rescue. Quilt Face paced back and forth, never taking her eyes off of Heath. It was as if she regretted letting him go back on the lawn. A German shepherd, probably a hiker's companion, was barking ceaselessly, mingling with the wolves like it was born to the pack. Its muzzle was stained red. The blood of its former master? Deer stepped fearlessly into the midst of killers. Smaller mammals—voles, squirrels, pikas, and forest rats—scurried across the rocks. The bigger animals sometimes stepped on them, ignorant of their presence. Every creature on the shore was fixated on the humans in the river. Watching and waiting for their chance to pounce.

"Have you got Heath?" Dunbar asked, the concern of a true friend in his voice. "Yes? Good."

Through double vision Heath watched two Dunbars wade quickly away through the water, elbows high, in Will's direction. When he reached him, Dunbar tossed a wild punch at Will. Will was startled, but as the quicker of the two boys, he managed to duck just as Dunbar's fist whiffed over his head. Dunbar lost his balance and fell forward into the water, resurfacing as Will dove on top of him and started to pummel his back and head. Every time Dunbar lifted his face and gasped for air, Will would plunge him down again.

"What's your problem, idiot?" Will snarled, dunking and punching. "If you want to die so badly, then you should have stayed in the livery!"

"Stop it!" Emily shouted. Molly was crying her eyes out. Theo was just standing there in shock, watching it all unfold.

Cricket, however, sprung into action. He half waded, half swam toward the fight. "Get off of him! He's gonna drown!"

"Help him . . . hurry," Heath croaked, still disoriented. Sylvester and Floaties passed Heath off to the Ems and jogged through the water after Cricket.

"Wait for us, stupid," Floaties called after him. He was so tall that his knees alternately broke the surface of the water as he ran.

When the three boys reached Will, he shoved Dunbar at them and escaped with a backstroke in the direction of the opposite shore. "He attacked me!" he claimed, pointing at Dunbar. "You all saw him. He's crazy!"

Sylvester yanked Dunbar above the waterline. Dunbar coughed a fit while Cricket asked repeatedly if he was okay.

Leaning on Em and Em for support, Heath managed to stand up. There was a shooting pain in his shoulder where he'd slammed against a rock during his tumble down the hill and his hand ached fiercely. When he looked at his upturned palm he saw a partial imprint of Onyx's horseshoe. He ran his other hand over the contour of his head, inspecting for divots like the one Mr. Soucandi had. His skull seemed solid. He'd survived the run in one piece, no thanks to Will.

"Dunbar's not crazy," Heath said. He slipped free of the twins, allowing the buoyancy of the water to act as a crutch. "Will set us up."

"What do you mean, Heath?" Emma asked, her eyes darting between the accuser and the accused.

"You're a liar!" Will snarled at Heath.

"Am I? You left your noisemaker in the livery! Admit it!"

"Why would he do that?" Floaties asked, furrowing his heavy brow as he strained to understand. "The noisemakers worked, right? They kept the animals off us."

"You think?" Heath said. "Look around, man! Or did you not notice that the group was cut in half? How about a head count now, Will? We left the livery with twenty-one. Ten of us made it to the river. The rest are dead. Dead! The only thing the noisemakers did was drive the animals even crazier. They went straight for the loudest of us."

Floaties still hadn't connected the dots. "Why would—?"

"Think, you guys!" Dunbar sputtered. "He did it so the

animals would attack us and not himself." He went into another coughing fit. He'd swallowed a lot of water.

"That's stupid." Will slapped the surface of the river sending spray into Dunbar's face. Dunbar, momentarily blinded, attempted to splash him back but missed by a mile.

"Where's your noisemaker, Will?" Emma demanded to know.

"I dropped it," he answered quickly.

"In the livery?" Emma asked.

"No, halfway to the river. Accidentally. I don't have to defend myself to any of you."

"You never had it," Dunbar insisted. "You were the last one out the door, so nobody noticed. You left yours behind; admit it."

"I don't get it." Floaties was still struggling to grasp the idea that Will may have betrayed them. "Are you saying he tried to kill us?"

"Not exactly," Heath said. "I'm saying he tried to save himself, and the best way to do that was by making the rest of us juicier targets. The animals weren't afraid of loud noises. After what just happened, it's pretty obvious they were drawn to them. When I saw that Will didn't have a noisemaker, I made Dunbar dump his. A pack of wolves ran right by us and bit the two kids ahead of us that still had theirs."

Emily was dumbfounded. "They ran past you?"

"Yeah, they did," Heath said, keeping his eyes on Will. "This whole thing was one of your chess moves, right, Stringer? Strategy to save your life at our expense?"

"Chess moves? What's he talking about, Will?" asked Sylvester.

"Nothing. You can't prove any of that, Heath," Will said, not in an offended way; it was more like a challenge.

Floaties plowed through the river toward Will. "He doesn't have to. I'll just drown you right now. We'll tell everyone the chipmunks did it."

Will swam a few yards farther out. "It's deep here, Floaties," he warned. "Come drown me if you can. I bet I can get that life jacket off you before I run out of air."

Floaties stopped in his tracks. He looked back at the group, helpless.

"Well, I can swim just fine," Emma said, wading out toward Will. "*I'll* drown him."

"You can't," Heath said.

"Sure I can. Watch me."

Heath grabbed her arm. "No, that's not what I mean. I mean *we need him*."

Emma was furious. "To do what? Offer us up as bait again? That's not gonna happen!"

He wouldn't let her go. "Emma, I hate to say this, but we'd be trapped in the lodge if we hadn't followed Will. We trusted his instincts and were smart to do so. And I think he was right about leaving the livery, too."

"How do you know?" Emma demanded. "Maybe those three kids we left behind in there'll be the only ones to survive this nightmare. Like a dozen kids are already dead because of Will. . . ."

"Em," Heath said in a soothing voice, "some of those animals were coming after us no matter what. Will's trick may have changed the outcome somewhat—maybe more people would have survived . . . maybe different ones would have died, like me and Dunbar, probably, but no one saw the wolves through the window. No one knew Onyx would free himself from the tree or that the raccoon would be hiding in the grass. You can't predict that stuff. And, yeah, I wouldn't trust Stringer as far as I can throw him, but I'd still rather be here in the river than in the livery or the lodge. Will was right—the animals *didn't* follow us into the water. We have a chance now as long as we stay in the river. We may not like it, but we have that chance because of him, even if he is a dangerous lunatic."

Emma stopped struggling against Heath's grip, but her body was still tense and there was wrath in her eyes. "How do you know he won't try to sacrifice us to save his own neck again?"

Heath thought for a moment. It was a fair question. He turned to Will. "Okay, how about this? If you try anything, anything at all, that results in one of us getting hurt or worse, we'll *all* drown you."

Will stared defiantly at Heath from across the slowly wandering water. His lips parted into a hint of a goading smile that said, *You can try.*

It was settled. At Heath's insistence, Will would be accepted as part of their group as they made their way downriver toward Granite Falls. Almost immediately after winning the argument, Heath wondered if he'd made a huge mistake. He doubted Will would be inclined to help them, and only after they'd left the shore of Camp Harmony behind them did he consider the possibility that the kid might even go out of his way to make things worse. There was something inside of Will that had troubled Heath from day one. A calculating ruthlessness. It was closer to the surface now, maybe even aimed at Heath and the others, like a loaded gun. He had a sick feeling in his gut that Will had a whole box of dirty tricks he'd use to survive, and so far they'd only blown the dust off the lid.

With the exception of Will, the campers clustered together to take one last look up the sloping lawn at the main lodge.

"There's so many of them." Sylvester could only be referring to the hundreds of squirrels that were swarming the cedar shake roof from soffit to peak.

"They're horrible," Emily said, her voice trembling.

"Do you guys think they'll get inside?" Cricket asked.

"Maybe not." Heath tried to sound hopeful, but in his heart he knew it was only a matter of time. He could see little splinters of wood raining over the side of the building and down into the bushes rimming the lodge below. The squirrels were tearing away at the roof shakes bit by bit. Uncle Bill had led a hundred campers into the building. Heath sickeningly sensed they'd never get out alive. It wasn't a good idea to stand around and watch the carnage unfold. "Let's get going," he prodded.

"Good idea," said Sylvester, slinging his bow over his shoulder. It came to rest at an angle across his back. "Everyone follow me."

This didn't sit well with Emma. "What, suddenly you're the boss? Now that we're out of danger? If I remember right, you didn't want the job."

"Look, I was just a little freaked out, that's all. We all were. I'm okay now. You saw how many animals I killed on the run."

"Yeah, you were awesome, Robin Hood." Emma snorted. "Too bad you didn't have the guts to lead when it mattered. If we'd waited on you to step up, we'd still be in the livery watching you tremble in the corner!"

"Emma, let him take charge," Emily said calmly. "Who cares now that we're in the river?"

Heath agreed with *both* of the twins, not that it was important enough for him to say so.

Dunbar, still smarting from his beating, said, "I don't care who's in charge, as long as it's not Will."

"Wait, where *is* Will?" Emma asked, panning around.

The answer was fifty yards down the river, negotiating his way over a nest of tree branches. He wasn't moving at a pace to abandon them, but he wasn't waiting on them either. If they planned to take advantage of Will's survival instincts, their job was to keep up with *him*.

"Jerk," Emma huffed.

"Don't let him get under your skin, Em," Heath said, wading in Will's direction. "C'mon, you guys. It's a long way to Granite Falls."

* * *

When they'd traveled a quarter mile or so down the river and the group had spread out a bit, Cricket asked Heath a question privately. "What you said back there . . . do you honestly think anyone at camp will survive?"

Heath glanced back up the river. Although Camp Harmony was now obscured from view by a flank of pine trees soldierly lining the shore, he could see several tiny black specs in the sky gliding in a halo formation. They were directly above the spot he knew the camp to be, a dozen or more vultures arriving to the feast. He remembered that a group of flying vultures was called a kettle. He'd never understood that name until now as he watched them slowly stirring the air, waiting for the meal below to be ready. He shuddered.

"Let's just focus on getting the girls to town safely, okay?" Heath said. "They're depending on us." He knew this would steel Cricket's courage.

"Sure," Cricket agreed, straightening to his full height of four foot eight. "I can do that."

"I know you can." Heath clapped his friend on the back. Then he noticed that Cricket looked worse in the sunlight than he did under the livery's fluorescent bulbs. "Are you feeling okay?"

"Yeah . . . just a little tired. I've never run that fast in my life. I didn't think I'd make it. I almost got bit twice. Counting the porcupine, that's three near misses in one day. And it's still early."

Heath thought of something. "Lift your left heel for a sec, will you?"

Cricket raised his foot out of the water and held it close to his bottom like a flamingo. "Why?"

The porcupine quill was gone. It had probably shimmied loose on the lawn or was washed away when Cricket hit the water. He scanned the river surface for it—Marshall said porcupine quills float—but he guessed the current would have carried it out of sight by now. He eyeballed Cricket's heel. The skin around the puncture mark was an angry pink color, like a bee sting, but didn't look too bad. Better a quill in the foot than a bite somewhere else.

"Nothing," Heath said. "Just checking to see if you had anything on your feet." He really meant *in* your feet.

"Not all of us were lucky enough to be wearing aqua-shoes."

"Yeah, it's my lucky day," Heath said.

"Good thing they don't make them for horses," Cricket added, and both boys laughed halfheartedly. Still, it was nice. Joking made things feel a little sane again, even though everything else in their world had gone topsy-turvy.

"They'll kill us if they get the chance," Cricket muttered bleakly, stripping the conversation of humor. The boys observed the two dozen or more rabid animals keeping pace with them on the west bank. There were some new ones since they'd started their journey and one or two additions joined the bizarre menagerie every few minutes. There was a coyote now. Heath had never seen one in person before. It didn't look anything like the pathetic one that was always trying to kill the Road Runner on TV. Although smaller than the wolves, it was still fierce and capable, a born hunter. The rabies gave it a disheveled, sinister appearance, like a beast from a fairy tale. It growled like one, too. In fact, all of the animals were noisy, barking, snarling, and chattering so loudly that collectively they muffled the gurgling of the river's flow. Heath hoped that deprived of drinking water their throats would dry up soon.

"They look like a twisted version of those Bible paintings," Cricket said. "You know? The ones of what Heaven is supposed to look like, where the lions and sheep are hanging out like they're best buds? But in the paintings they look so clean and peaceful. Fluffy. Not like these animals. These are ugly. They hate us, don't they, Heath? I mean, they really, truly hate us."

Heath searched Quilt Face's eyes for the answer. Maybe he'd been spending too much time with Cricket, the bug enthusiast, but the wolf's black pupils reminded him of ancient insects frozen forever in hardened amber. There was something else there, too, equally disturbing, deep inside her eyes.

"Yeah, Cricket," Heath replied. "I think they do."

FOUNDER'S POEM
From the Cascades so majestic,
an emerald river flows.
Ambulant waters tug my heart;
its languid beckon grows.
Peaceful and meandering,
the Dray carries hope aloft.
Not north, to fight like salmon.
Its southern nudge so soft.

IF THEY DISCOUNTED the parade of deadly animals keeping pace with them on the shore and the dismal mood of the group, it was a beautiful afternoon. It was hot out, but the heat wasn't as oppressive as it had been back at camp. The air was fresh, cooled by the flowing Dray. Whenever Heath got too sweaty he just bent at the knees and dipped to his neck or reached down and splashed water in his face. In fact, there was little concerning the journey itself to complain about besides the purpose for it. Physically Heath was feeling pretty good. Except for a throbbing ache in his hand where Onyx stepped on him, the pain had subsided. He felt okay.

Even his spirit was healing, nursed by the view. He'd come to Camp Harmony for a taste of nature, and now he was gorging on the scenery. Purple mountains met cobalt sky. Flamboyantly colored rhododendron bushes, honeysuckle, and wild roses broke up the monotony of the forest's abiding green. The river itself was beautiful, a deep blue-green color. Flecks of sunlight sparked across the surface. With the exception of the little plumes of silt that clouded around his feet as he walked, the water was crystal clear. It was easy to spot the crayfish ambling across the riverbed, dragging its outgrown carapace behind, searching for the perfect rock to hide under while it finished molting. Tiny fish everywhere shimmered in the sunlight, reminding Heath of coins in a wishing well. As a bonus there were very few bugs, just random mosquitoes, and those seemed to prefer Dunbar anyway.

"It's your blue shirt," Cricket offered in explanation when Dunbar complained. "Mosquitoes love the color blue. Take your shirt off and they won't bother you as much."

"I'm fine," Dunbar grumbled, winced, then swatted the back of his neck. He hadn't gone shirtless in public once since camp started and wasn't about to start in the presence of Em and Em. "Stupid Jersey bombers! Man, I hate bugs."

Cricket wouldn't stand for this. "They're survivors, you know. There's one and a half billion of them for every one of us. Bugs lived through the asteroid that killed the dinosaurs."

"Not interested," Dunbar grumped. "I'm too worried about my own survival right now to care."

For the first mile or so the water's depth seemed to hover between thigh- and stomach-deep, no more, no less. At these levels it was always faster to wade than swim, but when the water crept up past their hips there was a natural tendency to wade slightly sideways to reduce the drag created by the pelvis. Heath noticed that Floaties became increasingly agitated as the water level approached the bottom hem of his life jacket. When this happened, Floaties unwisely let his body drift closer to the shore where the water was shallower but the danger of being bitten was greater.

"I guess I've got hydrophobia, too," Floaties said, trying to make light of his fear.

"No, you've got aquaphobia," Will corrected him, speaking for the first time since his unofficial trial when they entered the river. He was back within conversation distance from the others but still preferred to be a satellite to the group, staying on the periphery, safely out of Emma's reach.

"Who asked you?" Floaties grunted.

Dunbar's curiosity outweighed his anger toward Will. "What's the difference?"

"*Hydrophobia* is a term people use when talking about rabies," Will explained. "It's a fear of water itself. People with aquaphobia, like Floaties, are afraid of drowning in it."

Emily chimed in. "That makes sense, Floaties. You're fine being in the river as long as it's not too deep and you've got your . . . um . . . floaties on, right?"

Floaties thought about it. "I guess so. It's not too bad

right now. I don't know how to swim, obviously. Every time I tried to learn I'd have a major freak-out. Something in the back of my mind kept telling me I was gonna drown."

"Why? Did you fall through ice or get tossed around by waves at the beach as a kid?" Heath asked.

"Maybe," Floaties replied. "I dunno. But you're right. I don't want to die that way . . . by drowning. That'd be the worst."

"Does anyone know how deep the Dray gets?" Sylvester asked.

No one did.

"The only thing I know for sure," Will said, "is that the Dray that runs by Camp Harmony is the same Dray that runs by Granite Falls. What happens to the river between those two points, I have no idea. Just watch your feet. We don't need any sprained ankles slowing us down. And be respectful of the river. After falls, drowning is the leading cause of death outdoors."

"I'm not worried. We'll make it to Granite Falls," said Dunbar, always the optimist. "I've seen a ton of shows about people that get stuck in the wilderness, and they all managed to survive."

"Great. Any tips for us?" Emily asked.

"Er . . . I don't know," Dunbar admitted. "Actually, most of those people had to deal with things like dehydration, starvation, or frostbite. This is a little different."

"It's *a lot* different," Sylvester said. "We're surrounded by fresh water. We have a fair amount of shade. And its summer so I highly doubt we'll freeze to death. Plus I'm pretty sure *most of us* can go half a day without eating, right?"

Everyone looked at Dunbar.

"We'll see." He shrugged. "Why starve when we're surrounded by sushi? And didn't I see a lobster back there? It's like we're trapped in a seafood buffet."

"That was a crayfish," Heath chuckled.

Dunbar licked his lips and rubbed his belly theatrically. "Yum! Crayfish are just Cajun-style lobsters."

"You guys do realize how much nutrition is packed inside a single dragonfly, right?" Cricket asked. "And they're easy to catch, too. So are mayflies, but those are super delicate. Their wings will tear right off in your fingers."

Emma made a look of great disgust. "Stop being gross."

"I wasn't trying to be," mumbled Cricket, offended.

"I wish the camp didn't have a no–cell phone policy," said Dunbar. "We could sure use Google Maps right about now."

"Yeah," Emma agreed. "Plus, you know, we could call for help."

"Oh, yeah. My phone can do so many cool things, sometimes I forget I can use it to make calls."

"There's nothing to worry about. I'll get us there safely," Sylvester announced, keeping his dubious leadership fresh in their minds. Heath figured Sylvester was angling for some undue credit when they reached Granite Falls and the story of their harrowing ordeal came to the media's attention. He's welcome to it, Heath thought. The last thing Heath wanted to do was talk to reporters about what happened back at Camp Harmony. He knew the media would come from all over the country, ravenous for the story—it *was* pretty sensational. But Heath had already been swarmed once that day and once was enough to last him a lifetime. As far as he was concerned, the reporters could just go there and see for themselves. And they would go, and they'd be sorry for it. Heath knew there were only four things to worry about when people are lost in the wilderness, and fame wasn't one of them. Water, food, shelter, and morale. The first two were covered, the third not needed. He'd try to focus on keeping their morale up, even if he wasn't feeling too cheerful himself.

"We'll be at Granite Falls by dark. So the longest we'll have to be out here is"—Sylvester considered the positioning of the sun—"another six hours? Other than turning into giant prunes from the waist down, I don't think we have much to worry about. Except for . . ."

The group gazed over at the west bank in unison. The wolves were picking their paths across the shore carefully to avoid the sharp pieces of splintered shale and the broken bottles left behind by careless fishermen, yet somehow they seemed to keep their orange eyes glued to their prey in the river. Dollops of saliva would occasionally fall from their flexing jaws and plop on the rocks. They growled constantly. It was a subdued growl now, quieter, like the rumble of an engine idling. It had become the sound track of their journey toward town. The growling was punctuated occasionally by a whimper, always a reminder to Heath that the wolves were in horrible pain. So were the rest of the animals on the shore.

"I feel sorry for them," Heath said.

"Yeah, boohoo." Floaties rubbed invisible tears from his eyes. "You know who I feel sorry for? All of those dead kids back at camp, and the ones trapped in the main lodge, if they're not dead already, too."

"The animals are sick," Heath said. "The disease attacks their brains. It's not their fault. Do you have a dog at home?"

"Sure," Floaties said. "A sheltie named Corker. Good dog."

"Barkly was a good dog, too," Heath reminded him.

Floaties let that sink in. "Okay, I get it. I'll knock off the hating, but just to be clear, I'm rooting for us, not them."

"Know your enemy," Will said, only Heath wasn't sure who or what he was referring to. In Will's case, he guessed it could be just about everyone. And it didn't escape Heath's attention either that Theo glanced over at Floaties right after Will spoke.

The chatter picked up from there, but most of it came from a single source, Dunbar the Question King: "If a plant like the Venus flytrap ate meat from a rabid animal, would the plant get rabies, too? What would happen if a dolphin got the virus since they live in water? What about other animals? Would they die from fear of their own pee?"

That last question was pretty stupid, but it got Heath thinking. He doubted the animals following them would be urinating much since they were refusing to drink and replenish themselves. If the Flash was similar to regular rabies in that regard, the animals should start to slow down and eventually die of dehydration. Worst case scenario, they could try waiting them out in the river until then. Unlike their situation in the livery, they had plenty of fresh water, and probably food, provided they were willing to get a little creative. How long would it take to outlast them? A few days at the most? But he doubted it would come to that. They'd find help in Granite Falls.

When Dunbar asked if the group thought a camel would be afraid of its own hump, since it's really just a built-in water tank, Floaties reached his breaking point.

"Would you shut up already? Man, how many questions can one kid have inside of him?"

"Loads more," Dunbar promised.

"Yeeesh, being in the river with you is like being stuck next to the guy on the plane who talks to you the whole flight. The only way to get away from either of you is to jump out and die."

Heath hid a smile. Floaties may be a jerk, he thought, but the kid had a point.

"I don't know what your problem is," Dunbar said. "It's not like I'm asking *you* questions."

"That's because you already know my answers: shut up, shut up, and shut up."

"Figures." Dunbar sniffed. "I'm sure you've got a lot to hide."

"I know what you're trying to do," Floaties snorted. "Reverse psychopathy."

"Reverse psychology, you mean," Emily corrected.

"Whatever. I'm not falling for it. Go ahead and ask me a question."

Heath and Emily glanced at each other and tried not to laugh. Poor Floaties. Dunbar's reverse psychology seemed to have worked just fine.

"Okay." Dunbar thought for a moment. "This is what I want to know. Why would you be best buddies with a butt-munch like Thumper?"

"Dunbar!" Emma snapped. "That was a rude question!"

"What? Why?" asked Dunbar, turning pink.

"Seems like a reasonable question to me," Theo said with surprising resentment in his voice.

"You're not supposed to talk bad about someone who just"—Emily paused before finishing—"died."

"It's all right. I'll answer his stupid question." Floaties took a few seconds to assemble his response, then said, "I knew Thumper—wait, it's not right to call him that now that he's gone. His name was Renny. If we're gonna talk about him, we'll call him Renny, okay?"

The others agreed.

"I sort of knew Renny from back home. We weren't friends or anything growing up, but when we were both sent off to Camp Harmony that first summer years ago, he found out my dad was in jail, same as his. They were in for very different reasons. Mine robbed a liquor store. His dad got drunk and plowed his car through a school crosswalk. A bunch of kids died."

"That's horrible," Emily gasped.

Heath was stunned. Will knew why Renny's dad was in prison and had used that information against him like a choke chain earlier that afternoon. Now that Heath had the whole story he felt pretty low. He'd rather have been Thumper's runner all summer than take advantage of such a tragic situation. Was there any line Will wouldn't cross? He was afraid they'd eventually find out. Knowing how Will had used the information to curb Thumper was just more evidence for his case against Will and the noisemakers. He vowed to keep a close eye on him.

"It was bad," Floaties agreed. "Renny's dad got sober in prison, but the whole town hates him now. They hated Renny, too. I think people resented him for being alive when the kids his dad ran over weren't. Maybe they wished Renny'd died in their place. It wasn't fair, but that's the way a lot of people are. I guess they got their wish today."

"People can be so cruel," Emma said, her eyes brimming with tears.

"Yeah, they can be. Renny figured I'd relate to what he was going through." Floaties thought back. "I couldn't though, not really. It was different for my family. People forgave my dad. Some people in our church even petitioned for his early release. They wrote letters to the judge saying that he was basically a good guy who was desperate to keep food on the table, which was true. What Renny's dad did . . . people don't forget . . . or forgive. You're right, Dunbar. Renny wasn't a nice guy to most people, but that's because most people weren't nice to him."

"That's a sad story," Theo murmured. "But it doesn't

excuse the way you two went around camp making life miserable for the smaller kids who were too weak to fight back." Something about Floaties was drawing hostility like a magnet from Theo. Heath had a feeling he knew what it was, and it was probably the reason that he was staying as far away from Floaties as possible without going ashore.

"Leave him alone!" Emma said sharply. "You too, Dunbar! Whatever happened before today is history. We need to get along now. You asked the question and he answered. Let it go!"

"No, let them keep talking," Floaties told her. "The animals go for the noisy ones first, remember?"

"Har, har. Okay, then," Dunbar said. "I'll get off your case. But I have one more question. For all of you."

"Dunbar . . ." Heath said, angling for some peace. "Maybe you should give it a rest with the questions, okay?"

"Well, no one else has asked this one, and it seems pretty important."

"Fine." Heath sighed. "Shoot."

Dunbar stopped wading. "What do we do if we get to Granite Falls, and everyone there is dead?"

The question rattled them. Heath wondered why it had never occurred to any of them before that Granite Falls might have been attacked, too. If the rabies virus was in the air, it stood to reason that the wind might have carried it into town. Or maybe, for all they knew, the virus *came from town*. Should Granite Falls prove unsafe, how far would they have to continue on down the river? Did the mild-mannered Dray eventually rejoin its source, the much wider, often turbulent, Skagit River, or did it run a course all the way to Puget Sound, thirty miles away, dumping out into the Pacific Ocean? Either scenario meant they'd eventually have to leave the Dray and take their chances on land. They had to cling to the hope that Granite Falls hadn't suffered an outbreak and there were people there who could help them.

No one had the answer for Dunbar or even the time to think about it.

Heath noticed when Will looked up sharply, scanned the trees, and narrowed his eyes. Will's whole body tensed. He'd obviously heard something, but all Heath picked up was the sound of rocks gargling water. Then he realized the wolves had stopped growling and were looking up, too, every muzzle aimed in the same direction as Will.

"Will?" Heath said. "What's wrong?"

He didn't reply. Instead, abruptly and without explanation, he burst through the water, charging at Floaties with a wild look in his eyes. Floaties lifted his arms to fend Will off, but Will slipped between them easily and before Floaties knew what had happened, Will had unsnapped the two plastic latches on the front of his life vest.

"What are you—? Knock it off!" Floaties grasped with wide-eyed fear that Will was trying to remove his life vest. He threw wild swings at Will, but Will was too fast and, Heath observed, too strong for Floaties to fend off. There was a lot of unexpected power in Will's body. He yanked the life vest over Floaties head and fed it to the river.

"He's trying to drown me!" Floaties screamed. The fear in his voice was palpable.

Will's attack didn't stop with the liberation of the life vest. He leapt on Floaties and dragged him forward onto his knees. The water splashed against Floaties's neck and chin, and he screamed bloody murder. All his strength left him. Will shoved Floaties onto his back and his whole body disappeared beneath the river except for his head, which Will yanked above the surface.

The group, realizing that Will might actually drown Floaties, finally woke up and rushed to stop him.

He's mad, Heath thought. Then, just as he tackled Will from behind, a chilling thought crossed his mind.

Humans aren't immune to the virus, after all.

"When Darkness Falls Upon Us"
(Sung at Camp Harmony's Agape
supper ceremony)

When darkness falls upon us,
We'll focus on the light,
And hide from gathered enemies,
Safe within plain sight.

"DON'T LET WILL BITE YOU!" Heath warned the others.
"He's like the animals now!" He tried to tie his cabinmate
up by hooking his arms through Will's, but both boys were
slippery wet and Will escaped easily. Sylvester jumped on
Will next, but Will grabbed the strap on Sylvester's quiver
and tugged it hard sideways, launching him headlong into
Heath, knocking them both stupid. Several of the arrows
spilled out of the quiver, and their fearless leader opted to
chase them in the current rather than return to the fray.

Cricket, emitting a primal war cry, ran at Will but froze in check when Will held his palms straight out and yelled, "Stop! I'm not sick! Listen, you idiots!"

It was a faint squeaking sound, like thousands of pieces of Styrofoam rubbing together, coming from somewhere above and beyond the black tips of the pine tree canopy.

"What's that noise?" Emily whispered.

Years ago, Heath's doctor suggested to his parents they vacation "someplace warm" to celebrate their son's renewed health. They took Heath to Mexico as part of a church mission team building a medical clinic in a poor, rural town. Every morning, Heath was roused from sleep by one of four things: the snarls of two dogs fighting; the mangled crowing of a sickly rooster; the drawn-out squeal of a pig being slaughtered for breakfast; or, most disturbingly of all, the dreadful chittering of bat swarms racing the sunrise to their caves. When you hear something like that, hundreds of flying rodents using screams as eyes, you never forget.

"Bats!" he shouted. "That sound is bats!"

The group tipped their faces to the sky.

"That can't be," said Emma, her eyes tracing the contour of the blue dome that lidded the forest. "Bats don't fly in the daytime."

"It's the rabies," Will explained, easing his weight off of Floaties, who was still too stunned to get up. "It tends to reverse their sleeping patterns. They're almost here. We have to hide."

"Hide where?" Emma turned a full three-sixty degrees in the water. "We can't leave the river!" As if in protest of this statement, the wolves started a new chorus of howls.

Will pulled out the drinking straws he'd scavenged in the livery. "I know. We have to hide *beneath* it." With a few quick yanks, he skinned the straws of their mushy paper wrappers then held them out to the group. "Snorkels," he explained. His gift to Heath in the livery finally made sense.

"You—you *predicted* this," Heath said, flabbergasted. He considered the kind of mind that could foresee something so random and realized that Will was operating on a whole different level than the rest of them, like Einstein or Batman.

"No, I *prepared* for this," Will clarified, as if the distinction made a difference. The group stared at him in an accusing way that suggested he probably *plotted* this. "Chess, Heath," Will said, his tone now pointedly defensive. "Play chess more and you'll see bats coming, too."

Heath doubted it. "All right then, we go underwater." He pulled out his own straw, yanked it at both ends to extend the flexible, ribbed bend.

Sylvester took the arrows out of his quiver, mined the river for a large, egg-shaped rock, and slipped it into the opening. He adjusted the strap so that it ran across his chest, the quiver itself snug in the valley of his spine. "For ballast," he explained.

"Good idea, boss." Will searched around for a rock, too. "The rest of us can set them on our chests."

"You mean he's not trying to kill me?" Floaties asked piteously from his seat on the river bottom.

"Your life vest would've kept you afloat. You'd be exposed to the bats." Heath plucked a good-sized chunk of shale from the bottom, sat down in the water, and clutched the rock to his stomach. "Will was right to get it off you. You wouldn't have done it yourself. I know this isn't going to be easy for you, buddy, but you have to submerge entirely. Even your head."

"I can't," Floaties whimpered. Horrified, he stared at the water lapping at his chest as if it were writhing maggots.

Emily eased into a sitting position in the water next to him. The water line was parallel to her collarbone. She placed her hand on Floaties's arm and squeezed it gently. "I'll keep my hand right here the whole time," she said. "You won't be alone."

Heath thought that was a bad idea, since the human body, full of gasses, had a tendency to float to the surface. He suspected they'd need every limb free and in motion to keep them anchored to the riverbed.

The Styrofoam squeaking sound was close now and deafeningly loud. The sheer number of bats required to make such a racket would dwarf the swarms Heath heard in Mexico. He realized the bats were probably a half mile away when Will first detected them, and in seconds they'd be breaking over the tree line.

Emma and Dunbar lugged rocks over to Emily and Floaties and set them carefully in their laps. Heath was pleased with the way the group was acting protectively toward one another. He'd experienced it himself when they'd saved him on the shore.

"Okay," Floaties mumbled and placed the bendy end of the straw into his mouth. Emily did the same, and then together they slowly leaned back into the water. Emily went straight under until only her hand on Floaties's arm and the top half of her straw were left exposed. Floaties went below at a much slower speed. When the river flooded his ear canals, he sniveled. Floaties took a deep, sucking breath through the straw, then finished his recline. Heath watched for a few moments to make sure he didn't resurface. He could hear Floaties hyperventilating through his straw, but thankfully he stayed down.

Theo and Molly must have submerged while Heath was watching Floaties. Good, he thought. Let Theo worry about the egg for awhile. Heath wiggled his rock up to his rib cage, rolled the straw on his tongue until it was in the middle of his lips, and waited. The others were submerged except for him and Will, a garden of straw tips sprouted up from the water between them.

When the bats fluttered over the tops of the pines, they came in numbers of thousands, flying in such tight ranks they reminded Heath of spilled ink seeping across the sky.

Heath and Will exchanged one final glance, and then Will melded into the river. Heath watched the bats spiral madly above, a living tornado, and then they plunged like a sword toward the Dray. He went under.

Even though most people referred to a group of bats as a swarm or a colony, there was another name for it, he remembered. Sometimes a group of bats is also called a camp. Heath processed the irony of that underwater as the blurry sun above was blotted out by a black cloud of roiling, screeching death.

The attack lasted maybe forty seconds. Heath had hoped that once his group was under the water, the bats would simply pass over. But he watched from beneath, eyes wide open, as a substantial piece of the massive swarm broke off and dive-bombed the Dray. He could hear the bats spearing the water with their echolocation, hunting for anything moving. They *knew* Heath and the others were there, he was sure of it.

Even with the stone weighing on his chest, Heath found it a challenge to stay in a supine position. No matter how hard he focused on staying glued to the bottom, some part of him would randomly buoy up toward the surface. When he felt a breeze on his kneecaps he seized them down so forcefully that the crown of his head broke the surface. Immediately he felt a shock of his hair twisted tightly and yanked by tiny grasping feet. A bat had landed on his head and tangled itself good. Heath plunged back down to the bottom, dragging the animal under with him. It thrashed against the side of his head, convulsing and flapping its paper-thin wings madly as it died of fear or drowning—he couldn't be certain which—before it could find purchase in Heath's flesh with its small fangs. He could hear the waterlogged howls of Quilt Face and her pack, either egging on the bats or in protest of being cheated out of their hard-earned kill.

Somehow Heath managed to keep the straw in his mouth, but during the struggle, it filled with water and was useless as a snorkel. He tore the dead bat from his hair, removed the straw from his lips, breached the surface, and spit the water out in a vertical spout, like a whale. In the few seconds he was above the water, he glimpsed the vastness of the attack. The swarm of bats was so thick that only slim shards of sky were visible through their collected mass. Most of them stayed above the river, but some of the bolder bats were strafing dangerously close to the surface. He killed two or three simply by splashing hard in their flight path.

He saw someone floating face down, drifting in the current. A dozen bats were crawling across the person's back, using their twiggy arms as crutches. They were stabbing their victim's skin with their ugly faces. He caught glimpses of identification . . . a tanned human leg maybe. A scrap of cloth. But that was all. It was too risky to stay above the surface any longer. He ducked back under just as another bat swooped in for his eyes.

Who was that? His mind raced. Molly? Floaties? They were the most likely to panic and surface prematurely. What if it was Emily? Please let her be okay. He had to know.

He took a long drag on his straw, capped the other end with his fingertip, and turned his head so that his left ear pressed into the slimy film of algae covering the rocks on the riverbed. He could see Dunbar easily enough, even though Heath was churning up silt with every twist of his body. His chunky friend was resting motionless, corpselike, beneath his rock. He made it look effortless, like Houdini. If it wasn't for the fact that the straw was still planted erect in his mouth, Heath would have thought him dead. How Dunbar was able to stay so sunken, he had no idea. He had to question the adage that muscle weighs more than fat. Heath couldn't see past Dunbar. He wished he'd thought to position himself next to Emily on the opposite side of Floaties, but hindsight is twenty-twenty.

Heath felt something cold and slimy wriggling against his armpit. Something trying to burrow. He lifted his head until his chin was pressed against his left shoulder. He saw a flicker of a mottled, dark-tipped tail wriggling under his arm and naturally assumed it was a trout. His instinct was to leap up out of the water, but he forced himself to stay calm. The fish would eventually swim away, but the bats would kill him for sure. Other than tickling his side, he knew the trout was harmless. Then, to his horror, the thing he thought was a fish crawled up between the rock on his chest and his chin and looked him right in the eye. It was a Pacific giant salamander, and a big one, maybe thirteen inches long. Heath knew they were in the Skagit River system, but had never seen one before. It was almost a folktale in these parts, like Bigfoot or a decent phone signal. If he'd come across a giant salamander before everything went nuts, it would have been the highlight of his summer—something to write home about, for sure. But flat on his back underwater, the king-size amphibian crawling brazenly toward his face was the cherry on his terror sundae. He'd forgotten most of what he'd read about the species, but not the scary stuff. Giant salamanders could growl like dogs. Bite like them, too—it could tear Heath's lip off and swallow it down. And when faced with capture they could emit a toxic secretion that would burn his skin. It wasn't rabid—amphibians were immune to the virus—but it was still notorious for being an aggressive hunter, the number one predator living in the river. He had no choice but to let it explore his face. Heath tucked his lips inside his mouth, just in case they looked too much like delicious earthworms. The salamander bumped its rounded snout against the straw, then tilted its head and wrapped its mouth around it. It jerked on the straw and for a few seconds the creature and Heath engaged in the strangest tug-of-war in history. Heath knew that if he lost, he'd be without his source of air, so he held his breath and bit down hard on the plastic tip, locking it in place. After a few tries to steal the straw, the salamander decided it wasn't worth the effort. It quickly lost interest and swam away. Heath had never been so happy to be deemed boring.

With the massive amphibian no longer blocking his view, he could once again make out the shapes of the bats as they crossed over the river—shadowy blades slicing the rays of the noon sun, which hovered bright and watery overhead. The effect was comparable to blinking rapidly while staring at a lightbulb. It was night attacking day.

And then, like a black veil yanked off a blue canvas, the bats were gone.

Heath stayed submerged for twenty Mississippis just to be safe. When he was positive the bats were gone, he sat up slowly, wiped the water off his face, and dumped the rock over the side of his lap. He was the third up—Will and Cricket had risen before him.

"You both okay?" he sputtered.

"Yeah." Cricket nodded.

"We're fine," said Will.

Theo and Molly popped up simultaneously like marionettes with their strings entangled. Molly was sobbing hysterically, frightened not to death, but as close as a little girl should ever have to come to that.

Emma came up next. She spit her straw out into her open palm and peered down into the water beside her. To Heath's relief, a grin spread across her face. Emily rose beside her, alive and well. Floaties followed. He sat hunched over in the river and cried like a baby while Emily rubbed his back to console him. Floaties kept repeating the same words over and over between heaving sobs: "I'd rather be buried alive."

Dunbar surfaced effortlessly, like Dracula from his coffin. That left . . .

Sylvester's body was bobbing in the current twenty feet down the river, snagged on an anchored piece of driftwood.

Molly started screaming, and it was a good long while before she was able to stop.

While the rest of the group fished for arrows and Floaties tossed rocks at the coyote shredding his lifejacket—it had washed up on shore—Will, Theo, and Heath freed Sylvester from the dead branch.

Will insisted they perform a visual autopsy. "This is our chance to get a close-up look at the Flash. Let's do it before the girls come back."

"Stop being such a creep," Theo said, disgusted by the suggestion that they treat their dead friend like a science experiment.

Sylvester was a human being, so it felt irreverent to

examine him in the same way Marshall had handled the porcupine in the health center. But Heath agreed with Will. They weren't exactly CSI detectives, but they might learn something useful. "Hurry up and get it over with."

Outvoted, Theo fumed. "Try not to enjoy yourself too much, Stringer."

Will went to work. After scraping the bat droppings off Sylvester with a piece of rigid bark, they looked him over closely. The most evident sign of the Flash was the dark purple, nearly black, tendrils covering every inch of his skin. They looked like veins that had risen to the surface, similar to blood poisoning, only much more prominent and densely woven.

"Dilated pupils," Heath said, holding Sylvester's eyelids open. "Same as the porcupine."

"No one should have to die like this," said Theo. "Bats. It's just not right."

"He should have stayed underwater." Will slipped the quiver from Sylvester's body and passed it to Theo. "Here. Wash the guano off of it. And don't let any get on you. I can't remember if rabies can be spread through contact with feces. Probably not, but better safe than dead."

Theo stared at the quiver balanced on Will's fingertips, as though it were a bomb. But reluctantly he took it anyway.

"What was he thinking?" Heath said, shaking his head. "Why'd he do it?"

Will lifted Sylvester's sopping shirt. "Who knows? Probably panicked."

The body was covered with dozens of tiny puncture wounds, raw and seeping runny blood.

"I didn't know bat colonies could get that big," Heath said.

"In Texas they do. They all migrate in from different parts of Mexico to breed," said Will. "There's a place called Bracken Cave between Austin and San Antonio that holds twenty million of them. The swarm that attacked us isn't natural for the Cascades. We were attacked by a super-colony. Multiple colonies joining into one big one, like Bracken Cave."

"Why would they do that?"

"Probably because there's no point in sticking to territories anymore," Will surmised. "Now that they're rabid, stuff like social groupings and food supplies don't matter. Like all the other mammals in the forest right now besides us, their only goal is to kill every human they find. They're more effective as a super-colony, like locusts attacking crops."

Will lifted Sylvester's right arm out of the water.

"He never let go of the bow," Heath said sadly as he watched Will pry the weapon from the dead boy's grip.

Theo returned with the cleaned quiver. Dunbar accompanied him, holding an arrow straight out in front of his chest. There was a dead bat impaled on the end of it. "We found a couple of these bat-kabobs in the water," Dunbar informed them.

"Well, now we know why Sylvester was killed," Will said. "He was trying to be a hero. Stupid."

"Man, he was a good shot," said Theo, and he and Dunbar left to show the bat to the girls.

"Not Molly!" Heath called after them.

"Yeah, Sylvester had skills. Too bad about him," Will said, slinging the bow around his own neck, claiming it as his prize. "We could have used him."

Heath was instantly furious. "Is that why you pulled the life vest off of Floaties? You wanted him alive in case you needed him, too, at some point? He *is* pretty strong. Maybe his muscles would come in handy along the way. He could move a log out of your path or keep Emma from pounding your face in. When you say we needed Sylvester, don't you really mean *you* needed him?"

Will's eyes were cold, the color of ice in the sunlight. Equally frigid was his reply. "Don't ever assume you know my motives. Not with the noisemakers and not with Floaties. You're not up to it." He waded away toward the arrow collectors leaving Heath alone with warmer company—Sylvester's corpse. Heath thought for a moment, then hollered after him, "We're people, Will, not chess pieces!" He received no response, not even a glance back. Either Will hadn't heard him, or he didn't care. It didn't take a genius to determine which it was.

It was near four o'clock (judging by the sun, since Dunbar's dunk in the river had rendered the only watch in the group useless) when they decided to push on. At Dunbar's insistence they discussed trying to haul Sylvester's body to Granite Falls, but in the end they agreed it was too dangerous. The effort would slow them down and the risk of not making it to town before dark was too great. Instead they secured him to the branch as best they could and said their good-byes. It was rough. Even Dunbar, who had called Sylvester a show-off at the archery range, couldn't help but tear up during Emma's eulogy. She was probably the last one who should have spoken on the group's behalf. Besides Will, she was the coldest cube in the freezer, a comparison Heath's dad used to describe the charge nurse who kicked visitors out of Heath's room not a second past eight. Emma's speech was clunky and quick, but still surprisingly touching, not the stoic words Heath had expected to hear. Emma showed she had a heart after all.

"He was a good dude," Cricket said when she'd finished. "Really cool."

"Amen," Heath added in agreement.

Heath tented Sylvester's cold hands over his still chest. Molly and Emily picked some flowers—purple foxgloves—growing tenaciously from a fissure in a boulder in the river and weaved them into his stiff fingers.

"We'll tell the authorities in Granite Falls where we left him," said Dunbar. "When everything goes back to normal, they'll come get him."

Back to normal. What was normal? Heath tried to remember. They'd gone maybe two miles, less than halfway there, and they'd already lost Sylvester. Dunbar was acting like someone—the mayor of Granite Falls, maybe—could flip a switch and it would be like nothing ever happened. Like the lights coming back on after a blackout. No, he thought. Things would never be normal again. Not for them, at least. Definitely not for Heath. The pain was back, gnawing at his body. He'd known worse, but, coupled with the onset of fatigue, it was making walking difficult. They still had at least three miles to go. For the first time since starting their journey, he questioned his ability to finish it, even if there were no more animal attacks to contend with.

Quilt Face growled hungrily from the shore. Heath met her determined gaze with his own. *One mile. You were supposed to pursue for one mile and then give up. That's what the expert on the nature show said. But that's not your plan, is it? You're coming all the way to Granite Falls, so you can kill us on the verge of rescue. But we've got something in common, Quilt Face—an early expiration date. Neither of us has much time left, do we? So if it comes down to it, then you and I are going to end each other's misery. Better to finish things up on the shore of Granite Falls than to wither away in some hospital bed in Seattle.*

The group waded south without much conversation. They were too tired to talk. The water was getting deeper, the effort to push through it was wearing them down.

Heath expected Dunbar to break the silence, but instead it was Floaties with a surprising plea.

"I have to learn how to swim." Floaties blurted the words out like they were dirt in his mouth. "If I don't, I'll drown, I know it. Can someone please teach me?"

Happy little buzzards, eating up the dead.
Chewing with their mouths full,
until they're nice and fed.
They swoop right in and feast,
these uninvited guests.
Leaving bones and wallets,
and nothing for the rest.

"HE'S NOT EVEN TRYING!" Will said, throwing his hands up in surrender, catapulting droplets of water onto the group. When the kids came upon a chest-deep pool in the river, they formed a circle around Floaties and started his swimming lesson. Will had insisted he could teach anyone to swim like a fish in five minutes, which was all the group was prepared to allot for it, since getting to Granite Falls by dark was vital. But Floaties was proving to be a difficult student, and the lesson had run into serious overtime. Will tried to instruct him on the Olympics-regulation breaststroke, but that was a complete disaster. Floaties just leaned over until his chest was touching the water, rotated his arms like a double-sided windmill, then asked if he was swimming. He looked ridiculous.

"Not really, buddy," Heath said, trying not to laugh and hurt his feelings. "You kinda gotta get your head wet, for starters."

"It's still wet from before," Floaties replied. He was serious.

"No, I mean you have to put your face in the water."

"This is getting annoying!" Emma nagged. "Will, you said you could teach him in five minutes. It's been close to half an hour now."

"I suppose *you* could do better?" Will scoffed.

"No, and that's my point," Emma said. "It's hopeless. We can't spend all day stuck between camp and town. Just teach him the freakin' doggie paddle and let's move on."

"The doggie paddle isn't really swimming, Em," Emily said. "It's more like . . . crawling on water."

"Teach it to me! That sounds perfect!" Floaties pleaded. He rationalized, "How hard can the doggie paddle be if *he* can do it?" then he pointed toward a grimy border collie that had joined the shore party.

Heath agreed with Emily. "I think we better teach you something more advanced. Just in case."

"Can I try?" Molly asked. Up to this point she'd been like someone on the subway, traveling in the same direction but keeping to herself. Heath had never noticed her before the livery because she was one of the junior campers and had a different schedule than he did. Uncle Bill came up with a naming system—kids Molly's age were called Chicks (both the boys and girls hated this title, but for different reasons), and older campers like Heath were called Fledglings, which Heath thought was stupid because in the bird world, chicks and fledglings were basically the same thing. Molly couldn't have been more than ten, the baby of the group.

"Where'd you come from, chicken nugget?" Will seemed ruffled by Molly's offer. "I didn't know you could speak. Thought all you could do is whimper and cry."

"Be nice," Emily reprimanded him.

"Let her try," Emma insisted. "She can't do much worse than you, Will."

He directed his ire at the little red-headed girl. "If I can't get through his thick head, how the heck can you? If you think you can pull off a miracle," Will grumbled, fed up with it, "then be my guest."

Molly positioned herself right in front of her student, as if initiating a dance. She was shorter than Cricket; the water-line was at her chin. "First things first. Blowing bubbles."

Will snickered.

"Ignore him," Molly told Floaties. "The hardest part of learning how to swim is putting your face in the water. This will help." She dipped down until her mouth was below the waterline, then she blew bubbles, little ones that popped on the surface. She came up, took a breath, and smiled. "Fish farts."

"Okay, that doesn't seem so hard," Floaties agreed, then mimicked Molly.

"Easy peasy?" she asked.

Floaties nodded his head, continuing to blow bubbles.

Heath couldn't help but feel a little cheerier watching big Floaties making silly motorboat sounds in the middle of the Dray. Even Quilt Face seemed to relax some. She stopped growling and cocked her head to one side as she watched.

"Okay, that was perfect." Molly laughed when Floaties came up sporting a huge grin. "As long as you're blowing air *out*, nothing gets *in*. Make sense?"

"I like the way you teach," Floaties said, then shot Will a look of contempt.

"The next part is simple, too." Molly placed her hand on Floaties shoulder. "We put our whole face in the water."

"I don't think—"

"Great," Molly cut him off, "you're not supposed to think. You're just supposed to relax and get your face wet. Watch." She bent her head down, easing her face into the water, just past her ears. Her long red hair spread out like kelp across the surface. She blew bubbles that way for five seconds and then came up for air. "Not very different, but hold your mouth shut and blow the bubbles from your nose this time."

"Not your butt," Cricket added helpfully.

"Hush," Molly scolded. "Ready? On the count of three?"

"I'll count," Floaties insisted. "One . . . two . . . . three."

He took a huge gulp of air and plunged his face into the water like he was bobbing for apples. A cloud of giant-sized bubbles spread out around Floaties head.

"Whale farts." Cricket chuckled.

Floaties stayed under for a full twenty seconds, at least. When he came up, he took another big gasp and squeegeed his face with his hands.

Molly clapped excitedly and the group joined in.

"Take a picture and put in on the fridge," Will said, his eyes rolling in their sockets.

"Now what?" Floaties asked, encouraged by the applause and eager for more success.

"This part may seem kinda silly, but I swear it works. Have you ever heard the song *'Noah Had a Submarine'*?"

"I don't think so," said Floaties.

"I have," Dunbar chimed in. "They used to sing it at body image camp. It always got me thinking about submarine sandwiches. I really hated that place."

"I know the words," Theo said.

"You guys can help me sing it. Everyone can. It's easy peasy.

"Some say Noah had a boat, but I have to disagree.
Instead it was a submarine that went beneath the sea.
In forty days and forty nights, the problem to be
    solved?
They wanted to play shuffleboard, so the animals
    evolved.
The horse became the seahorse. Ney glub, glub, ney,
    ney.
The chimp became a sea monkey. Ooh glub, glub,
    ooh, ooh.

The snake became a sea snake. Hiss glub, glub, hiss, hiss.

The dinosaur became extinct, because it wasn't on the list."

Heath thought Molly had a tin ear for music, but she could definitely make a living doing animal voices for cartoons. Her mer-chimp was spot-on.

"Got it? Sorta?" she asked.

"I think so," Floaties said. "But I feel stupid."

"My dad taught my little sister and me to swim by having us sing to each other underwater. It really works."

"That's sweet. Your dad taught you . . . that's really . . ." Emily breathed wistfully, then trailed off.

Molly said, "Time to put your whole head in the water, Floaties. I'll go first and start the song. Ready?"

"I'm ready," Floaties said apprehensively.

"Down we go." Molly sang the first verse above water and then took the second verse below. Floaties sang, too, fumbling with the words. With a pained expression on his face, he joined her, continuing their duet underwater. When it looked as if he might be starting to panic, Emily dropped down and made it a trio.

"C'mon," Heath said, sinking with a smile on his lips. "This looks fun."

Soon the whole group was under the river, holding the circle around Floaties, singing in exhalation. No one had expected Will to add his voice, but that was his style, to do the unexpected; he graced their choir with a pitchy tenor. Will did a lot of things well, but singing wasn't one of them.

Heath thought about what Dunbar said. About things getting back to normal. He had to admit, things felt pretty normal at that moment. Not because they were singing a stupid campfire song beneath a river. It was that they were being kids. Having fun. Making friends. If he didn't need oxygen for his lungs, he would have stayed below, singing their silly song until Quilt Face and the rest of them died of old age.

The next half hour saw Floaties enjoying one breakthrough after another. He was able to float with his whole body, then glide while leading with his head. Molly introduced his arms into the lesson, and Floaties propelled himself forward. When he incorporated Will's breaststroke on his own volition, and did it with passing ability, the group celebrated by howling together at the sun. Quilt Face did not like this at all, and she and her family broke into a new bout of rapid pacing. The group didn't care.

Floaties hugged Molly tight, and she squeaked like a mouse.

"Good job, Molly," Will admitted.

"Thanks." She giggled shyly.

"We need to get going," Dunbar said. "It's getting late."

"Last one to Granite Falls stays in the river!" Floaties proclaimed, taking the lead with newfound confidence.

And that, Heath thought, is how you teach someone to swim.

* * *

They progressed another half mile down the Dray, stopping abruptly when Emily froze midstep and gasped. She stared straight down into the water. "Oh, oh."

"What? What is it," Heath quickly waded toward her.

"Keep back," she warned.

"Em, what's wrong?" Emma asked.

Demurely, Emily replied, "I have to pee." She looked mortified.

"Oh," Heath said, relieved it wasn't anything serious. "Go ahead."

"What! Here?" She turned on him with the comparable fury of Onyx. "I'm not doing that! Here! Surrounded by . . . *YOU*!"

Heath assumed *you* encompassed everyone, but he still didn't appreciate the sour way in which she'd aimed the word at him.

"The ladies room is just past the coyote, up the stairs and to the left," Will needled. "We'll wait here for you."

"Shut up!" the twins said in stereo.

"Okay, okay." Heath tried to calm Emily. "What would you like us to do?"

"I don't know!" she panicked. "What are *you* gonna do when *you* have to go?"

Heath looked away, a sheepish expression on his face. Emily's eyes got owlishly wide. *"You've been peeing in the river?"*

"Yeah," Cricket said with a casual shrug. "That's what dudes do."

"No, that's what gross animals do!" Emily flared. She

was turning beet red. Heath wasn't sure if her color change was triggered by anger or embarrassment—probably both.

"There's a game we always played at Lake Tupso," Cricket shared, despite Heath's attempt to shush him. "Whoever takes a whiz in the water has to impersonate a birdcall. You know, as a warning."

"*That's* why you've been making those stupid chicken noises?" she seethed.

"Um . . . actually, I was a barn swallow." Heath felt foolish as soon as he'd said it.

"Don't tell me you didn't recognize my perfect mourning dove impression," Dunbar said with an indignant air.

"You guys sounded like chickens to me, too." Heath suspected Will was attempting to exclude himself from Emily's wrath.

"Don't act so innocent," Emily cut into Will. "I heard your chickadee."

"Well"—he hazarded a chuckle—"at least you could tell what my impression was."

"*I* was the only one actually trying to imitate a chicken," Emma declared proudly.

"Ugh! You too, Em?" Emily covered her face with her forearms to make the group disappear.

Heath had an idea. "What if the rest of us head down the river a bit? We could give you some privacy?"

Emily opened a crack between her arms and peeked through. "Not too far?"

"Not too far." Heath gave her a gentle smile. "There's a bend up ahead. We'll wait for you on the other side."

"Want me to stay?" Emma asked dutifully.

"Go!" Emily snapped.

"You're ridiculous sometimes, you know that?"

"Um, shouldn't we be headed *upstream* from her?" Dunbar asked the group. "Because you know, the river flows downstream and—"

Heath prodded him forward. "Just come on."

The group moseyed away from Emily. When they'd gotten to the elbow of the river bend, Cricket waved to her and hollered a warning, "Be careful if any porcupines come floating by! They're crazy for salt."

With the group slowed and waiting on Emily, Heath seized the opportunity to take Theo aside. He needed to talk to the boy. He wanted to confirm a suspicion. Theo didn't like being singled out, but he followed Heath to a shaded spot not far from the shore and they talked.

"You don't like Floaties very much, do you?" Heath was blunt and straight to the point.

Theo looked uncomfortable, but he answered the question. "No. I hate him."

"Because he made you his runner last summer, didn't he?"

Theo's expression was dark and not because of the shade.

"Did he hit you?"

"Once. Slapped me on the side of the face pretty hard. And he shoved me a couple times. Knocked me down. Why are you asking me this stuff?"

Heath glanced over at Floaties, who was chasing a trout through the water for Molly's amusement. "Floaties and Thumper had my summer planned out, but Will put the brakes on that. I was lucky. I'm sorry Floaties made life hard for you, Theo. But do you think maybe you can let your anger go? Hanging on to resentment isn't good for your health. Trust me, I know."

Theo pondered this advice, then replied, "I don't hate him because he hurt me."

"Really? Then why?"

"I hate him because after all he and Thumper put me through, the kid doesn't even recognize me! It's bad enough he ruined my summer last year, but he doesn't even remember my face! It's like I wasn't even a person to him, just some robot to push around and do his bidding!" Theo was so angry he was shaking.

"Yeah," Heath said with a drawn-out sigh. "That would tick me off, too."

They watched their bully in silence. Floaties actually caught the darn fish and offered it headfirst to Molly for a kiss. She obliged, giggled, and then insisted he put it back into the water, causing Dunbar heartbreak as he watched his potential lunch swim away.

"Look at him, Theo. Floaties isn't a bad guy. Not at the core. He's just had a bad life."

"So maybe he's destined to have a bad death, too." Theo had no intention of letting go of his anger. Heath could see that now. Floaties had done too much damage.

"That won't happen. We'll get to Granite Falls," Heath assured him. "We'll be okay. But you should forgive him. It's the right thing to do."

"You think, huh?" Theo was done. He waded backward

toward the group and pointed to the rabid animals watching them from the bank. "You said not to blame the animals because they're sick. It's not their fault that they've become monsters, because they had no choice, right? Well, Floaties *had a choice*. He didn't have to become a jerk like his dad. Maybe you can forgive him for that, but I can't."

Heath watched Theo go, sad for him. Then he considered the "monsters" on the shore. Most of the animals had followed the group, except for the wolves, who stayed put across from Emily, the straggler. They must have thought the group was leaving her behind because she was sick or had been cast out. This made Heath nervous, but he knew that as long as Emily stayed in the water she'd be okay. Still, when he heard her scream his first thought was of Quilt Face sinking her teeth into Emily's flesh.

The group ran back toward Emily's position, twisting wide at their waists to cut through the water faster.

"Emily!" Heath and Emma shouted in rounds.

"I'm okay!" she hollered back. "Hurry!"

They found her where they'd left her. She was facing the east bank, shivering. She pointed a trembling finger at a thicket of brush. "Over there."

Cricket wished he'd hadn't looked, because his immediate and reflexive reaction was to vomit in the river.

"Oh, sick!" Dunbar choked, then dry heaved a few times himself.

A man was lying under the bushes. His clothes were tattered and covered with blood. He was wearing a yellow helmet, shorts, and a life jacket that had been torn open in several spots. He was dead, they knew that immediately. The corpse was gruesome, too, but that wasn't what sucked such a strong reaction from the group. A huge vulture was perched on the body, tearing away at it, swallowing whole chunks of flesh.

"Rough luck," Will muttered.

"What was he doing out here?" Emma asked, wincing when the bird started playing tug-of-war with an extra stretchy piece of meat.

"That's a kayaker's helmet," Heath pointed out. His family had four well-used kayaks hanging from hooks in their garage. He knew what the gear looked like.

Floaties glanced up and down the river. "Where's his boat?"

"It's not here," Will said. "The current must have carried it away."

"If we find it, we can use it," Theo said excitedly. "Someone can kayak to Granite Falls and send help back for the rest. I've kayaked before."

"Me too," Heath said, but when Emily glanced at him, he quickly added, "You can go, Theo. If we find the kayak, I mean."

The vulture extracted its bloody beak from the corpse and hopped down to the river. It flapped its huge black wings, floated a foot off the ground, and then dropped like a rock back into the weeds. It did this several times, but couldn't take off.

"What's wrong with it?" Molly asked. "Do you think it got rabies from eating . . . ?" She couldn't finish the question.

"No, that's not it." Will watched the vulture with fascination. "Birds are immune to rabies."

Heath fished a rock out of the water, just in case. "We don't know if that's true with the Flash. Maybe it affects—"

"It's not ill," Will insisted, then after a pause he said, "It's too full to fly."

Cricket threw up again. He looked whiter than Heath had ever seen him before, which was saying something, because the boy nearly glowed in the dark.

"Vultures are gluttons," Will told them. "They eat until they're so heavy they can't get off the ground. They're nature's cleanup crew, which is a good thing during an outbreak of rabies. They dispose of the infected dead carcasses before other mammals come along, eat them, and ingest the virus too. It's a pretty efficient disposal system, if you think about it. Eating the dead."

"Ghoulish." Molly shuddered. Heath wasn't sure if she was referring to the bird or Will.

Emma took her sister's hand. "Did you go?" When Emily nodded slowly, Emma sympathetically mirrored the gesture. "Then let's get out of here."

As the group waded away from the grisly scene, Heath noticed that Will was not among them. He looked back and saw his cabinmate fixed in place, engaged in a staring contest with the vulture. Will's eyes were vacant and his jaw hung slack. He was slowly cocking his head from side to side, mimicking the bird's movements exactly. It looked to Heath almost as if Will and the vulture were communicating, but what could Will be asking it? *How's the grub?* Heath had seen a lot of creepy things today, but Will silently communing with the engorged vulture took the cake.

"Let's go, Stringer!" Heath called out, attempting to end Will's morbid behavior.

It took Will a few seconds to unlock from his trance. When he finally did, he turned and flashed Heath a wide but humorless smile. "Sure thing," he said, then pushed through the water past him.

Deciding it wasn't quite full after all, the vulture returned to the corpse for a second helping. Sometimes an idea slips into your mind that you just wish hadn't. The bird had feasted well on the dead kayaker, but as Heath took a last, disgusted look at the vile creature he wondered if there was any Sylvester in its stomach, too.

(Sung to the tune of "There Ain't No Bugs
on Me")

Oh, there ain't no squirrels on me, on me.
There ain't no squirrels on me.
There may be squirrels on some of you girls,
But there ain't no squirrels on me.

By six o'clock, the sun was lolling toward the west bank, starting its descent into the Pacific Ocean. It was still fairly bright out, but now the forest shadows were creeping across the river, crawling over the group, chilling the perspiration on their skin. The summer's fat cicadas were chirping so loudly they could be mistaken for car alarms. Cricket felt the need to discuss them, of course. "Did you guys know that cicadas are one of the few insects that can perspire?" Nobody pretended to care. Cricket looked especially tired. He dropped the topic of bug sweat quickly.

They'd been in the water for almost three hours and were starting to feel the effects. Heath thought it would be heaven to have a shower and put on a clean pair of socks. At Christmas his aunt Wanda always gave him socks and every year he'd smile politely and act like they'd been at the top of his wish list. What he wouldn't give to be lounging by the fire, wearing a pair of warm, dry Aunt Wanda socks now.

He thought about his socks back at the cabin, too. The ones wrapped around his vial of OxyContin. He wanted *those* socks even more.

Heath was exhausted. Although the current was consistently mild, it was still pushing them along like a cattle driver. He had to constantly adjust his body to stay in synch with it, a physically draining proposition. Water had weight, he knew that, and it was fairly heavy. He'd already plodded through millions of gallons, and it was starting to grind him down, as it had done to the polished rocks below his feet. There'd been points when the river became a riffle, where the water was white, shallow, and turbulent. It took effort to avoid being swept off his feet. At other times the river stepped down sharply and the kids had to help each other descend between boulders, mindful not to slip and bash their heads open on the rocks. And even with his aqua-shoes on, he was bleeding where shards of rock had pierced his skin through the mesh. Little red streamers of blood trailed from his heels, diluting and fading in the current.

He felt saturated and irritable, like when he was a little kid, anxious to get out of the tub. At least they weren't in salt water. That would be a hundred times worse. He'd seen a TV show about a guy who was lost in the sea for two days. First, his skin dried out, even though he was submerged in water. Then the salt worked its way into his pores and started to burn. After that, his skin started to rot. Finally he suffered something called skin-slip, which is when the skin gets soupy and slides out of place. By comparison, the river didn't seem so bad. And on the bright side, the Dray had been more or less shallow for over three miles with an occasional pocket of deeper water, which they were able to swim over or maneuver around. Heath noticed that when the banks got steeper and the shoreline narrowed, the river between them got deeper, too. It was a good way to gauge the depth of the water ahead, which was rarely more than chest-high. They'd been spoiled. Which is why, when they came around a bend—the east bank becoming the south bank—and saw that the shore disappeared completely, the banks rising up sharply as clay bluffs, it came as a surprise to all. The shift in the riverscape meant two critical changes. First, the shores were no longer wide enough for their quad-ruped stalkers to traverse, not even in single file formation. Heath watched in relief when Quilt Face was forced to turn away, leading her pack back toward Camp Harmony. She glanced over her shoulder several times, her eyes always on Heath, until she and her family disappeared around the bend. "I think she has a crush on you," Will said, which Heath didn't find amusing at all.

The other mammals seemed confused and frustrated by the tapering of the shoreline. One of the deer tried to step its way across the base of the bluffs, struggled in the soft clay, tipped over into the water, and died. Now that Floaties could swim with some competency, the new U-shaped channel was the perfect opportunity to give the animals the slip.

The second noticeable change was not in their favor.

"That's not good." Dunbar pointed out at the slender trees jutting out from the sides of the bluffs. A web of partially exposed roots anchored them there with questionable integrity. The tops of some of the trees bowed like fishing poles so that they arced out a good ways over the river. Already dozens of filthy, manic squirrels had loaded the boughs, chattering excitedly, constantly repositioning their heavy tails for counterbalance as the trunks swayed under their weight.

"There's so many of them," Emily whispered.

"They can't reach us," Heath reassured them. "The trees are too far overhead. We should be able to swim right under them."

"I've got another question," Dunbar said, but it didn't need asking since it was already on everyone's mind.

What if the squirrels jump down on us?

"Are you sure you're going to be okay?" Molly asked Floaties for the fourth time. "This part is deeper than last time. The water will be over your head."

"Everything's over his head," Will joked.

"Shut it," Floaties said.

"Molly . . ." Heath sighed. "He has to be okay. This is the only way to town."

"He could wait here," she bargained. "We could send help back for him."

Heath thought it ironic that the egg had become the mother hen. He knew why she was so freaked out. If Floaties went into the channel and drowned, as his swim teacher she would feel responsible. "He'll be okay," Heath said. He hoped. The fact was, if Floaties panicked and started to drown, it would be dangerous for anyone to attempt a rescue. At over two hundred pounds, Floaties weighed almost twice as much as him and three times as much as Molly. He'd probably drag his rescuer under with him. Now Heath wished they'd taught him the doggie paddle, like Emma suggested. It was an easy stroke he could transition to if he got into trouble. But they were out of time. They had to keep going forward.

"Let's just get it over with," Floaties said. "I know how to float now. I'll be fine."

"That's the spirit." Heath flashed an encouraging smile. "Although we can't really call you Floaties anymore, can we?"

"He's Aquaman now," Molly giggled. Even her laugh sounded cartoon worthy.

"Yeah, from now on we'll call you Aquaman," said Dunbar.

Floaties grinned. He clearly liked this newfound acceptance. "Why don't you just call me Miles? That's my real name."

"Miles it is," Heath agreed. "From now on this is a no-nickname zone."

"Seriously?" Cricket pouted. "I like mine."

"You would," Dunbar snorted.

"Let's go swimming, Miles," Emma said, and with all the grace of a mermaid she dove down and torpedoed into the channel.

Em and Em made it look easy. They glided below the surface, coming up quickly for gasps of air then going deep where nothing could touch them. Theo and Dunbar were competent swimmers, too. Cricket stopped often to bob in the water and catch his breath. His white skin was starting to turn an angry red from the sun. He looked miserable. It came as no surprise to anyone that Will was the fastest swimmer; he'd shown off his skill during Miles's swimming lesson. Miles and Molly swam together. This time Heath brought up the rear, keeping an eye on everyone.

It was eerie. The constant chattering from the squirrels echoed horrifically in the channel. The rabid rodents quickly figured out that if they congregated closer to the highest limbs, they could bend the supple trees farther out over the river, coming within a ten-foot drop of the group's swim path.

A squirrel fell in front of Miles, but he didn't panic. He calmly watched it die, then he swam over it. He was doing great. It was Molly that Heath was worried about. When a squirrel splashed down a yard away she screamed at the top of her lungs until it stopped thrashing and sank in a clump to the bottom. Molly, badly shaken, nearly went under with the squirrel, but she managed to fix herself with Miles's help.

Two more squirrels splashed close to the bluffs.

"They're jumping!" Dunbar shouted.

"No, they're not!" Heath replied. "I see them. They're falling! Just keep swimming!" From his vantage point at the rear he observed the rodents scurrying up to the thinnest branch tips, bunching there together like grapes. The squirrels would either jostle one another off, or the branches would break under the strain of their collective weight. They were raining down around the group, dying in the river. Heath knew that squirrels could swim if they absolutely had to, so they weren't drowning. It was their fear of water that was killing them.

"Don't panic!" Heath called to his friends. "Remember, the Dray is like lava to them! If you can swim underwater, do it now!"

Theo submerged. A squirrel landed where he'd been a second before. Heath watched the spot like a hawk until Theo popped up five yards ahead. Heath exhaled, relieved, just as a squirrel fell inches from his ear, hit the water, and twisted so violently from the agony he could hear its little bones crack beneath its fur. They were leaping down from the top of the bluffs, landing on the trees, or in the river if they weren't as lucky. The dead ones were quickly replaced by more from the woods above. Wave after wave of squirrels poured over the crest in a follow-the-leader mentality that was better suited to lemmings. Heath had never seen so many squirrels in one place before, not even during a school field trip to Lafayette Park, across from the White House, which people called the Squirrel Capital of the World. "Keep swimming!" he ordered.

A ratty-looking black one with a hairless, torn tail landed on Will's shoulder, but he rolled in the water so fast that it couldn't hang on. Will was a true athlete.

A loud creaking sound was followed by a splash and the rustle of leaves swatting water. A whole tree had torn away from the east bluff directly behind Heath. Twenty or more squirrels died when it crashed with a leafy rustle.

Swim.

Heath was exhausted, but he knew resting meant death.

Swim.

Splash!

He felt fur against his leg and jerked it away.

Just a dead one.

His lungs burned.

Swim.

The bluffs were heaving with gray fur.

Pain ripped through his thigh.

Not a bite—just a cramp. He fought through the sting, kicking harder with his other leg to compensate.

Swim.

A scream. Molly.

She's okay, he saw.

Splash!

Swim.

Breathe.

Swim.

Breathe.

Swim.

After a tenth of a mile the river widened and the bluffs flattened out. The shore returned. Heath's toes glanced off something hard. Cobbles—flat, rounded stones on the riverbed. The rubber soles of his aqua-shoes skidded across their surfaces. He dug his heels down and slowed to a drift. The group was an octopus, many arms reaching out and pulling him close. "We're alive," sobbed the octopus. "We're all alive."

Behind them a roar of frustrated squeaks echoed through the gauntlet.

The group carried on, their mood was funereal. Molly's spirit had been fractured by her near-death experience in the channel. Her eyes wouldn't stop leaking, her lips trembled ceaselessly. It didn't help that Miles kept hovering over her in concern like a dog with a sick master, worried, useless, and pressing into her space. She'd come so close to dying, Heath realized. So had Theo. So had he. It was just dumb luck that had brought them all through the channel alive.

After a long spell of glum silence, Dunbar had had enough. "If someone doesn't say something, I'm gonna pull my hair out."

"I hate to admit it," Miles said, "but for once I agree with the chatterbox. We need to get our minds off what happened back there." He gestured with his brow to let the others know he meant Molly, then said, "We all do."

Heath thought that was the smartest thing Miles had

said all day. They needed to get their mind off the squirrels, the massacre at camp, the animals they'd left at the mouth of the gauntlet . . . basically everything that had happened since lunch.

"Anyone know any travel games?" Dunbar asked.

"What? You mean like Punch Buggy?" Miles asked. "Tell you what, if you see a Volkswagen bug out here, I'll let you punch me in the face."

Emily offered a suggestion. "We could play Wonder Woman's Lasso."

Emma nixed the idea. "That game's only fun with cute guys."

"Hey!" the boys cried in unison.

"Sorry! Sorry! I meant, guys that are cute to me," she clarified.

"Emma, stop while you're ahead," Emily suggested. "I swear—you can be so insensitive sometimes."

"Who cares what the Queen of the Nile thinks?" Dunbar grunted. "What's Wonder Woman's Lasso, Emily?"

She mimed like she had a length of rope in her hands. "It's simple." She twirled the imaginary lasso overhead, then tossed it in Theo's direction. Theo stared at her as if she were nuts.

"I just tangled you in Wonder Woman's lasso," Emily explained. "It's magical. It makes people tell the truth. Now you have to answer honestly, no matter what I ask."

Theo sighed. "So it's like truth or dare. Minus the dare option."

"Right, I think we've had enough dares for one day," said

Emily. "It might be fun. But you have to answer honestly, or it'll be boring. We can wade and play at the same time."

"Sounds okay," Cricket said. "I'm in."

Theo, pretending to lift the rope's slack, said, "Sure, go ahead. Ask me a question."

Emily looked up at the clear sky and thought for a moment. "Hmm. All right, what's the most embarrassing thing that's ever happened to you?"

It was obvious that Theo had an instant answer, but he was reluctant to share it. "Seriously? I don't want to say."

"I understand," Emily said with a smile, "but unfortunately, you've got the lasso around you."

Theo refused at first, but the group teased him until he caved. "Fine. You want to know my most embarrassing moment? Here it is: I farted in church."

The group had a good laugh. At first Theo looked angry, but their laughter was infectious and he started chuckling, too. "During prayer!" he added, and the kids laughed harder. "Right when our pastor was thanking God for fresh water, abundant food and"—he could barely finish—"CLEAN AIR!"

They couldn't stop laughing. Tears rolled down their cheeks, and they gasped for breath. Heath wondered if this is what happened to people right when they started going crazy. If so, he decided, crazy felt pretty good.

"Oh man." Dunbar gasped for air. "I love this game already."

When they finally calmed down, Emily thanked Theo

for his honesty and told him it was his turn to "lasso" some-one and ask whatever he wanted.

Theo tossed the invisible hoop around Molly.

"I don't want to play," she said. She was on the verge of sobbing.

"Nah." Miles stepped in and pretended to wind the lasso around his arm. "Ask me something instead."

Heath saw immediately how awkward this was for Theo. The boy wasn't happy to be tethered to his bully, even by an imaginary rope.

"What's your favorite color?" Theo muttered, throwing his turn away.

"Black," Miles answered. "And blue."

"Figures," Theo said under his breath so that only Heath, who was closest, could hear him.

Miles roped Cricket and asked why he was so obsessed with bugs even though it probably dropped him a few rungs on the popularity ladder.

Cricket answered honestly. "I admire them. They're able to live anywhere, get by on hardly any food, and not only survive but do pretty well for themselves. There're very few bugs I don't like."

"How about cockroaches? You live in the city, right?" Miles asked. "You probably see lots of cockroaches."

"There's a few, yeah."

"I bet you invite them home for dinner, huh?"

"Shut up!" Cricket snapped, surprising everyone but Heath, who knew exactly what line Miles had crossed.

"What'd I say?" Miles asked the group. "I was just messing around. It's a game, dude."

Cricket was fuming, his whole body rigid.

"What, Cricket?" Miles said throwing his hand out to his sides.

"You can tell them, Cricket," Heath said. "I think it'd be okay. They won't make fun of you."

"Okay, fine." Cricket sighed, allowing the tension to seep out of him.

"Well?" Miles asked.

"There aren't any bugs in my house because . . . because I don't have a house. Or an apartment. Or even a tent. Happy now?"

"Oh," Miles said, blushing redder than the sumac growing on the banks. "You're homeless? I—I didn't know. Sorry, man."

"We're sorry to hear that, too, Cricket," Emily said, speaking for the group.

Cricket shrugged. "It's temporary. My dad left a few months ago after a bad fight with my mom. He packed a suitcase . . . said he needed a night to cool off, but never came home. He wasn't exactly Father of the Year before that, but he was our only source of income. Our landlord eventually evicted us. We got some hotel vouchers from the Salvation Army, and when those ran out, we moved into the mission. But things are getting better. A job opportunity opened up for my mom, but they wanted her to go to California for training. Our church offered to pay for me to come to Camp Harmony for the summer while she's away."

"That's rough," Miles said, patting Cricket on the back. The size difference between the two boys was so great that they reminded Heath of a parent burping a baby.

"I see why you like bugs," Emily said, her tone soothing and sympathetic.

"You do?" Cricket raised one eyebrow guardedly.

"Yes. They're adaptable, like you. Strong and determined. When the going gets tough, bugs get tougher."

Cricket's lips spread out slightly at the corners. "Yeah . . . exactly. Thanks, Em."

"Well, you can stay with us if you ever need to," Emma offered. "Although I bet your mom will be able to afford a place soon."

"You can crash with me, too," Miles said. "We don't have much either, but *mi casa es su casa.*"

Having already made a similar offer to Cricket, Heath remained quiet, basking in the warmth the others were showering on his friend.

"My turn," Cricket said. He lassoed Dunbar and somehow that segued into a discussion about eating contests, which led to another conversation about who could belch the loudest, which led to an impromptu belching contest that Emma won soundly. She burped so loudly a flock of songbirds rose from the trees, fleeing into the sky for dear life.

"Impressive *and* disgusting," Dunbar said with admiration. He roped Emma and asked if she really meant it when she said that none of the boys in the group were cute. It wasn't the answer he was hoping for, but Emma admitted she had a "tiny crush" on Will. "He has pretty eyes," she noted.

Will didn't seem to care, and when Emma roped him next, probably with the intent of asking him if he liked her back, he formed invisible scissors with his fingers and cut the lasso in two. "It's a stupid game," he said cruelly, hurting Emma's feelings.

Although Heath felt badly for Emma, he was relieved Will had refused to play. He was worried Will might rope him next and make him reveal to the group that he was sick. The pain was back, getting worse by the second. He might have to come clean eventually, but he didn't want to be forced to do it now.

"Congratulations, Will," Emma sulked. "You win the prize for the shortest crush I've ever had."

"Whatever." Will swatted a horsefly off his chest. "I'd never date a twin."

"That's stupid," said Dunbar. "Who doesn't want to date a twin? It's like having a spare tire in case one blows out on the road."

"NO, IT IS NOT!" Emily screeched. "You're as big an idiot as he is!"

Emma went after Will. "What's so horrible about dating a twin, huh? Are you so used to being a loner that you can't stand to be around more than one person at a time? I bet you're just jealous. You see the great relationship that Em and I have and you—"

"I would never date a twin," Will repeated, his jaw

muscles twitching, "because *I have a twin*. My sister, Wren."

"No way!" Miles laughed. "You mean there's a Xerox of you somewhere, running around with girl parts? That's hilarious!"

"You do not have a twin!" Emma accused.

"I do, too."

"Where is she?" Emily asked. "How come she didn't come with you to camp?"

Will shrugged. "Last I heard she was living in Seattle with our aunt."

"Last you heard?" Heath was confused. "You don't know?"

Will's eyes narrowed and his gaze drifted down the river as he spoke. "No. We haven't talked in two years. And I don't ask about her."

"Why not?" Emily asked. "I couldn't imagine not talking to Emma for more than a day, and even that's difficult to do. Don't you feel a natural bond to your twin?"

"'Natural bond'?" he scoffed. "I can't stand her."

"What's wrong with you, Will?" Emma demanded.

Heath suspected there was no honey in that particular bees' nest, and they were best off not shaking it.

"What's so special about being a twin?" Will asked. "In your case it's just one zygote splitting off to form two people. Big deal."

"What's a . . . *zygote*?" Miles looked confused. "Is that like . . . some kind of farm animal?"

"If anything," Will continued, "I'd say twins are even less special than normal people because right from the beginning they have to share *everything*, even their mother's womb. And I can't stand how some twins even dress alike."

"These are equestrian outfits!" Emma argued. "They *all* look like this!"

"Look," Heath started, always the peacemaker. "Let's just agree that everyone's born unique and leave it at that." His line of thinking pleased no one.

"Twins *are* special," Emma insisted, poking Will in the chest. "But to be honest, I'm not surprised that you can't get along with yours. *Nobody* likes you, Will Stringer, and you know why?"

"Tell me." He chuckled. "This should be good."

She pressed her finger into his sternum hard and screwed it there. "Because everything that comes out of your mouth is as germy and nasty as those squirrels we left back in the channel. Your brain is just as diseased as they were, but at least *they* have an excuse. What's yours? Huh?" When she received no reply she demanded, "Answer me!"

Will glared down at Emma's finger, then up into her watering eyes. Then back down at her finger again. "Do you *see* a lasso around me?"

"Em . . ." Emily said softly. "Who cares what he thinks? He's an idiot. Just let it go."

"She's right. You're not even worth it . . . *jerk*." Emma gave Will a flimsy shove, then trudged quickly through the river, returning to Emily's side.

"Oookay, that was fun," Dunbar said. "Whose turn is it next? Or is it still Emma's?"

"I think it's probably Heath's," Cricket said. "Unless Emma wants—"

"Have any of you ever heard of the Greek goddess Lyssa?" Will asked his perplexing question in a voice so cold it was creepy.

"What are you talking about now?" Emma dried her eyes with her palms.

"The goddess Lyssa," Will repeated. "When my grandfather's dog got rabies I wanted to understand the disease. Learn everything I could about it. So I searched the Internet for days. Found tons of info. It's how I knew the Flash was airborne just by watching the squirrels. And how I predicted we'd probably have to deal with bats, the biggest carriers of rabies."

"Know your enemy," Heath said, quoting Will's earlier sentiment.

"That's right," Will nodded. "Anyways, that's when I found out about Lyssa. She was the daughter of Gaia, the Earth goddess, and Aether, the god of the—"

"Yawn," said Miles. "We don't need a history lesson. Get to the point."

"Fine. Lyssa was known as the goddess of mad rage and frenzy . . . and rabies. She wasn't a lot of fun to be around."

"So she was kinda like Emma," Dunbar muttered under his breath.

"Shut it!" Emma ordered, flicking water off her fingertips into Dunbar's face.

Will ignored them. "There was a hunter named Actaeon

who traveled with a pack of hunting dogs. One day he saw the goddess Artemis naked and to punish him for not looking away, Lyssa gave the pack rabies and they tore their master to bits."

The group quieted. Heath felt uneasy. This wasn't the kind of story they needed to hear in their current situation, but he was curious to see where Will was going with it.

"Lyssa is also mentioned in the story of Hercules," Will said. "Her mother, Gaia, had a grudge against Hercules. Hated his guts. So she ordered Lyssa to punish him. See, even though Lyssa was the personification of mad rage, she was actually one of the more levelheaded gods. She tried to talk Gaia out of it, but Gaia wouldn't listen, and since she outranked her daughter, Lyssa had to do as Gaia commanded. But Hercules was Lyssa's stepbrother, and she didn't want to kill him. So rather than siccing rabid animals on him like she did to Actaeon, she gave Hercules rabies instead. She drove him mad. I guess she figured if anyone could beat the virus, Hercules could. And he did. But before he cleared it out of his system, he murdered his wife and kids. Tore them limb from limb. Ripped them apart with his—"

"Stop it!" Emily cried out. "Can't you see you're making Molly miserable?"

Molly was hiding her face in her hands. Her body was shaking in little jumps.

"You're such a loser, Will," Miles said, wrapping an arm around Molly's shoulder to comfort her. "If it was a different day, I'd knock your teeth out."

"What's the point of your story?" Heath was ready to pound Will, too. "There *was* a point to it besides making Molly cry, right?"

"Of course there's a moral to the story," Will said. "Think about it."

Before Heath could reply, Cricket started swishing ahead through the water excitedly. Pointing downriver, he hollered, "Look! Over there! Isn't that—?"

Heath saw it, too. Bright yellow and a sight for sore eyes, like a taxi waiting to take them home after their long, grueling day.

It was the dead man's kayak.

There's something wrong with me,
    I'm not doing well.
A busted, rusted truck is hardly
    worth the sell.
But it's not how long I lasted,
    or the miles that I went.
It's the beauty in my rearview mirror
    that makes my life well spent.

THE KAYAK WAS collared between two small boulders, bobbing slightly in the crack. It was a two-man boat with two cockpits. Both were empty.

"Do you think he was alone?" Cricket asked as Miles and Heath clambered up on top of the boulders and shifted the kayak free.

Heath looked down into the rear seat hole and saw a pink

sandal with a plastic daisy on the thong sloshing around in a broth of red water. "I don't think so."

It felt like Christmas when they found the paddle bobbing close by, not trying to escape at all.

Heath told Molly not to look while they prepared the kayak. After the blood was poured out and the boat was set and balanced in the river, the group helped Theo and Molly inside. The choice of passengers went undisputed. Theo knew how to kayak and for some unspoken reason it just seemed right that Molly should go with him—nautical etiquette maybe: women and children first, and she was the youngest girl in the group.

"Forty to fifty minutes," Theo guessed. "We'll be in Granite Falls in less than an hour."

"Don't forget about us," Dunbar said, only half joking.

"You'll be all right now." Heath patted Molly's arm. He was relieved because he believed his own words. "You know what you look like, Molly, all snug in that seat?"

With her chin tucked to her chest, she shook her head.

"You look like a perfectly good egg, safely back inside its carton."

She lifted her eyes to his, reached out from her seat, and pulled Heath in for a hug. He hugged her tight.

"We'll send help back right away," Theo assured them.

"I know you will," Heath said.

Will gave them last-minute advice. "Keep your ears open. If you hear bats, flip the kayak and wait under it until they're gone. There'll be plenty of air in the seat holes. And don't get out of the boat when you reach Granite Falls. Hyde Street runs parallel to the river. If people are alive in town, you'll see them. But don't get out of the boat until you know for sure how things are there."

"Listen for bats and don't get out of the boat," Molly parroted absently while picking at coils of shredded fiberglass where something big made claw marks on the side of the kayak.

"See you soon, Moll." Miles wrapped her in a careful hug, then swished away from the group, sniffling.

"Good luck," Will said, then he, Dunbar, and Heath launched the kayak off down the river. The remainders followed them, wading in the boat's gentle wake. Theo stabbed the water with his paddle and they quickly pulled away.

The Dray's course ran straight for quite a ways, so the group was able to track the kayak for several minutes until it was no more than a tiny fleck of yellow. Then it rounded a dash of land and was gone.

Unexpected sadness gripped Heath tightly. He felt so friable, as if a gentle breeze could crumble him into dust. Tears spilled from his eyes, skated down his cheeks, and slipped between his trembling lips. He washed the evidence away with a splash of river to the face.

"That Theo kid doesn't like me very much, does he?" Miles said, still staring off at the spot the kayak had vanished, his eyes veiny and pink.

"You made him your runner last year." Heath spoke softly because he knew his words were hard. "You weren't very nice to him."

Miles was taken aback by this. "I did? Oh. I guess that explains it."

"He's mad that you don't remember. Can't really blame him."

"Me neither." Miles gave a heaving sigh. "I suck."

Heath thought back to his first encounter with Miles earlier in the day. And then again later in the forest, before the porcupine charged. Mere hours ago, the kid had seemed so dangerous. Shivering in the water, shoulders sagging, full of self-loathing, Miles was the most pitiful creature Heath had ever seen.

Heath put his hand on the boy's shoulder. "Don't worry. You'll see him again."

"Hope so," said Miles. "I'll do better."

"I believe you. Talk to Theo at Granite Falls."

Dunbar caught the tail end of this exchange and repeated his earlier prognosis. "Granite Falls is fine. The virus couldn't have made it that far. It's not even windy today."

Heath's reply, if he'd felt like stealing Dunbar's brightness, which he didn't, would have been, *Bats don't need wind to get to Granite Falls.*

It was sometime around seven o'clock when Heath felt the first pangs of hunger. He'd forgotten all about the chicken salad sandwich he'd tucked into his pocket, had even napped with it, and now that he'd remembered, it was mushy and inedible like his mother's meat loaf. He dropped it into the water and watched little fish weave in and out of the pieces, nibbling the soggy chicken. Birds are supposed to eat fish, he thought irritably. Nobody minds the food chain anymore. He was tired. So tired, in fact, that when Dunbar nudged him he nearly fell over.

"You should talk to her," Dunbar said with a wink.

"Who?"

"Emily. I think she likes you. Lucky jerk."

Heath squinched his face and considered this. "She does not. Besides, that'd be weird, don't you think? Under the circumstances?"

"It's kinda weird that you seem to be talking to everyone *but* her."

Heath glanced over at Emily. She smiled at him, and he felt his ears warm and prickle.

"It's stupid," Heath hissed. "If she likes me, it's only because we're in this mess and she's not thinking right—"

"I agree," Dunbar sniffed.

"Stressful situations mess with peoples' emotions. Besides, Camp Harmony is done. It's not like we'll have a chance to spend time together, assuming we survive. She lives all the way in Portland."

Dunbar put it another way. "So what if we don't survive? Shouldn't you try to get to know her a little bit? For that reason alone? Emma's fighting with Will again. Now's your chance."

"Okay," Heath surrendered. "But not this second. It'll look like you put me up to it."

He shooed Dunbar away, waited thirty Mississippis, then waded sideways, gradually, until he was beside her. At that point he realized he didn't have a clue as to what to say.

For a few uncomfortable seconds they walked side by side silently like two horses pulling a wagon.

"I like your shoes," Emily said finally.

"Thanks," he replied, and they watched his fascinating feet for quite awhile until more words came to him. "Are your boots comfortable?"

He could feel Dunbar rolling his eyes behind him.

"Not really. They're leather so they're getting tighter in the water. If the rubber grip soles didn't make it easier to walk on the rocks, I'd probably ditch them and go barefoot."

"Mine have rubber soles, too."

"That's nice."

"Yeah."

More painful silence.

"Oh, I know what I wanted to ask," Heath blurted, excited to have a topic. "It's about what happened back in the livery. When you and Emma went off to decide whether to stay or head to the river."

"What about it?"

"I didn't think you'd win that one. Your sister seemed to have made up her mind. What did you say to her?"

"Not much," Emily said. "Just three words."

"That's it? Really?"

She smiled. "Rock, paper, scissors."

Heath laughed. "It all came down to—"

"Paper. Paper smothers rock."

"Sweet."

"Being twins isn't as fun as people might think. I mean, we're not as bad as Will and his sister. I love Em a lot, but we argue too much. It's gotten better though. When we were little we used to get into horrible fights. Bloody noses, scratching, hair pulling . . . over the littlest thing. Our mom got sick of having to be our referee so she taught us rock, paper, scissors. She said we had to use it to decide all of our arguments. It worked pretty well. Even now, we use it on a daily basis. But . . . if I'd lost in the livery . . . if I'd picked scissors . . . I would have asked for best-two-out-of-three. And if I'd lost that, I'd have argued the point with her some more. Anyway, I got lucky, and that saved a lot of time and hard feelings between Em and me. I knew that going to the river was the right choice. And I still think that. It's not anyone's fault that some of us didn't make it." Heath knew that what she meant was it wasn't *his* fault. Was he that transparent, that she could read his mind and sense his guilt over the deaths of the ones who died on the run to the river? After all, he'd helped talk them into leaving the livery. "You know that, right, Heath?"

"Yeah, I guess so," he said, nodding. He glanced down at his feet again, but this time he noticed a snail had hitched a ride on his shoe. He lifted his foot and plucked it loose.

"Looks like you found a friend," Emily said.

"I guess he's a good judge of character." Heath chuckled. He'd heard somewhere that girls liked confident guys. It seemed to work.

"Oh, is that so?" she said and touched his arm in a flirty gesture.

Heath ran his finger along the spiral pattern on the snail's grainy shell. "Or maybe he just had to get somewhere quicker than one foot per minute. That's how fast they go on land, anyway."

"You know a lot about nature and stuff," Emily said. "I think it's cool that you're so smart. I'm jealous. Sometimes I wish I'd spent more time hitting the books growing up and less time mucking horse stalls."

"But you love horses," Heath reminded her. "You and Emma are amazing riders. Everyone knows that. I saw it while I was watching you at the arena. The way you and Sweet Pea seemed to understand each other . . . it was impressive. I may know a lot about animals, but that's just from watching TV and reading books. The bond you have with Sweet Pea is something most people never experience with an animal. *I'm* jealous of *you*."

He felt himself melt just a bit from the warmth of her smile.

"Thanks," she said. "Heath . . ."

"Yeah?"

"Can I ask you a question?"

From her tone he could tell it wasn't about the snail. "Without a lasso?" he joked, setting the tiny gastropod free in the river.

"I don't know you very well, but you seem so mature. You're not all crazy like most boys your age. You're different somehow. I can't explain it."

"You can ask me anything, Em."

"Well, I was wondering . . . do your parents get along?"

Heath didn't have to think about his answer. "Yes, they love each other. They've been though a lot together, good and bad. The bad stuff probably brought them closer than the good stuff. Funny how that works, isn't it? Why do you ask?"

"My parents are splitting up. They told Em and me on the drive to camp."

"Oh." Heath felt a bit blindsided and woefully unqualified to offer advice. "I'm sorry."

"I wish the bad stuff had brought my parents closer, too. Instead Dad's moving to Hawaii to manage some resort there. I don't want him to leave. I've always gotten along better with him than I do with my mom. And now I'll only get to see him in the summer and holidays."

"Well . . . surfing on Christmas could be kinda fun," was all he could think to say.

"Yeah," Emily said, her frown fading into a slight smile. "I hadn't thought of that. That might be nice." Heath noticed that her nose *did* lean a little to the left. Cricket was right; the imperfection was cute.

"It'll be okay," he promised. "Your situation at home and the one we're in now. You'll see."

"Thanks, Heath."

"No problem."

"So how are *you* doing?" She took his hand in hers, and he felt his heart skip a beat. Until she turned it over, and he realized she only wanted to inspect the horseshoe scar Onyx had left on his palm. "Onyx really did a number on you."

"Oh. That. I'm okay. Besides, horseshoes are supposed to be lucky, right?"

"It depends. If the horseshoe is facing up, like a *U*, then yes. If you turn it over, the luck runs out." She let his hand go, breaking their connection far too soon for Heath.

He felt a sudden surge of bravery. "Listen, Em . . . Dunbar thinks you maybe . . . like me a little."

Her face softened and her brow rose and puckered in the middle. "Oh. I don't know why he would—I guess it's not Dunbar's fault. I never talk about Josh."

"Josh." Heath didn't know *who* Josh was, but he knew *what* Josh was.

"My boyfriend. In Portland."

"Right . . . right!" Heath backpedaled. "That's what I told Dunbar. That you probably had a boyfriend, and I wanted to make sure he didn't say anything stupid to you . . . you know . . . since you probably had a boyfriend. I'm just looking out for him. Being a buddy."

"Oh. That's nice of you." She looked uncomfortable.

"I'll go tell him now."

"I . . . okay."

"Okay."

"Heath?"

"Yeah?"

"That snail was a good judge of character. You're a really nice person."

"Thanks," he said in an overly cheery pitch. "You are, too."

Heath turned and high-stepped in Dunbar's direction. *Stupid, stupid, stupid.* He felt like an idiot.

He stared at the scarred hand dangling limply at his side. The horseshoe was upside down.

If you turn it over, the luck runs out, Emily had said.

It sure does, he thought, and like the molting crayfish, he searched the river's bottom for a suitable rock to hide under.

Shortly after, the group saw an overpass bridge up ahead. It was resting on four massive concrete pylons that rose twenty feet above the river.

"That must be the Mountain Loop Highway," Will deduced. "It's the road that runs between Granite Falls and Darrington. We should go up and check it out."

"For what?" Miles asked. "It's not safe. We should stay in the river."

"There're no animals following us," Will pointed out. "We lost them all at the bluffs. I'm going to check it out. Maybe I can wave down a car. For all we know, we're past the outbreak area. It's the Loop—someone could be along any minute. Don't you think that's worth the risk?"

Heath's surveyed the contour of the steep hill leading up to the bridge, looking for a footpath. He found one that seemed relatively safe. "It's a good plan. I'll go with you."

"It's settled then," Will announced. "Let's head up."

While the others waited in the water under the bridge, Heath and Will climbed the weedy slope to the guardrail. They straddled over it. The metal felt scorching against Heath's inner thighs. They found the road empty with the unexpected exception of an old pickup truck parked on the center line a quarter mile down the way. It was just sitting in the road, idling with its brake lights on.

"Let's check it out," Will said.

The boys jogged for a several yards, but the slapping noises their wet shoes made on the road were loud, and rather than attract animals, they decided it would be safer to walk. Through his waterlogged shoes Heath could feel the warm pavement flattening out the soles of his feet. It felt wonderful.

They eyed the hills around them for any sign of movement, but other than an eagle circling its nesting tree, the Cascades were as still as a painting. Any other time Heath probably wouldn't have noticed the sheet-like clouds creeping in from the west, but he noticed them now. He pointed them out to Will. "See those? They're cirrostratus."

"What does that mean?" Will asked. "Weather isn't really my area of expertise."

"It means rain is coming."

"Are you sure?"

"Yeah, I'm sure."

"That's awesome! When the animals get wet they'll—"

"Don't get your hopes up. It'll be awhile," said Heath. "Cirrostratus clouds usually appear a day or so before a storm. We'll be home by then."

"Oh." Will sounded disappointed. "Still, it's nice to know that it's coming."

"Agreed."

"So, loverboy . . ." Will grinned slyly. "Things didn't go so well with Emily, huh?"

Heath shouldn't have been surprised that Will had been eavesdropping on his conversation earlier—violating privacy was basically his "thing"—but he was caught off guard anyway. "Not that it's any of your business, Stringer. It went fine. Emily and I are friends, and that's more than we were when I woke up this morning. But weren't you a little preoccupied at the time? Looked to me like you were busy getting under Emma's skin. You're not exactly smooth with the ladies yourself."

"Actually she's the one who drew my attention to your awesome crash and burn. She was ignoring me. Seemed fixated on you, in fact."

"On me?"

"Or maybe on her sister. She's very protective of Emily. Probably doesn't appreciate a loser like you hitting on her twin, especially when Mr. Perfect is waiting on her back in Portland."

Heath was ready to pounce until he realized Will was just ribbing him.

"Lighten up, Heath. It's not the end of the world. There's plenty of fish in the river."

"I guess so." Heath thought for a moment, then said, "I need to ask you something."

"I'll trade you. A question for a question."

"Nothing's ever easy with you, is it?" Heath sighed.

"Never."

"You go first."

"How bad is it?"

It was a vague question. Heath wasn't sure which "it" Will was referring to: The general attitude of the group toward Will, their chances of survival, his crush on Emily—

"Your cancer," Will clarified.

"Oh. That."

"So I'm right," Will said, and he was, although for once he didn't seem happy about it.

"Yes. I have cancer. The doctor's call it lymphoblastic lymphoma."

"That's a mouthful."

"It's a cancer that attacks all over . . . the lymph nodes, the chest, the central nervous system . . . even bone marrow. I had it when I was eight. I went through the treatments. A mix of radiation and chemotherapy. It was bad. My hair fell out. I couldn't eat. I lost thirty pounds—I didn't weigh much to begin with. But I fought hard and it went into remission. I got better."

"And now it's back?"

"Worse than before. I'm stage four, which means that even if I go through all of the painful treatments again, I may still die."

Will stopped for a moment and looked around. They were almost to the truck now. If an animal came after them, or blocked the road back to the bridge, they'd be in big trouble.

"What's wrong?" Heath asked.

"The truck's brake lights just went off. Someone's in there."

"I don't see anyone through the back window, do you?"

"No. The driver may still be in the cab though. Maybe he's hurt and lying down on the seat."

"Or maybe he's dead."

"He could have run off into the woods."

"If he had a death wish, maybe."

"Like you?"

"What's *that* supposed to mean?"

Will said, "For starters, why did you even come to Camp Harmony? Shouldn't you be in a hospital getting better? OxyContin is a painkiller, not a cure. And I notice the way you seem to place everyone's safety above your own. Self-preservation isn't really your thing right now, is it?"

"Not really," Heath admitted. He didn't want to talk about it anymore, but a deal was a deal. "I'm not accepting treatment for the cancer this time."

"That's stupid!" Will shoved him. "Why not?"

"That's more like two or three questions."

"It's one question in multiple parts. Let's start with why you're trying to get yourself killed for the others."

"I'm not *trying* to get killed for anyone. I'm trying to make sure that everyone survives. It has a lot to do with beating cancer as a kid. Going through something like that, cheating death, it changed me. I started to appreciate life and stopped caring about all the petty stuff I faced every day. I focused on what's important, like my family and friends. After I was discharged from the cancer wing of the hospital, I made it a point to go back every weekend to visit the kids that were still sick and the nurses who were fighting to get them well. I'd bake stuff for them, like cupcakes or lemon bars. I got to be pretty good at it. It wasn't a huge deal, but I could tell they appreciated it. And it made me feel good, too. So, yeah, maybe that's why we're all here, Will. To care for one another. Maybe we owe that to each other."

"You don't owe me anything," Will said quickly.

"Yeah, I do," Heath insisted. "I owe you. And so do the others. Dunbar, and Miles and Molly . . . We all owe you. And I owe them. *And you owe us.* It's called *being human.* We draw from each other's strength and give it back when someone needs it more. I came face-to-face with death and realized I'd almost missed the entire point of my existence. Cancer led to a more meaningful life than I ever thought possible. Even if I only got another six years out of the deal. I'm grateful for that. A second chance was worth fighting for then."

"Wow, that's deep, Heath."

"You're making fun of me."

"A little. And now? What's changed this time around?"

"Now? I just can't do it again. I don't have any fight left in me. I know it, and I've accepted it. It's as simple as that."

They walked along in silence for a bit, then Will said, "You're totally lame, but whatever. It's your life. Your turn. What do you want to know?"

Heath approached his question as cautiously as they were approaching the truck. "I need you to tell me the truth. Did you leave your noisemaker in the livery or did you really lose it on the lawn like you claimed?"

Will stopped and turned to face Heath. "I—"

The answer, denial or confession, was interrupted by the sound of a man groaning in pain. It was coming from the front side of the pickup. The boys ran toward it. In a million years, they wouldn't have expected what they found.

The truck was parked on top of a horse, the passenger-side tires were resting on her broken front legs, the bumper was pinning her flanks and hind legs to the ground. It was a camp horse; the one Emily had been riding earlier in the day. Her favorite. Sweet Pea. She was still wearing the blindfold Dunbar said Mr. Soucandi had tied over her eyes to calm her down. There was a lather of gooey salvia caked into the fur on her muzzle. Burgundy blood was streaming in rivulets down her brown neck and turning deep pink where it soaked into the shag of her white mane. Her eyes were glassy and vacant. Trapped beneath the horse, still tucked up on the saddle, was her trainer, Mr. Soucandi, and he, on the other hand, was alive.

"Boys . . ." he groaned, lifting his head off the pavement. The skin on the left side of his face was scraped badly, road rash. There was a gash above his left eyebrow. But it was evident that his lower half was worse for wear. "My leg. I can't get it free."

A truck on top of a horse, on top of Mr. Soucandi. It wasn't going to be easy to free him, but Heath felt they had to try.

"We'll each take an arm and see if we can't pull him out."

"You know he's going to slow us down," Will said.

Heath glared at him.

"Fine." Will squatted. "He's *your* package though. *You* can deliver him to Granite Falls."

That prospect was daunting—the pain was slowing Heath down. He was tired, near exhaustion. But he would hang in as long as he physically could. Heath stepped around Mr. Soucandi's head and gripped his right wrist tightly. He felt Soup Can's pulse pounding beneath his fingertips.

"Hurry..." Mr. Soucandi pleaded, but he flinched when Will took hold of his left arm, causing the boys to hesitate. "My shoulder... I think it's dislocated."

Will said, "Sorry, but if we're going to pull you free we can't afford to be gentle. Okay?"

Mr. Soucandi blinked twice in acceptance.

"Count of three?"

Heath nodded.

"One... two... three!"

Heath should have seen what was coming next. Bad things seemed to happen at the end of Will Stringer's three-counts.

Sweet Pea's head launched up from the pavement, and the horse swung it like a hammer at Will, chomping furiously at the air, her teeth clacking together loudly. Will fell onto his back. "It's still alive!"

The horse whinnied, then snorted a spray of blood and foam. She was still trapped by the truck but was determined to get at them, twisting her neck to an unnatural degree. She moved like a downed power line, thrashing against the blacktop, spewing spit into the air. Laden with the virus, her saliva was just as deadly as electrical sparks. Every time Will and Heath tried to grab hold of Mr. Soucandi, the horse would launch her head at them, cobralike, biting air, snorting and blowing snot through her enormous nostrils. There were cracking noises, too. Sweet Pea was breaking the vertebrae in her neck and withers in an effort to reach a little farther with each strike.

"Go get some water from the river!" Heath ordered

Will. "We'll toss it on her. She's suffering, hurry!"

Will shook his head and grabbed Mr. Soucani's wrist again. "There's no time for that. We have to pull him free now!"

A thumping noise inside the truck grabbed Heath's attention. "I think the driver's still inside," he said. "We could use some extra muscle. Maybe the person can help us." Despite Will's protest, Heath let go of Mr. Soucandi's arm and circled behind the truck to the passenger door. The window was filthy, he could barely see through it. He grabbed the door latch and lifted. *Click*. But a voice in his head told him to wait. He released the latch and leaned against the door. It clicked again.

Heath cupped his hands against the window, then pressed his forehead against them. He could make out the keys swinging from the ignition. Something had just jostled them.

"Hello? Anyone in there?"

He jumped back from the truck as a boney cat bounded from the floorboard beneath the steering wheel column and attacked the glass in a spectacular fit of violence. It scratched furiously at the window, hissing and emitting a horrific *reeeeeeee* sound from its contorted, hate-filled face. One of its claws caught in the rubber seal around the window and tore out of its paw, but it continued its attack. Right before the window became too opaque with cat blood to see through, Heath spied a hump of cloth and denim, the cat's owner, still inside of the truck, slumped into the leg space on the passenger side.

"The driver is dead!" Heath yelled to Will. "And there's a freakin' cat in there!"

"Then get back here, dummy! I can't do this by myself!"

Heath circled around the front, leaving a wide berth between himself and Sweet Pea's striking range, which was extending by inches with every crack of her neck bones. He clasped the horse trainer's wrist with both of his hands.

"You—you have to pull harder," Mr. Soucandi grunted, then gasped for air. He was in great pain. "Just grab my arms and pull like hell."

Heath nodded. "Okay."

This time Soup Can led the count. It was quick. "Three, two, one, pull!"

Mr. Soucandi screamed in agony. But he'd budged a bit.

Sweet Pea's jaw was creaking as it opened abnormally wide, unhinging like a snake's, mere inches from Will's ankle.

"One, two, three, pull!"

Soup Can's knee slipped free of Sweet Pea's body.

"One, two, three, pull!"

He left a boot beneath the horse, but Soup Can was free at last. They dragged him to the safety of the road's shoulder. He thanked them. "Bless you, boys," he said, then exhaled in sweet relief. "Bless you both."

Mr. Soucandi used Will and Heath as crutches as they hobbled back to the bridge. "Sweet Pea went crazy in the barn. . . ." Mr. Soucandi told them the story between winces and groans. "I'd blindfolded her to calm her down, but she was bad. I couldn't control the old girl. I never should've gotten on her back. I knew better. It was stupid. She kept trying to twist around to bite me, but she couldn't reach. Horses aren't built like owls, you know. Their necks only turn so far. She took off running. Guess she can see a bit—the blindfold is flimsy."

"And the truck?" Will asked.

"It came barreling down the road at us, sliding all over, bouncing against the guardrail. Sweet Pea wasn't even scared of it. Charged it head-on. You saw the results of that little joust. Poor fellow in the truck . . ."

"I think he was already dead before the crash," Heath said, trying to lift any burden of blame off Mr. Soucandi's conscience. He hoped that would make the man feel better, even if just a bit. "There was a cat inside the cab. It was rabid, like Sweet Pea."

"Rabies . . ." Soup Can said.

"Yeah," said Will.

"I saw a bear," Mr. Soucandi recalled suddenly. "It was on the road. It tried to run alongside Sweet Pea, but she was too fast for it. It was a little one, maybe three hundred pounds. Little, but it could have easily killed Sweet Pea with one swipe if it caught her."

Heath and Will exchanged looks across Mr. Soucandi's chest.

"It wasn't after Sweet Pea, sir," Heath said. "It was after you."

"Me?" Soup Can said, perplexed.

"We'll get you down to the river, and then Will can fill you in on what's happening."

"Where are you going?" Will asked.

"First to get some water. Then I'll come back up to . . . you know . . . *help* Sweet Pea."

"It's just an animal!" Will said sharply.

Heath threw his head back, exasperated. "Why are you so okay with leaving her behind? Letting everyone and everything suffer? I'll be five minutes! You can't wait five stinking minutes?"

"Use your brain!" Will refused to back down. "If you want to die so bad, then die helping the group, not putting down some stupid horse that's on its way out anyway. You'll get your chance to be a martyr, I'm sure."

"I should never have told you."

"Yeah, well you did," said Will.

"Boys . . . don't argue," Mr. Soucandi muttered.

"Not to use against me! It was a secret, Will, not a tool for your stupid 'chess set.'"

Will seemed genuinely wounded. "I won't tell the others. I promise."

"Yeah, like I believe that." Heath was livid, but that didn't change the fact that Will was right, as usual. He didn't want to leave Sweet Pea to suffer, but getting the others to safety was more important than risking his life for a horse. Even one that Emily—*Josh's* girlfriend—loved. Heath glanced back at the truck. "Fine, let's get out of here."

They carefully maneuvered Mr. Soucandi down the hill

and into the river, setting him down on one of the thick concrete supports reinforcing the bridge columns. Em and Em rushed to hug him, but Heath interceded. "He's banged up. Let him rest for a minute."

"Strangest thing, what happened to—" Soup Can started, but Heath cut him off.

"It's everywhere, sir." He didn't want Emily knowing that Sweet Pea was on the road above, dying a slow, painful death. That was the last thing she needed to hear, as unbearable as the situation was already. "It's a new strain of rabies. We think it's in the air. The woods aren't safe. The road either, obviously." He didn't think it prudent to mention the bear to the others. "You're okay now though. The animals are afraid of water."

Mr. Soucandi's eyes lit up. "You—you came all this way in the river?"

"We sure did," Dunbar said proudly.

Mr. Soucandi looked puzzled. He was working something out in his mind. He shook his head spastically a few times, reminding Heath of the fox he'd observed outside the livery window.

"We're going to Granite Falls," Emma said. "Following the river's course."

The horse trainer blinked, straightened up, and furrowed his brow. Then, in a buoyant voice, he said the strangest thing.

"We're off to see the Wizard?"

Reset.

My neighbor works real hard,
Day and night, like a fool,
Landscaping in his yard,
Cleaning his swimming pool.
What makes him tick is stacking his sticks,
Earning his keep while his neighbors sleep.
His teeth are his only tool.

WRITING POSTCARDS. Judging from the position of the sun drifting through the nearly solid sheet of clouds, that's what they'd be doing now if Camp Harmony hadn't been overrun by rabid mammals. It was past the dinner hour, and the schedule demanded some quiet time for reflecting on the events of the day and writing notes to their parents about them. Campers were each required to fill out the entire back of one postcard before they were freed to leave their cabins and head to the main lodge for games and shameless flirting. Heath resented Postcard Time more than anything.

He never knew what to say. Or more accurately, he couldn't say what his parents would want to hear. They didn't care that he'd spent the day waterskiing or playing tennis with Cricket or making boomerangs with Dunbar in the craft hut. He knew they skimmed every card, eagerly searching for one line of very specific information: had he changed his mind about accepting treatment for his cancer?

Weeks ago, when Dr. Wiley broke the news that the disease had returned, worse than before, there was a kind of emotional frenzy that infiltrated his home life. His mom quit her job to stay home and prepare for the treatment and recovery process, calling doctors, arranging consultations, reading up on new drug therapies (after all, she'd reminded him incessantly, it had been six years since the disease went into remission and medical breakthroughs happened every day). Then there was the ugly skirmish with their insurance company. It had refused to cover the battery of treatments Heath would need to get better. This skirmish lasted right up until the "heartless thieves," as his mom called them, got a letter from his dad's lawyer. But in the end, the most draining part of it all was the tug-of-war that ensued between Heath and his parents when he told them he wasn't accepting treatment this time. That he didn't want to do it all over again. That it wasn't a war he wanted to wage any-more. That he'd rather die than suffer through the physical torment of the radiation and the drugs. His parents didn't get it. His mom, through heaving sobs, asked Heath if it was because he didn't want to lose his hair again. It was a silly question, but he'd been patient with them because he had to be. Because they loved him and deserved to be handled tenderly, he calmly and repeatedly explained that it had nothing to do with his stupid hair—which was just a bunch of soft quills, when you thought about it—and everything to do with leaving the world on his terms. He was ready to go. Peacefully, not fighting and tearing to consume every ounce of life like Quilt Face, Onyx, and Sweet Pea. Like Will, in a way. But after awhile, he got tired of explaining and just started making plans. Coming to Camp Harmony was his last chance to experience life the way he wanted, out in nature, surrounded by kids who didn't have a care in the world beyond who would win the Color War at the end of the summer, Team Purple or Team Orange. So every time he was faced with a fresh postcard he wrote in space-wasting, colossal letters. And even though he made an effort to toss in a few specifics about his routine, his underlying message was always the same.

I love you both. I'm having the time of my life.

Besides, today was really the first day he had anything interesting to report:

Dear Mom and Dad,
The camp was attacked by rabid animals. I'm currently wading five miles down a river with seven other people,

heading toward the nearest town.

Everything outside the river is trying to kill us, but I suspect my cabinmate, Will, is doing a better job at it. You'll be happy to know we are now under adult supervision, but he's a little mental and thinks we're on our way to the City of Oz. I'll write again tomorrow. If I'm still alive.

　　Love,

　　Heath (a.k.a. the Scarecrow)

In order to convince Mr. Soucandi to leave with them, they had to play along with his latest delusion. This is how things appeared in the old man's addled brain: Miles was the Cowardly Lion; Heath was the Scarecrow; Will, as pale as he was, looked like the Tin Man, and Soup Can fused the Ems together to make up Dorothy Gale. Thankfully there was no Toto among them, rabid or otherwise. It was hard to say, since Soup Can's delusion was so far out there this time, but Dunbar and Cricket may have been members of the Lollipop Guild, even though he got his movies crossed and called them Oompa-Loompas. They led the horse trainer carefully through the river—the Yellow Brick Road—on their way to the Emerald City—Granite Falls—to find him the heart he said he needed. Like the Scarecrow, it was clearly a new brain that he should have been petitioning the Wizard for.

The animals came back slowly. The first to show up

was a western spotted skunk. The group smelled him five minutes before they saw his portly body shuffle through the curtain of tall grass ahead of them on the east bank. When the skunk saw the group, it bounded quickly toward them along the shore in a gait that was half waddle and half hop. Heath always wondered why the skunk in the Looney Tunes cartoons bounced up and down when he ran, and now he knew it's because they do in real life. The skunk was rabid, too. They were still within the outbreak zone. Heath imagined what would happen if the virus escaped Washington and spread across the country. Across the world. There were four hundred billion mammals on the planet. That meant that for every human there'd be sixty-five animals eager to kill them. It was a sobering thought. As they continued on, they were joined by deer, a few dogs (all former pets with collars and tags that jangled as they barked incessantly), a different coyote, wood rats, a family of marmots, a porcupine that was much larger than the one Heath had killed back at camp, raccoons, and, most disturbing of all, a milk cow that had escaped its pasture by charging straight through barbed wire. She still had a loop of it tangled around her neck and brisket.

"A freakin' cow." Miles moaned, shaking his head as she joined the animal parade. "Even the cows want to kill us now."

"*Them* I don't blame," said Emma. "I'm surprised they didn't rise up against us years ago."

"Especially Dunbar," Will said with a self-amused chuckle.

Dunbar licked his lips. "So I like a juicy burger once in awhile. What of it?"

The cow let out an angry *mrurrrrrrrrrrrrr* sound and snorted in punctuation.

Heath kept an eye out for Quilt Face. It seemed unlikely that she'd find a way around the channel and past the bridge, but when she didn't return he felt a little let down. He'd expected more from her. Maybe it had been his imagination, but he'd come to see her as the alpha of not just her pack but of the whole herd of animals. No, *herd* wasn't a term you could use for zombies or for the odd collection of creatures that had followed them on the shore. What do you call dozens of different species coming together with the sole purpose of killing you? Like a group of crows, Heath decided, you'd call them a murder. He'd pegged Quilt Face as their leader. The head murderer. Maybe he'd been wrong.

After they found Mr. Soucandi, the journey was uneventful up until what should have been the last mile before Granite Falls. The current seemed stronger, but the water was shallower, which meant more walk, less wade. It was, fortunately, still deep enough for a kayak to travel upon, although Theo and Molly would have had to carry the boat over gravel bars in a few spots where slight shoaling occurred.

Heath wished they could run the last mile, especially since it seemed more animals were joining the cavalcade with every passing minute, but Mr. Soucandi's leg was hurting, and with his right boot still planted under Sweet Pea, he had a hard time hobbling across the Dray's rocky bottom.

And then they reached the fork. They saw it coming, but hoped that when they reached the bifurcation, it would present itself as a short-lived thing, with the water rejoining again within range of sight. That wasn't the case. The river separated into two distinct directions. The group huddled together and debated their options.

"I say we go to the right," Will said. "The left looks narrow, shallower, like it wants to be a creek. I don't trust it."

Heath agreed.

"But if we go to the left, we'll shake most of the animals," Dunbar said, and he was correct, too. The animals on the right bank had no way of crossing over to the banks of the left. If they tried, they'd die.

Will said, "If we pick the one that doesn't run by Granite Falls, it might dry up out in the woods and that could get us killed."

In a show of solidarity, Emily and Emma decided to keep the animals and go to the right, so the rock, paper, and scissors stayed stored away.

Hands were raised and counted. Cricket and Dunbar were outvoted. They headed right, but before they got more than a hundred yards they heard a familiar growl. Quilt Face had found them. But she and her pack were on the far side of the left branch, with no way to cross over. The agitation in her face was clear even through the wooded peninsula that divided the two streams.

"Your girlfriend's back," Will said, clapping Heath on the shoulder. Then he turned to Emily and said, "Bet you didn't know he was two-timing you, huh?"

Emily blushed, but Heath was too focused on Quilt Face to care. He'd underestimated the wolf again. He had a feeling that might end up as the epitaph on his tombstone when all was said and done. "She must have crossed over the bridge and climbed down to the west bank," he said, a tinge of admiration in his voice.

"Well, she screwed up, didn't she?" Miles hurled a rock in Quilt Face's direction. It skidded at her feet, and she jumped sideways to avoid it.

"Knock it off," Heath said. "It's not their fault, remember?"

"Relax, I was just firing a warning shot. I wasn't aiming to hit her."

"There's a nice little café in town I'm sure you two will love," Will crooned. Then he cupped his hands to his mouth and yelled over at Quilt Face, "Don't worry! Heath'll meet you for dinner at Bella Vita on Stanley Street!"

Miles thought this was hilarious and joined in. "You two can share a meatball like Lady and the Tramp! Ooh la la!"

"Keep shouting, morons. Really smart," Heath admonished them.

Will grinned. "Are you the lady or the tramp? Or is it Beauty and the Beast?"

Heath was irked. He didn't want anyone hurtling rocks *or* insults at the pathetic creatures. They weren't in their right mind. He glanced over at Mr. Soucandi, who was babbling to himself about ruby slippers. Right minds were becoming a dwindling commodity.

Will held up Sylvester's bow. "Want me to kill her? That'd shake up the pack."

"Quit it," Heath said. "She's harmless."

"For now," said Will.

Heath kept walking. "C'mon. Let's get out of here."

Quilt Face split the air between them with one last mournful cry. Will quoted ninth-grade Shakespeare. "Parting is such sweet sorrow."

The animals followed for as long as they could, cursing the kids with growls, barks, yaps, and howls. It was quite a send-off. But soon they'd faded from sight, and the forest became blissfully quiet. The water in the branch they'd picked grew steadily deeper and when it seemed to taper off at waist-level, Emma said, "I think we made the right choice." Even those on the other side of the vote, Cricket and Dunbar, had to agree.

"It feels like the old Dray again," Cricket said. He hadn't been very talkative for awhile. In fact, Heath noticed, he looked very ill.

"You okay, man?"

"Not really," Cricket answered, his voice weak. "Are you cold? The river's cold, right?"

The water still felt fairly warm to Heath. But dusk had arrived, and he knew that with the sun dunking past the tree line the Dray would start to cool rapidly. "Not really. Maybe you're coming down with a fever or something. It's probably not healthy to stay in a river this long. It's been, what, five hours?"

Cricket considered the length of his shadow. "Yeah,

that's about right. I hope we get there soon. I'd kill for a hot cup of coffee."

This remark set off a round of the First Thing I'll Do When We Reach Granite Falls game. Dunbar surprised no one with: "Eat a gallon of ice cream." Emily wanted to call her dad. Emma went into detail about the joys of shampoo. Miles said he'd order a thick, juicy steak, then he stuck his tongue out at the cow (amazingly, she was keeping up with them despite having to negotiate her bulky body across loose, shifting rocks). Heath mentioned socks. Will didn't play, although Heath knew exactly what his cabinmate *should* do when they reached Granite Falls—write a confession.

They expected the forest to dwindle as they approached the town, but instead it seemed to thicken. The river current slowed to a crawl and the water got deep fast. Their feet still touched the bottom, except for Cricket's, who hitched a piggyback ride on Miles. The river widened, too, spreading out laterally, invading the tree line, drowning the shrubbery.

"This is a *pond*," Heath declared with alarm.

"It can't be," Emily said. "The Dray runs by Granite Falls, right?"

"This isn't the Dray," Will groaned. "We picked the wrong branch."

"We better not have!" Miles threatened, but he was as much to blame as anyone, since he'd voted for the right side, too.

When they waded through a tarp of lily pads it became obvious that Heath was right. A nubby turtle head poking up from below cinched his case.

"We could double back right now," Cricket insisted. "It's a half mile to the split."

"Yeah, let's go," Miles agreed with his sickly passenger.

"How did this happen?" Emma asked, on the verge of despair.

"There's your answer." Will pointed to a wall of downed and stacked trees in the distance.

"It's a beaver dam!" Dunbar said. "Wow, I always wanted to see one of those."

"It's huge," Heath noted. Eyeballing the structure he estimated its size. "It has to be forty feet long. Maybe ten feet high."

"That'd stop the river's flow, for sure," Emily marveled.

"That's gotta be the biggest dam ever," added Miles.

"Nope." Dunbar set him straight. "There's one in Alberta, Canada, that you can see from space. It's half a mile long."

"Oh," Miles said.

"But it's still impressive. Beavers sometimes leave drainage holes in the dams so the water can get through. Maybe we'll pick up the river again on the other side." Dunbar set out toward the dam. "Let's go check it out."

"No!" Miles gripped Dunbar's arm. "What if the beavers are home?"

Dunbar tried to put his mind at ease. "Beavers don't live inside of dams. They live in the tunnels they dig in the mud along the banks. *Underwater* tunnels, which means they're either dead from hydrophobia, or they abandoned their homes and are staying on the shore like the rest of the animals. We'll be fine."

Miles loosened his grip and Dunbar waded away. The group followed, with the Ems taking a turn assisting Mr. Soucandi through a film of algae that floated on the surface of the pond like cold soup skin.

"Musty." Heath sniffed the air. The pond had an earthy smell, a mix of minerals, dead plants, and something else. Rotting fish, maybe. It overpowered the pine scent of the forest that he'd come to enjoy.

As they neared the dam, the sound of trickling water returned.

Dunbar seemed thrilled. "Hear that? I think the river is getting through!"

"So this may lead to town after all?" Miles asked.

"Maybe," Dunbar nodded. "But we need to get past the dam if we're going to follow it."

A faint moo called to them from back near the vague entrance of the pond.

"We lost the cow," Emma said. "The rest of them, too."

Swack!

Heads swiveled.

The noise was like a wet towel slapping against the surface of the water. The group turned in the direction of the east bank, which was difficult to demarcate since the water seemed to spread without definable boundaries into the forest.

"What was that?" asked Emily.

They scanned the pond but saw nothing moving.

"A fish jumping, maybe," Will said, tossing out an explanation.

"Yes! A fish!" Dunbar accepted it eagerly.

Swack! Swack!

This time they traced the sound to the source, a chevron shaped series of ripples coming toward them on the water. At the point of the V they saw two nostrils, two eyes, and two round ears jutting up from the water. A broad, flat, scaly tail rose up behind the head and smacked the water hard.

SWACK!

More ripples formed, a dozen maybe, starting at a thin line of mud that Heath now recognized as the bank. The Vs fanned out and approached like torpedoes in their direction. They slapped their tails again and again.

"Flying monkeys," Mr. Soucandi said under his breath. "Evil . . ."

Emma presented a more accurate identification. "Those are beavers."

Dunbar was baffled. "How are they able to—?"

"They must not be infected," Will said. "They're not afraid of the water."

"Then why are they swimming toward us?" Emily asked. It was a good question.

Heath set the group in motion. "They've got the Flash! Let's go. Over the dam. Hurry!"

Will said, "I second that motion," and the two boys took Mr. Soucandi from the twins and half-walked, half-dragged him toward the dam.

Even with Cricket on his back, his long, powerful legs carried Miles into the lead.

They could hear the beavers snorting and making weird

grunting noises. They sounded like humans with duct tape over their mouths trying to talk. *Errr Errr. Mrm mrm.*

"Move it!" Will ordered. "They're almost here!"

The beavers' swim path curled to intersect the group, but the kids and Soup Can reached the dam ahead of them. It was taller than Heath had guessed, maybe fourteen feet high, a treacherous climb to the summit.

"Guys, Cricket doesn't look good at all," Miles said, lowering his passenger carefully into the water.

Cricket's legs crumpled beneath him, and he sank against the dam's spongy outer casing of smaller branches. "I don't feel so hot," he mumbled.

Heath took the entire burden of the old horse trainer and motioned for Will to climb. "You and Miles get to the top. Dunbar in the middle. I'll pass up Cricket and Soup Can. Em and Em, just get over as fast as you can! Go!"

The four kids scampered up the dam, choosing branches that seemed sturdy enough to support their weight.

Will made it to the top first. "Send someone up!"

Heath had a split second to make a decision and chose Cricket, figuring that if Mr. Soucandi was in his right mind, that's the way he'd want it. Heath draped Cricket over his shoulder and stepped up onto a thick bough. He was scanning the stack for a handhold when he heard a splash directly below his foot. He looked down into the face of a huge beaver, its eyes wild and swimming with disease. With every ounce of strength he possessed, he tossed Cricket up the dam as far as he could. Dunbar and Miles caught Cricket and hauled his limp body to the peak. Heath lost his footing and started to fall back into the water but grasped a branch at the last second. The beaver was snorting furiously, shimmying up the dam to get at Heath.

"Get away from that boy!" Mr. Soucandi cried out as he grabbed the beaver's powerful tail, dragging the rodent back down into the water.

Reset.

The beaver objected with a loud hiss, jerked around, and bit Mr. Soucandi on his boney forearm. Purple vines erupted at the bite and spread out across the poor man's wrinkly skin. He fell back into the water with the beaver still on top of him, still biting away, tearing at his flesh, mad beyond madness. Soup Can died without uttering another sound.

An arrow pierced the beaver straight through the neck and pinned it to the horse trainer's chest. The animal struggled briefly, then wheezed out its final breath.

Heath found Will at the top, loading a second arrow into Sylvester's bow. There was a look of determination in the boy's eyes. Heath wondered if he'd judged Will too harshly. How many times had Will saved them so far? He'd led them to the livery. Then to the river. He'd saved them from the bats. He'd risked his own life to pull Mr. Soucandi out from under Sweet Pea. Sure, he'd been reluctant, but he still did it. And now he was watching over Heath, protecting him once again. Were these the acts of the kind of monster who would use kids as bait during their run from the livery to the river? He wasn't so sure anymore.

"Heath!" Emma cried out. "They're on you!"

A half dozen beavers reached the bottom of the dam

and set to climbing, hissing and snorting as they wriggled upward. Another half dozen swam in behind the first wave. Heath didn't know much about beavers, but he'd never associated them with their cousin the rat until now, as their wet, bulky bodies slithered vulgarly across the branches. They grunted at him, baring their sharp, chisel teeth. Strands of lethal saliva stretched between the maxilla and the mandible halves of their jaws. Their wide black eyes were locked on his exposed flesh, eager to tear meat away from his body. Wet and diseased, like the rats throughout history that slipped off so many boats in so many ports and spread so many plagues across the world.

This wasn't the beavers' fault, he knew that, but he loathed them anyway. He *despised* them. They wanted him dead and it wasn't fair. What had he done to them? Nothing! The beavers—all the animals—were relentless, attacking and attacking, trying to destroy him, and he'd finally had ENOUGH!

Heath found a branch as thick as a chair leg, yanked it free, and squeezed it so tightly that wet bark crumbled through his fingers. Mr. Soucandi had been right—Heath was a scarecrow, but there was no straw inside of him. He was a scarecrow stuffed with anger, resentment, bitterness, and grief.

"GET AWAY FROM ME!" Heath raised his spear above his head and thrust it downward with power.

"JUST."

Stab.

"LET."

Stab.

"ME."

Stab.

"BE!"

When he saw the animal was dead, he turned and climbed as the next beaver in line growled with vengeful fury.

"Help him, Dunbar!" Emily ordered. "You're the closest!" She tried to pull a branch out to use as a spear, but it was lodged firmly, so she yanked on another and that one slipped loose. "Here!" She tossed it to Dunbar. He caught it and made his way back down the dam.

Three beavers were homing in on Heath, the nearest only a body length away. He tried to outclimb it, but he'd reached a section of the dam where the branches beneath his feet were thin and weak. They cracked under his weight, and he couldn't pull himself up. Will put an arrow through the beaver's tail, but it barely noticed—it was consumed by its need to reach and kill Heath. His next arrow went wide and disappeared through a gap in the dam.

"Do better!" Emma shouted.

"Shut up, Emma!" Will bristled. "I don't want to hit Heath! I'm not the shot Sylvester was!"

The thought of their dead friend set off a trigger in Heath's mind. He found renewed energy and, more importantly, a secure foothold. He climbed until he was next to Dunbar at the middle.

The beavers were faster, covering twice the distance in the same time.

Heath went to make a leap up to a thick shaft of pine when he realized his foot was jammed tightly between two rigid branches. He gripped his ankle with his free hand and tugged but couldn't pull it loose. He was twisted at an angle that denied him the balance he needed to strike with his spear. "I'm stuck!" he told the others.

"What?" Dunbar panicked. He was already heading back to the top.

The beavers were so close that Heath could hear their sucking, raspy breaths.

"Use that thing!" Heath said, pointing at Dunbar's spear.

Dunbar froze. "I—I've never killed anything before. I don't think I can."

The dam was now covered with the huge rodents, all grunting and chirring, spitting foam, and reeking of mud, rotted plants, and death.

Heath tried a new approach. "Dunbar, remember the Zombie Apocalypse game? You said when you kill a zombie, it's a merciful thing, remember? It's the same thing here! The beavers are in pain, Dunbar! It's okay to end their pain!"

Heath's words connected. Dunbar took a deep breath and exhaled loudly through puffed cheeks. A beaver lunged at Heath and found itself skewered on the end of Dunbar's lance.

While Emily watched over Cricket, Emma and Miles slid down to Heath and attempted to pry his foot loose. Miles grunted and his muscles bulged as he strained to pull apart the two branches that were locked like a vise around Heath's ankle. Will killed two more beavers with the bow, but there were still eight on the dam—six were after Heath, the other two were climbing straight to the top.

Dunbar shook his spear vigorously until the dead beaver slid off the end and tumbled down into the pond, knocking another off the dam as it fell. Dunbar let loose a guttural cry and lanced a third beaver in the heart. Then he slew another. Blood spattered up his striking arm and across his face, but he kept on jabbing, pausing only to shake dead beavers off his weapon.

"He's out!" Emma shouted when Heath's foot finally slipped free. "Let's go, Dunbar! To the top!"

Dunbar blinked and woke up, released from his bloodlust. He saw the dripping red spear in his hand, then tossed it into the pond in disgust. "I'm coming."

Miles hit the peak first. With impressive ease he yanked the others up and over, one at a time. Will ran out of arrows, so he flung the bow at a beaver and actually hit it. The beaver slipped and fell through a wide gap into the dam. With Cricket draped over Miles's shoulder the group made it down the backside of the dam in seconds, miraculously without breaking their necks.

The structure had drainage holes like Dunbar guessed; they landed in knee-deep, flowing water. Will, Heath, and Emma each freed a spear, took a Spartan-like stance in the shallow river, and waited while Miles carried Cricket to safety. Emily ran alongside of him.

The seconds ticked by.

Swack! Swack! Swack! They could hear the beavers swimming away from the dam, back toward their lodges in the bank, spanking the water with their tales in frustration.

"They're gone." Will dropped to his knees in the water. Dunbar collapsed down next to him. The spilling current rinsed the beaver blood off his hands and arms, dyeing the water around them a deep red wine color. Heath knelt down and massaged his bruised ankle. The three boys kept their eyes on the crest of the dam, just in case the beavers doubled back.

Emma's shoulders sagged and she cried. Emily dropped to her knees and hugged her twin tight. They mourned for their friend and instructor, Mr. Soucandi.

"We have two problems," Miles said behind them. "One of them is really big."

"No more problems, *please*," Heath begged. He turned around to see for himself. Cricket was cradled in Miles arms, unconscious. His feet were dangling in the air.

"Oh, God," Heath gasped. Cricket's heel—the one that had been punctured by the porcupine quill—was an angry purple color. Tendrils of infection had wound up his leg like grape vines, disappearing beneath his shorts. Although he was still alive, it was clear that Cricket had the Flash. That sure seemed like a *very* big problem, but he knew that wasn't what Miles was referring to.

No, the winner of the Big Problem Award belonged to the pair of eight-hundred-pound grizzly bears, mouths agape and dripping with foam, staring at them from the west bank with hate-filled eyes.

Does a bear knit in the woods?
Do we really give a darn?
Who cares if a bear can sew?
Just where did he get that yarn?

CRICKET'S BREATHS came in shallow, wheezing gasps, scarier than any growl, snarl, or howl the group had heard all day, scarier even than the sounds the grizzlies were making—the resonating grunts and the disturbing clanking of teeth. The sounds coming from Cricket terrified his friends because they meant that he was dying.

The quill, once lodged in his heel, had injected the Flash into his bloodstream and now the virus was slowly coursing through his body. Heath remembered Marshall explaining how the odor produced by the patch of skin on the porcupine's back—the rosette—would travel up the quill's hollow core. Heath believed the virus had passed from the sick porcupine into Cricket's body in the same way, the quill acting as a needle. (He'd once read that the spines of sea urchins were sometimes substituted for needles when blood transfusions were needed in emergency situations, and they were just a smaller version of porcupine quills.) Why Cricket didn't die instantly like the other victims was a mystery. Maybe it was because the virus hadn't been passed in a liquid such as animal saliva. He wasn't sure. Whatever the case, the results would eventually be the same unless they could find a way to save Cricket's life.

Miles's face was beet red and drenched with sweat. He was huffing huge snorts of air. "Can someone tell me where the heck Granite Falls went?" he grumbled. "Did they move it on us?"

"You sure you don't want me to carry him for a bit?" Heath offered, jogging to keep up. They'd gone another half mile since leaving the beaver dam, and Miles had carried Cricket in his arms every step of the way. The exertion was taking its toll, not that Miles would admit it.

"For the tenth time," Miles snapped, "I said I've got him!"

"Will, what happened back there?" Heath asked, looking for answers. "The beavers aren't afraid of water."

"I know!" Will bristled. "I'm thinking, I'm thinking."

"I have a theory," Emily said, surprising everyone, including her twin.

Emma looked at her as if she were a stranger. "You do?"

"Don't look so shocked, Em. I do have a brain, you know."

"Let's hear it," Heath said.

"I think it has to do with the reason why beavers build dams in the first place," Emily explained. "Our family went to a nature preserve in upstate New York a few years back and the trail guide gave a lecture about beaver dams—"

"I don't remember that," Emma interrupted.

"Of course you don't," said Emily. "You were pretending to be sick so you could stay home and hang out with that boy across the street. The one who got expelled for smoking. You really do have a thing for bad boys."

"Oh, yeah," Emma remembered. "Well, maybe that's because the good guys always fall for you."

Heath was surprised to find Emma looking directly at him when she said this, and not in the salty way he'd grown accustomed to. He wasn't sure what that implied. Emma had admitted to having a crush on Will, but from her tone she almost seemed envious of her sister, which was super weird. He hadn't gleaned much about Emma from their time in the river—she was a walking suit of armor. But maybe she wasn't as invulnerable as he'd thought. He promised himself he'd find out if they survived their ordeal. The way the pain was racking his body, he wondered if he'd make it at all. The battle on the dam had taken its toll, and without his medication he wasn't sure he could keep up with the group for much longer. He'd never felt so fatigued before, like he was wading through drying mud instead of water.

"Whatever," Emily said dismissively. "The guide said beavers are stimulated to build dams by the sound of moving water. It irritates them for some reason, so they start cutting down trees, dragging them into the river to block off the current and stop the noise."

Heath nodded. "I think I understand. Beavers already have a weird psychological issue with water, so maybe that overrides the hydrophobia?"

"It's just a theory. I mean, if this is a new strain of the rabies virus, different mammals may be affected differently, right?"

"Maybe." Heath looked down into the water and noticed clusters of frog eggs attached to underwater plants. They looked like tiny pale balloons. Inside the eggs were squirming tadpoles, eager to slip free and begin their lives. They were so blissfully ignorant of the death taking place all around them. It ticked Heath off. He wanted to shred the eggs apart, or stomp them into jelly with his pruned and peeling feet. He needed to feel like a predator again. He was sick of being prey. Instead he looked to the west bank, saw the two grizzly bears keeping pace with them, moving in powerful, ambling strides, and was correctively reminded that no matter how badly he wished otherwise, prey was exactly what they were.

"I should've saved a couple of arrows for those two," Will said, kicking water in the bears' direction. "I used them all up on the beavers. They probably weren't designed to kill a bear anyway. They were target arrows with bullet-headed tips, not bladed for big game."

"Is it just me, or is the water getting shallower?" Dunbar asked.

"That's exactly what it's doing." Heath noticed it, too.

"This can't be the river that runs by town. This is barely a creek."

"Maybe it'll rejoin the main branch," Emma said.

"Yeah," Will scoffed. "And maybe someone'll come by on a Jet Ski and offer us a lift."

Heath didn't think either scenario was likely. He suspected the stream would run its course, choked to death by the forest in the end. They'd gone the wrong way after all, and that meant backtracking the half mile, climbing over the dam, swimming across the beaver pond—it was exhausting to think about. And they'd have to deal with the beavers again.

"We should go back," Heath said, shrinking as he heard his own pronouncement. "I know that's not what you guys want to hear, but we made a mistake. We should have gone left at the fork."

The group eased to a stop.

"That was my vote," Dunbar reminded everyone. "At least Theo had the good sense to go left. I didn't see the kayak in the pond, and he never would have gotten it over the dam, just him and Molly."

"I don't know," Heath said. "I just wish we'd let Theo take Cricket instead. He needs a doctor. . . ."

"He won't survive the trip back." Will tossed this comment out so casually it made Heath flinch.

Emma had had enough. "Maybe you can feed him to the bears, Will! That'll keep them busy while you escape! Is that what you had in mind?"

"Overreact much?" Will fired back.

Heath stepped between them. "Emma, relax. Will's just stating the obvious, even if it was insensitive. Cricket's really sick. It's getting dark. In half an hour we won't be able to see. Backtracking all the way to the fork will take twice as long, and then we'll still have to get to Granite Falls from there."

"Figures you'd defend him," Emma said with a sneer.

Heath didn't like what she was implying. "If you have something to say, then just say it, Em."

"Fine. It's more than a little weird, Heath, that you're always defending Will. You two have been buddied up since we were in the livery. Mr Soucandi had you two pegged— the Tin Man without a heart and the brainless scarecrow that's always got his back."

"Shut up, Emma," said Dunbar.

She wouldn't. "You said the wolves ran right past you and Dunbar? Right, Heath? That's odd. I thought they were attracted to noise. Where was *your* noisemaker? I don't recall you having it when we dragged your sorry butt into the river."

Heath was unbalanced by her insinuation. "Mine was—"

"I suppose you could've hung on to yours if Onyx was using you as a doormat?" Dunbar leapt to Heath's defense. "And besides, it's not Heath's fault he's smart enough to figure out what the rest of you couldn't. And if he hadn't, he'd be dead and so would I! So I'll say it again—shut up, Emma!"

"Emma . . ." Emily said, gently taking her sister into custody.

"Fine!" Emma snapped, allowing herself to be separated from the group, but as a parting shot she said, "If Cricket dies, just remember who talked him into getting into this stupid river in the first place"—she made a V with her fingers and stabbed them in the air at Will and Heath—"*you two idiots.*"

This didn't sit well with Dunbar. "And when you're shampooing your *stupid* hair at your *stupid* home in *stupid* Portland just remember who saved *your* STUPID life."

"*Shut up, Dunbar!*" was her tight, over-the-shoulder response as she stormed back in the direction of the dam with Emily trotting after her.

Heath put his hand on Dunbar's shoulder. "Smooth, buddy," he whispered.

"Yeah, well . . ." Dunbar scowled. "She's stupid."

"So I heard."

"You know what? Emily *is* prettier."

"It's because her nose leans slightly to the left," Heath reminded him.

"Yeah. That's right. Cricket was right."

"Cricket . . ." Heath exhaled deeply.

"What the heck are you two yapping about?" Miles said, sick of the juvenile bickering. "Emily's nose? Quit gossiping like old ladies and make a decision!" He sounded tough, but Heath could tell by his expression that Miles was feeling brittle, spent, on the verge of a breakdown. The giant carefully shifted the sick boy in his arms to relieve some of the strain that had built up in his back while he'd stood around waiting for a decision. Heath would never have suspected Miles of being capable of such gentleness. Cricket looked smaller than usual in his hulking arms. Doll-like, even.

"We can't let him die, Heath," Dunbar said with determination in his voice.

"We won't," Heath promised.

The boys followed in the general direction of the Ems, but not too close, with Miles bringing up the rear. The bears weren't sure what to do. They just growled in complaint and shook their massive heads, frustrated by their inability to reach prey that was not only moving at a turtle's pace but was now reversing direction for no apparent reason.

Miles, who was having the absolute most miserable day of his life, growled back at them, "If you're coming, hurry the hell up. We're not waiting on you."

The group didn't get far.

A gunshot rattled the air.

"That was close by!" Will said excitedly. He and Dunbar skipped through the river sideways ten yards or so, searching for a window through the woods, hoping to see the source of the blast.

"There!" Dunbar pointed. "I can't believe we didn't see that!"

A hundred yards off through the forest was a large facility. It looked almost like a Walmart, gray and boxy, except there were no signs adorning the facade. The group's view of it was partially obstructed by trees, but they could see a Jeep parked in front of the entrance. A man was loading something into the back of the vehicle. He was wearing a khaki uniform, a baseball cap (a silver ponytail trailed from the back of it), and a pair of mirrored sunglasses. A rifle was slung over his back.

"Hey! Mister!" Dunbar shouted. He waved his arms frantically. "Yo! We need help over here!"

The man ignored them.

"Save your breath—he's too far away." Will put two fingers in his mouth and whistled loudly. The man whipped his head in their direction. Then he slowly turned his whole body. He took a few steps toward the stream and stopped.

"He sees us!" Dunbar said, doing jumping jacks in the water.

He *had* seen them, Heath was sure of it. But something was wrong. Instead of acknowledging the group, the man went back to his Jeep, slammed the back hatch shut, and climbed in behind the steering wheel. The brake lights glowed, then dimmed, and the Jeep lurched forward. It turned and headed away from the river, down a service road, disappearing into the forest.

"Where's he going?" Emma asked. "He's getting help, right?"

"The guy had all the help he needed slung across his back," Will said and spat in the river. "He's leaving us out here with Yogi and Boo-Boo."

The grim reality that they'd been abandoned by an adult, even if he was a stranger, came as an unexpected blow to their already fragile spirits.

"Hey! Come back!" But it was too late, he was already gone.

"Are you sure he saw us?" Emily asked.

"He saw us," Will replied.

"Loser!" Emma yelled after the Jeep.

"It's fine," Will said bitterly. "We'll go to the building. There's gotta be a phone inside. Maybe other useful stuff, too, like food, a TV so we can see if this mess is on the news yet. Maybe even guns. The place has a military feel to it."

"I agree," said Heath. "You think that guy was a soldier?"

"No," Will said. "A soldier would have stayed to help us."

Will's plan—to get inside the building, check to make sure it was secure from wildlife, and then contact help—had one major flaw. Two if you counted each bear individually. "It'll be easy enough," he assured them. "The fastest runner— that'd be me—will head down the river while the rest of you wait here. The bears should stay with the group since you pose a more tempting target as long as we're all in the water. When I've got a good head start on them, I'll head onshore and take off running. They'll come after me then, I guarantee it."

Heath shook his head. "No way! It's too dangerous. Grizzlies can go from zero to twenty-five in six seconds. They can hit thirty miles an hour when they sprint. They'll catch you, Will."

"No, they won't. I'll stay close to the river and just before they reach me, I'll jump back into the water. Maybe if they're busy with me, they won't even notice you leaving."

"And then what?" Miles asked. "You're stuck in the river."

"Yeah," Will conceded the fact. "But not for long. You guys will call in the cavalry and we'll all be home in no time. Easy peasy, as Molly would say."

The group admitted it was as good a plan as any. Before they put it into action Heath asked Will for a moment to talk in private.

"I thought I should tell you, in case something happens . . . to either of us . . . that I was wrong. Will, you can be a total jerk sometimes—"

"Agreed."

"—but now that I know you better . . . now that you've stuck with us and got us out of some pretty hairy situations . . . and here you are, about to do it again . . . I know there's no way you would have put our lives at risk coming out of the livery. I believe you. I'm sure you had your noisemaker and just lost it on the lawn. Things got pretty crazy and—"

"Listen." Will stopped him. He looked Heath in the eyes and said, "Remember after the bats attacked? I told you to never assume you know my motives, because you're not up to it."

"Yeah. I remember."

"I didn't mean that as an insult. I meant you're too nice to understand how a kid like me operates. Even now you're trying to absolve me of sins without knowing for sure whether I committed them or not. I'm not saying I tricked you all, but let's assume I *did* know that loud noises drive rabid animals crazy. Let's say your original instinct was right and I *did* leave mine inside the livery. . . ."

"You knew . . ." Heath whispered.

"Again, I'm not saying I did and I'm not saying I didn't. This is all just hypothetical, Heath. I'm teaching you a lesson here, so keep an open mind. Let's say you were right about another thing, and I *was* trying to keep certain people alive because I knew they might aid in my survival: Sylvester because of his skill with a bow—although it didn't help him any in the end. Miles for his strength—sure it was Cricket he ended up carrying, but if I'd gotten hurt, I could count on Miles to get me home. And then there's you, Heath. Let's say I *deliberately* gave you a broken noisemaker to keep you safe on the run to the river. Let's say you were the most important key to my survival right from the beginning."

"Me?" Heath was lost. "Why would I be—?"

"Because you're likable and I'm not. I know that, and I'm okay with it. But likability is a severely underrated trait. A necessary trait for a good leader."

Heath was starting to get the picture and the picture was ugly. "You used me! To get the others to do what you wanted . . . like when I tried to persuade them to leave the livery. And I convinced the survivors in the river to let you come along. I see it now. I've been agreeing with you at every turn."

"You think I was manipulating you? Really? No. . . ." Will shook his head. "You were agreeing with me because I was always right. And you've survived this long because of me and only me. But yeah, *maybe* I knew the group would listen to you, and that you'd listen to me. Not because you were weak-minded, but because you're *smart*, another reason you mattered. Nobody's come as close to beating me at chess as you did, and you've barely played before. That's not luck. That's intuition. Your intuition told you to follow me, and that kept you alive."

Heath was stunned. He didn't know what to say. Or think. He just held himself up against the current and tried to process Will's *hypothetical* confession. "What's wrong with you?" he asked, not as an insult, but because he truly needed to know.

Will gave a sad sigh. "Emma asked me the same thing earlier, remember? I told her about Lyssa. Did you ever figure out the moral?"

"Yeah, I think so." He'd been mulling the story over since he'd heard it. "It's better to be the hunter, Actaeon, torn to bits by animals, than to be like Hercules, driven crazy, forced to do things you don't want to do. Like you did today."

"No. You're still trying to find the good inside me . . . some crumb of compassion that you shouldn't assume is there." Will placed his hand on Heath's shoulder, his icy eyes darting side to side, scanning Heath's for understanding. "You with your cancer should know better than anyone what I'm saying. The world is out to get us. That's its job, dude. There's madness all around us, not just here. Get it? We all have to make choices, Heath. I made some and so did you. Our choices kept the group alive. Uncle Bill made choices, too, and look where it got him. Look where it got the other campers. He led them to a tomb. We led our group here. Think about that."

Heath felt the urge to shrug Will's hands off, but he couldn't find the strength. "What are you saying, Stringer?"

"I'm *saying* it's better to be *Gaia*. It's better to be the one controlling the madness than to be the one controlled by it."

Having delivered one final shocking lesson, Will gave his cabinmate some parting advice before sloshing away toward the shore. "Watch out for squirrels, okay? Try to stay alive, Heath."

"One, two, three, go."

This time the plan went off exactly as Will figured. He waded downstream, pacing off twenty yards. Then he marched onto the shore, hooting and hollering. The bears charged after him. Right before they caught up to him he ducked back into the river. The grizzlies were furious, pawing at the ground, standing up and slamming back down, driving deep tracks into the mud. They were fierce. They made Onyx look like a wimp. Will did a victory dance, then broke into a fit of insane laughter. His antics held the bears' attention.

Heath, Dunbar, Em and Em, and Miles, with Cricket cradled in his arms, ran close together through the trees, across the service road, and up to the front of the building. While they were running, it dawned on Heath that they might need a key to get inside, but instead they found the left side of the glass double doors propped wide open. There was a dead man lying across the threshold keeping it from closing. He wore a white lab coat, ruined by a bullet hole in his back. Blood was pooling out around him. There was no time to be horrified.

"Get him out of there," said Emma.

Dunbar and Heath cleared the door, dragging the body into the foyer.

"I'm starting to think it's a good thing the guy with the gun left," Dunbar said.

Heath nodded slowly. "Yeah, I think you're right."

"I'd have preferred if you'd dragged him *outside*," said Emma, disgusted.

"So his smell can attract the animals?" Dunbar stood up and faced her. "Way to use your head, Em."

With everyone safely inside, the door closed and the lock clicked. They were in a long, rectangular room that ran the width of the building front. On the wall opposite the entrance was an unmarked metal door with a small porthole-sized window. To the right of it was a check-in station. There was no one inside to greet them. Although it was obviously a waiting room—there were several padded benches lining the walls—it was barren of any creature comforts like magazines, a television, or even plants.

"Is Will okay?" Emily asked.

Emma pressed up against the glass. She grinned. "I can see the crazy boy. He's okay."

Will was standing in the middle of the stream, looking back at them. He'd whipped the bears into a fury. They were guarding the shore carefully, bellowing in challenge, aching for him to come on land again. Will flashed the group a relaxed smile.

"Man, he's fearless," Dunbar marveled.

Heath signaled Will with a halfhearted wave. He understood what the group didn't—they were looking at three very dangerous creatures.

Miles laid Cricket down on the bench closest to the metal door, positioning his limbs so he wouldn't fall off. He stretched tall, then did some bends and twists until his back cracked in three places. Considering that he'd had Cricket's weight on him since they entered the beaver pond, he'd definitely earned the break.

"Help me flip this guy," Heath recruited Dunbar.

"I wish we had a giant spatula," Dunbar whined. "We're kids, not coroners. We shouldn't have to do this stuff."

"Just help me, dude." He was nearly spent and doubted he could do it alone.

The boys rolled the dead man over onto his back. He looked to be about forty or so with bad teeth, but otherwise unremarkable. His skin was still warm, but his face was frozen in a look of deep surprise. There was no bullet hole in his front; the man in the Jeep had callously shot him in the back, then stepped over his corpse to leave the building.

"I think we just entered a whole new world of weird," Miles said.

The dead man was wearing an ID badge. Heath unclipped it from his lab coat and read it out loud. "'Carl Schroeder. Microbiologist. U.S. Army.' Will was right—I think this *is* a military complex. Probably some kind of laboratory."

"I bet there's a phone at the check-in desk," Emily said. "I'll see if I can't find an address to this place and let the Granite Falls police know where we are."

"Great," Heath said. "Tell them we need an ambulance, too."

Emily tugged on the metal door, but it wouldn't budge. "I think the lock is computerized."

"Try this." Heath handed her a plastic card he'd pilfered from the lab coat's pocket.

Emily slid it through a magnetic reader and a little green light blinked on. They heard a *beep* and a *clack*. She lifted the handle and the door opened. Emily peered inside. "It's dark," she said nervously. "Anyone want to come with me? Em?"

"Sure." Emma reluctantly peeled her eyes off the scientist. "I'm tired of dead bodies, anyway. I didn't wake up this morning thinking I'd be looking at dead bodies all day."

"It's getting to all of us," Emily empathized. "Hopefully his is the last one we'll see for a long time."

"When I die—of old age, of course—I'll understand if you guys want to skip my wake." Leave it to Dunbar to make a joke out of it.

"Nope, I'll be there with bells on, dancing a jig," said Emma wryly.

"You're evil." Dunbar grinned. "I admire that."

To an outside observer who hadn't been through their ordeal, it may have seemed odd that they could make light at that moment, but Heath understood perfectly. Their playfulness was a sign of relief. It was probable that they were out of the woods now, literally and figuratively. Being inside a building, especially one solidly built, felt instantly soothing, like aloe on a nagging burn. They'd seen enough bodies that day to fill a small-town cemetery. One more wouldn't break them and it certainly wouldn't taint their freshened spirits.

"C'mon." Emily tugged at her sister's arm. "Let's go find a phone."

"Dunbar and I will come, too," Heath said. "Miles can wait here with Cricket."

"Hurry," Miles pleaded.

The door had a stopper at the bottom that Heath used to prop it open for light. The group filed into a long, shadowy corridor. The entrance to the check-in room was the first room off to the right, but it was vacant except for a desk, a chair, and an empty corkboard hanging on the wall. It was the same in all the rooms. None of them had doors. The place had been designed for collaboration, not privacy.

They came to another metal door at the end of the hallway, but unlike the one in the foyer, it had no handle or card reader and it swung open easily when Heath pushed on it. A nasty smell like boiling soap wafted over them. The group cringed and took a step back to let the brunt of it pass on by into the hallway.

"That's bad," said Emma, gagging against the back of her wrist.

"The worst. Let's find a light." Heath led them into the room beyond.

Suddenly laughter echoed through the darkness. Not a normal laugh either. It was a maniacal, whooping giggle. The kind that blares over speakers in a fun house or from the mouth of an insane villain on a cartoon.

Heath had heard that laugh before. He recognized it from when he was in the hospital as a kid. He never expected to hear it again, especially not here, of all places. It made no sense. No sense at all. He knew exactly what it was and why they had to flee.

Heath lifted his arms warningly and whispered, "Back away toward the door."

"Heath?" said Emily.

"If we don't leave *right now*," he told them, *"we are all going to die."*

We're off to the comedy show.
We love a good laugh, hee ha ho!
Each bug got a ticket, except for the cricket.
For the cricket was late, don't you know.
For the cricket was late, don't you know.

SUDDENLY HEATH WAS eight years old again, back in room 309 of the pediatric wing of the Providence Sacred Heart Medical Center. His father had somehow managed to fall asleep in the torturously shaped plastic chair next to Heath's bed. His mother was standing outside in the hallway crying. *Again.* If she kept it up, the hospital janitor would have to set one of those CAUTION: WET FLOOR signs at her feet.

Although the room was dimly lit, the glow from the television mounted on the wall still made him squint; sensitivity to light was one of the side effects of the chemotherapy. The National Geographic Channel was broadcasting a show about the wildlife of the Serengeti, and he'd decided an escape to the African grasslands was worth a little discomfort.

Nurse Kevin came in and fussed about, checked Heath's IV, scribbled on his chart, and pretended to be interested in the elephants gorging on tree bark on TV. "They could use a little less roughage in their diet," joked the young man, nodding at the screen. "And you, my friend, could stand to eat a little more."

"Okay," Heath said. "I'll try." He'd discovered over the past few weeks that being agreeable meant less hassle from the hospital staff, especially Nurse Kevin, who was constantly on his case about keeping his strength up.

"Good. And it wouldn't kill you to watch a cartoon once in awhile. It's hard to feel sorry for tree bark, but usually when I drop in it's nothing but animals eating one another on TV. Try to watch something less grim occasionally. It's a corny expression, but it's true: laughter is the best medicine."

"Okay."

Nurse Kevin smiled warmly and jiggled Heath's big toe through the fleece blanket. "See you tomorrow, buddy." He headed for the door, paused, and pointed with his pen up at the screen. "See? Now there's a guy who enjoys a good laugh."

As the door to his room eased shut, Heath watched the television with fascination. A creature that looked to be part dog and part cat, but bigger than both, trotted across sun-scorched grass. It had a coarse brownish coat, a black muzzle, and black spots on its legs. Its lower jaw hung slack, as if dangling from a broken hinge, giving the animal a sickly, dull-witted appearance, even though the narrator of the show declared it to be healthy and cunning. Heath had never seen one of these creatures before, but he disliked it instantly and intensely. Not just because it looked mangy and evil, or because it was an opportunistic scavenger, but because it had a creepy, high-pitched laugh, like the annoying clown that stopped by on Saturdays to make lame balloon animals and squirt sick kids in the face with his boutonniere. The animal on TV had a 3-D guffaw that blasted out of the screen, mocking Heath for being sick. It was a horrid, vile thing.

Even the creature's name was weird.

Hy-e-na.

Hyena.

He shuddered.

Heath took Nurse Kevin's advice and flipped through the channels, setting the remote down on the nightstand when a lovesick skunk in a beret came bouncing across the screen. He tucked the blanket up under his chin.

Better.

The laughter stopped as lights flickered on.

"They must run on motion sensors," Dunbar determined.

Heath scanned the room for danger and found none at all. "I don't get it," he said, deeply confused. "I know what I heard. . . ."

Seeing no cause for alarm, Emma brushed Heath's arm aside and moved deeper into the room. "What is this place? It looks like a laboratory."

That's exactly what it was. The room was large and clean. The tile floor had been freshly waxed. There were two rows of workstations, with a dozen stations in each row. A third and middle row consisted of five stands, each with a large printer on it. Almost every piece of furniture was white, metal, and on wheels, giving Heath the impression the room was designed to be easily cleared and cleaned quickly, if anyone had stuck around to do it, which they hadn't. The place was a ghost town. Heath listened intently for the weird laughter, but all he heard was the electrical hum of computers still processing data that would go unread.

"Check it out." Emily motioned them over to one of the desks. The computer screen set on it was glowing, displaying video feed from four different cameras positioned at different areas of the facility. The screen was quartered to monitor the following: a room with high-tech equipment, like centrifuges and microscopes. A room with several impressive freezers that looked nothing like the ones he'd seen in the appliance sections of Lowe's or Home Depot. An even larger laboratory, with animal cages lining the walls— every cage was occupied. And finally, a view of the area surrounding the facility, which seemed to be the only one constantly changing. In this quarter, the video feed passed around a network of cameras fixed somewhere on the roof, and Heath determined that one full orbit around the building took maybe ninety seconds.

"Look!" Emily pointed. "There's the river!"

The monitor displayed the last spot they'd seen Will. He was gone.

"What's that idiot up to now?" Emma asked. "And where are the bears?"

"I don't know." Heath studied the image for clues. "Let's keep watching. Maybe he'll pop up."

They waited anxiously as the feed jumped from camera to camera, returning once more to the river, revealing no sign of Will.

"Do you think the bears ate him?" Dunbar asked.

Emma smacked him on the back of the head. "Don't say that!"

"Hey!" Dunbar protested. "Sorry! I thought you said you were over him!"

She smacked him again.

"What was that one for?"

"For not knowing a thing about girls," Emma said crossly.

"I'm sure Will's okay. Maybe he walked the bears farther downstream for some reason," Heath speculated. "If he did, we wouldn't be able to see him through the trees, right? Or maybe he's already inside the building and the bears wandered off. Let's not jump to conclusions."

They heard the laughter again. It was louder and more pronounced.

"What the heck *is* that?" Dunbar asked.

"That"—Heath pointed to one of the cages on the bottom left corner of the split screen—"is a hyena."

"Are you serious?" Emily asked, leaning in for a closer look.

"A real, live hyena?" said Dunbar. "In this building? Right now?"

"We're not watching reruns." Heath straightened and

headed toward a set of heavy glass airlocked doors at the back of the room, which had been wide open. "Guess we should say hello."

"Hideous thing, isn't he?" Emma commented, studying the hyena through the thick bars of its cage.

"Yeah," Dunbar agreed. "His nose *is* pretty straight."

"What does *that* have to do with anything?" Emma demanded to know.

"Nothing," Dunbar said. "Forget it."

The hyena paced nervously with a low, tight gait, watching the kids. It seemed agitated, but that struck Heath as normal behavior. It didn't appear sick at all. Its eyes were clear and alert, and its mouth was free of foam. It was a male, much bigger than Heath thought he'd be judging by the one he'd seen on the nature show. The beast was almost as big as Quilt Face, but he was built differently, with hind legs that were shorter than the front, a back that sloped noticeably toward his stubby neck and broad, flat skull. His tail resembled a lion's, sporting a pom-pom at the end. And his legs were spotted, which is why, unlike the three other types of hyenas in the world, he was called a spotted hyena. There was a clipboard on top of the cage with a thick stack of pages clamped to it. Heath started reading.

"At least now we know where that smell's coming from," Dunbar said, pinching his nose shut. The foul stink emitted from the hyena's rump gland had a pungent burning, soapy quality. Even with dozens of other animals in the room, it was the dominant odor.

"Look at them all," Emily said, wandering from cage to cage. "It's a zoo in here."

"They're indigenous," Heath pointed out, remembering the placard Dunbar had found in the livery. "Except for the hyena, every animal in here can be found in the Cascade Mountains."

"You're right," Emily said. She pointed some out. "There's a woodchuck. And a chipmunk. I think that's a bobcat."

A booming grunt brought their attention to a huge cage at the back of the room. Inside was a male moose. Heath estimated the beast was seven feet tall at the shoulders and weighed close to a ton. He could take a nap between the far tips of its antlers. Heath had read somewhere that the moose didn't have many natural enemies besides man, with the exception of Siberian tigers, bears, and on the rare occasion, killer whales hunting around islands near North America's northwest coast. Only a super-predator could mess with a moose and come out on top. The one in the room with them stood in his paddock with his back to them, completely uninterested, which was fine by Heath.

"Why are they so quiet?" Emily peered into a long cage. Whatever was at the back, bunched against the bars, wasn't moving.

"They're probably drugged," said Dunbar.

Emily tapped the cage.

"Em, don't—!" Heath's warning came too late. The wolverine inside came to life, lunging at her, snarling and gnashing the wire. Foam bubbled from its mouth. Emily screamed and trotted backward toward the center of the room.

Heath caught her. "Did it bite you?"

Emily inspected her shaking hands for teeth marks. "No—no, I'm okay. It just scared me."

The wolverine emitted a long hiss, then backed up as far as the cage allowed and lay down on its belly.

"It has the Flash," Heath said. "I bet they all do. Even this guy." He tapped on the hyena's cage, but the animal didn't react aggressively as the wolverine had. In fact, the creature shrunk back a bit. It was fearful. Heath suspected it might have been abused.

"Are you sure it has the virus?" Dunbar asked. "It seems okay to me."

"Look." Heath pointed to a handwritten note card clipped to the side of the hyena's cage.

Dunbar read it aloud. "'Spotted Hyena—*Crocuta crocuta*.'"

Below the animal's two names, common and scientific, were the words *Patient Zero*.

Dunbar was confused. "What's that supposed to mean? Patient Zero?"

Since beating cancer the first time, Heath had developed an interest in diseases and read a lot of books on the subject, specifically about their cures and origins. He'd even thought about becoming a medical researcher one day. "Patient Zero is what scientists call the first known carrier of new diseases," he explained. "Usually the term refers to a human, but I guess it can apply to an animal, too. This hyena is Patient Zero for the mutated rabies virus."

Dunbar took a healthy step away from the hyena's cage. "So you're saying *he's* the cause of everything? The reason why everyone back at camp is probably dead? Sylvester and Soup Can, too?"

"I don't think the hyena is directly to blame." A dour expression settled on Heath's face. "I don't want to believe it, but I think the people here, the scientists, *gave* him the disease. On purpose."

Emily knelt down to get a better look at the hyena. It was rubbing its side against the bars, struggling to scratch an itch. "Why would anyone do something so horrible?"

"I don't understand most of this report." Heath bit his lip and flipped through the papers. "I'm not a microbiologist. It's over my head. But I bet I know why they chose the hyena as Patient Zero. It's because hyenas are special. They're the only known mammal that can carry the regular rabies virus without showing any of the symptoms or dying from it. In fact, thirty percent of hyenas in the wild probably have rabies."

Dunbar said, "So?"

"So, I can't be sure, but it looks like the military was deliberately trying to create a new strain of rabies and chose a hyena to host it because it wouldn't die or go psycho on them. They could run it through trials for years, if they needed to."

"That poor thing," said Emily.

"I feel sorry for it, too," Heath said. "Just don't get too close to him. Rabies or not, hyenas can be vicious."

As if on cue the hyena belted out a long, loony laugh.

"That's not funny," Emma scolded him. "Bad dog. Bad."

Heath continued reading. "It looks like the scientists started with some kind of airborne super flu that only affects water buffalo in Southeast Asia—I remember seeing that on the news. It killed off thousands of the animals in less than a month. They combined the water buffalo flu with regular rabies and then kept tinkering with it. I think the scientists also engineered the new rabies to be harmless to humans in the airborne form." Heath wrinkled his brow, squinted at the congested writing and confusing equations on the pages. "I don't know . . . this document . . . it's so technical, it's almost like reading a foreign language."

"Remember, in the gazebo?" Dunbar chimed in. "Will said that regular rabies can't get a foothold in possums because their temperature is too low."

"Yeah," Heath nodded. "I think it's a similar idea. There's a list of mammals . . . with their temperatures next to each. They're all just a few degree points different than the standard human ninety-eight point six. It says here they tested the virus on chimpanzees and they all survived. Chimps are primates, like humans, and they have the same body temperature we do. That's probably why we didn't get sick either."

"I don't see any monkeys around," Emma said. "Where'd they go?"

"They probably destroyed the chimps once they had their results. Burned the bodies in an incinerator or something." Heath wasn't certain that was true, but it seemed the most likely explanation.

Emma pointed out the flaw in the scientists' plan. "Looks like someone forgot to carry the one, because people *are* dying from the new virus."

"Maybe that was all part of their plan," noted Emily. "The airborne form of the virus doesn't seem to affect us, but—"

"When it's passed to humans in a heated liquid like saliva . . . instant death!" Emma finished her sister's thought.

"Right," said Heath. "I'm not sure how it'd work, exactly, but if they wanted to kill a lot of people without making it obvious that it was a military strike, releasing the virus into the surrounding woods would be an efficient way to make it happen. Let the animals tear the people apart and no one gets blamed but the local wildlife."

"They were making a weapon!" Dunbar slammed his fist into his palm. The gesture looked silly, but his anger was understandable. "Just like in the movies. Dude! They were messing with nature, thinking they could control it, and then things blew up in their faces! Somehow the virus escaped into the open. Out into the woods. And then the cowards abandoned ship. Marshall . . . Uncle Bill . . . Camp Harmony is a graveyard because these idiots let this nightmare loose."

"Probably so," Heath said.

"So why'd they give all of the other animals in here rabies, too?" Emma asked.

Heath had an answer for that. "I think the hyena unintentionally infected them all. The virus went airborne through his scent glands—that soapy smell—and these other animals were just put here to see what'd happen to them."

The group was stunned by the thought that all of this madness was orchestrated on purpose. Heath felt that together they'd worked out a pretty plausible picture of what had happened, and it was disturbing on so many levels.

"We have to find a phone," Emma said. "Did anyone see—?"

The sound of tiny paws running across glass jerked their attention to the ceiling. What they saw above sent them into a panic.

"This place has skylights!" Emily gasped. "The whole ceiling is glass!"

They'd been so preoccupied with the hyena that they hadn't noticed the large panes above their heads. In the dusk's fading light, squirrels were crisscrossing over them, occasionally stopping to peer down inside. Little pools of drool were collecting on the surface directly beneath their dark faces. The light of the room reflected in their beady eyes and illuminated the white fur of their rapidly heaving underbellies. Every few seconds, one of them would try to chip at the glass with its teeth or rake the surface with its claws. The squirrels could see them and they wanted in.

"Forget the phone," Heath said, leading the group back

toward the doors. "We need to find someplace safe to hide. This room isn't it."

Miles came bursting into the lab. "Hey! You need to come quick, I think . . ." He looked around with wide eyes. "Ooookay. Is that a freakin' moose?"

"What's wrong?" Heath said, snapping his fingers to draw Miles's attention.

"It's Cricket," Miles panted. "He's having a seizure. It's like every muscle in his body is locking up."

Heath remembered Marshall's list of the final stages of rabies: *paralysis, coma, and then finally death.*

"Guys, I think this is it," Miles said. "We're losing him."

The group followed Miles in a sprint out the door and through the lab beyond. There were skylights in this room, too. As they were passing the video surveillance monitor strange moving shapes in the exterior feed caught Heath's attention. Hoping it was Will, he circled around the desk and leaned into the screen. The cameras had automatically switched to night mode. The light from the monitor washed Heath's face in a ghostly green glow. The camera was recording at the back of the building, aimed at a pine tree a few feet away from the facility's back wall. The lower, thicker boughs seemed to stretch out over the roof, past the camera's mount.

"Is that live?" Miles asked, leaning over Heath's shoulder.

"Of course it's live," Heath told him.

Miles jaw sagged open. "Then that means—"

"Yeah." Heath nodded. He tapped the screen. "It means

that our two grizzly bears are climbing that tree right now. And it means they'll be on the roof in seconds."

Emma whispered, "Can the skylights—"

"Can they hold the weight of two full-grown grizzly bears without breaking?" Heath's head felt so heavy with despair he could barely shake it. "I really doubt it."

The ghost of Miner Bill
Came tapping at my door.
He'd left his gold in a till
Deep beneath my floor.

I didn't open to look,
Not even just a sliver.
I overheard when Old Bill swore
He'd drown me in the river.

EMMA SHOVED THE BOYS aside and hogged the screen. She had one thought on her mind and everyone knew it. "If the bears are on top of the building, then where's Will?"

The first bear had passed by the video camera and pulled itself onto the roof. The second bear was chewing on the camera, and the group got a good look at its cavities before the lens cracked and the image turned to static. "Do you think he led them up there?"

"Why would he do that?" Dunbar rejected the idea. "He'd be trapped. Easy pickings. Maybe they just got bored of waiting for him to come out of the river and followed our scent to the building."

Heath reminded them, "We didn't see him the last time the river was on the screen."

"You have to use the arrow keys." Miles leaned in and tapped the keyboard and the live exterior feed blew up to fill the whole screen, shunting the other three boxes out of sight. Then with every tap of the arrow key, a new view replaced the old. "There's probably a letter key assigned to each of the cameras, but the arrow keys will control them, too."

Heath was impressed. "How do you know all this?"

"Dude, I told you my dad was in prison, right? They only allowed one visitor at a time, so when my mom was with him, I'd wait by the guard cage. I'd love to be a guard someday. Those guys are pretty cool. They showed me how the prison's surveillance system worked and even let me play with it a little. It was the same basic setup as this one. Aaaand here we go. Voilà!"

The river popped onscreen.

"No Will," Heath said. "He's gone."

"I'll keep looking for him," Miles said, sweeping Emma away from the monitor. "You guys go help Cricket."

The foursome turned to leave but stopped when Miles jerked back from the desk with a startled, "Whoa!"

The camera he'd tapped into was positioned on a pole facing the front entrance to the building. They could see Cricket through the glass. He'd fallen off the bench and was lying facedown, sprawled out on the floor. Outside the building, a gathering of animals larger than any that had followed them before was milling about the small parking lot. Several animals were pacing in front of the glass, like customers window-shopping at a butcher's store. Cricket was the daily special.

Heath's heart raced. He wanted to scream when he saw the scarred wolf. He pointed at a collection of pixels in the bottom corner. "There's the alpha. The leader."

"Are you sure?" Dunbar asked.

"Yeah, I'm sure. Look at the scars on her muzzle." It was Quilt Face all right.

"No way," Emma said. "Her pack found us?"

"Not just *her* pack." Heath moved his finger around the screen, pointing out several dark shapes around the she-wolf. "There're a dozen or more of them out there. Her family must have merged with another. A super-pack, like the bat swarm."

It wasn't just wolves stalking Cricket. There were deer, dogs, three mountain lions, a lynx, a red fox, coyotes, small ferrety creatures that were either ermines or minks, and an enormous animal that resembled a deer but was much larger and therefore had to be an elk.

"Look at the rack on that thing!" Miles whistled.

Its antlers weren't quite as large as the moose's, but they looked more dangerous with their many sharpened points. Heath thought of Marshall, skewered like a roasted pig on the rack of the buck back at camp.

Almost as if it sensed it was in the spotlight, the elk charged the building, ramming its head against the window with a loud bang.

"I didn't know the camera feed had sound," Heath said.

Miles shook his head. "It doesn't. We heard that from all the way down the hallway."

The elk shook off the pain and trotted away, revealing a hairline fracture in the glass.

"That window is tough, but it isn't bulletproof," Emily noted. "If the elk rams it again, it'll shatter."

Heath sprinted toward the exit. "I'll get Cricket. You guys find a place we can hide. Hurry!"

He ran down the long corridor and stopped at the open door to the foyer. He hung back in the shadows for a moment, took a deep breath, then raced into the room. As soon as Quilt Face saw him she went berserk. She rose up on her hind legs and began scratching and biting feverishly at the glass. Her tongue folded against the window, her face blurred behind her smearing spit. The other wolves sprinted back and forth across the parking lot, growling in support of their leader.

"You can't have us!" Heath hollered at the she-wolf, which only provoked her further. She rammed the side of her face hard against the window and a tiny web of cracks appeared, but she was dazed and paused to recover. Quilt Face never took her eyes off Heath, not even when a trickle of blood traveled down her forehead, ran the length of her nose, and dripped into her mouth, between her sharp teeth.

If anything, the taste of her own blood seemed to make her crazier.

Heath knelt down and scooped Cricket up in his arms. The vines of infection were spreading across his belly, toward his heart. It was time to go.

A mountain lion slammed against the glass door with its oversized paws, but the door didn't budge. The big cat swished its tail and growled angrily. Only at the last moment did Heath see the elk behind it, charging again, head down, antlers aimed like a dozen spears in his direction. The mountain lion's head squished like a grape beneath the elk's heavy hoof.

Heath carried Cricket into the hallway and kicked the doorstop loose just as the elk exploded into the room, smashing the door to a million bits of glass, which showered down around the animal. A large shard sliced into the elk's neck, killing it instantly. The beast fell to the carpet with a tremendous thud and the sound of crunching glass. Quilt Face leapt into the foyer, bounded over the elk's body, and reached the metal door to the hallway just as it slammed shut in her furious patchwork face. She rose up on her hind legs and glared at Heath through the tiny porthole. He leaned in until only a thick square of glass and a few inches of air separated their faces. He was so close he could see the scarred black skin on her snout where her fur had refused to grow back. Despite her wounds, she was quite magnificent. They both stared into each others' eyes for several seconds, their breath fogging the glass. Then the wolf dropped from sight and the porthole was empty. "You blinked," Heath said triumphantly. "I win."

Heath met Miles in the hallway and passed Cricket off to him.

"We found a place!"

"Where?" Heath asked.

"There's another hallway off the lab. It leads to the back end of the building. There's a bunch of rooms there—offices, more labs, a kitchen. They've all got skylights, too, though."

"You found the kitchen? With the heavy duty freezers?" Heath hoped it was the room he'd seen in the surveillance monitor.

"Yeah, why?"

"Show me."

As the boys jogged through the winding hallway, Miles continued, "There's a warehouse area. Steel doors that lock from the inside. Metal roof. No glass anywhere."

"Great! Is it safe?"

"Well, there's a bay door that leads to the back parking lot, but it's chained and locked. We couldn't see any other way inside. We should be okay."

"Take Cricket there," Heath instructed.

"You're coming, right, dude?"

"I'll catch up. I need to check something first."

"This is it." Miles stopped at a small room on the right. "That's the kitchen. You *are* coming, Heath?"

"I'll be there in a minute," he promised. "Get Cricket

into the warehouse and lock the door. I'll knock when I get there."

"How will we know it's you?" Miles asked.

"Because animals don't knock." Heath gave him a weak smile.

"Oh, yeah. Sorry. I'm not thinking straight."

"I know the feeling. Now get going, Miles. I'll be right behind you."

Heath entered the kitchen and started rummaging through drawers and cabinets. It didn't take him long before he found a prize, several kinds of painkillers, including OxyContin. It was a lab that dealt in pain, so he wasn't too surprised. He squinched the sides of the cap and twisted, popping it open. Two pills rolled out into his palm. He'd been in near constant agony for hours, although he'd tried his best to shove it from his mind. The pills would make the pain go away. He lifted them to his mouth and dropped them between his lips. And immediately spit them out. The pills would make him drowsy. Slow. A common side effect. This was another fork in the river. He could fix himself, or he could live with the pain and stay alert. In fact, the pain was keeping him sharp, on edge. An edge he might need to save his friends. He knew what Will would do, but for Heath there wasn't really a choice at all. He dropped the pills back into the vial and slipped the vial into the pocket of his swim trunks. For later.

He kept searching. What had looked like a row of individual freezers on the monitor was actually one big freezer with several doors. The entire contraption was on wheels, just like everything else in the building. They were high-tech. Above each handle was a computer keypad. They weren't meant to keep people out, just to keep the freezers sealed tightly when in use, and the symbols on the buttons were easy enough to decipher. He found the UNLOCK button and pressed it. A puff of icy air escaped from the seal. He yanked the door open and checked the freezer's contents but didn't find what he was looking for. He fared no better at the next door. When he checked the third, he saw a clear plastic case on the top shelf. The contents were visible inside.

"You *do* exist." He smiled, pleased with himself. He was starting to think like a chess player.

He took the case and headed back into the hallway, where he ran headlong into Dunbar. The others were following closely behind him, shaken and panting. Miles was hugging Cricket tightly to his broad chest to keep him from thrashing around. Cricket was breathing in dry, raspy gasps through blue lips, like a fish out of water.

"The warehouse has an air duct," Dunbar explained. "We didn't see it until squirrels started pouring through it and dropping to the floor. We barely made it out in time."

"Okay, we'll keep looking," Heath said. He led them back into the room with the animal cages. They could hear Quilt Face and the other wolves howling in the foyer. The bears were still pounding away at the skylight. The hyena was finding the whole show hilarious.

"Cricket!" Miles shouted. Their friend's eyes had opened, but they were rolled back into his head. He was making a strange burbling sound, like his lungs were filtering water.

"Set him down!" Heath said. When Miles had Cricket prostrate on the tile floor, Heath knelt down beside him and opened the plastic case. Inside were six glass bottles with flat, metal screw caps. The centers of the caps were made of rubber. There was also a syringe inside the case. Heath took one of the bottles and carefully slid the needle through the cap to get at the liquid inside. He'd seen this done a hundred times before at the hospital.

"What *is* that?" Miles asked. The label glued to the sides had nothing telling on it except a bar code and *Immunirhabdoviridae X* handwritten above it.

"I don't know," Heath answered truthfully. "But I think it'll stop the virus from killing him."

"They made a cure?" A hopeful expression flitted onto Miles's sweaty face.

"They'd be stupid to make a biological weapon as horrible as the Flash without a cure that reacts just as fast. At least I hope not."

Heath bent forward to inject Cricket with the needle.

Miles gripped Heath's arm. "Wait! You can't stick him with that! What if you're wrong? It could be some other virus, like bird flu or smallpox!"

Heath held up the little bottle. "*Immuni*. Sounds like *immune*, right?"

Miles dug his fingers deeper into Heath's arm. "You could kill him!"

"Maybe." Heath looked down into Cricket's blue face.

The boy's life was quickly fading away. "But at this point I don't think it really matters, do you?"

Miles slowly released his grip. "Okay. I trust you."

Heath jabbed the needle into Cricket's arm and squeezed down on the plunger. When every last bit of the liquid inside the syringe was gone, he extracted the needle. They waited.

The thumping above grew louder. The bears roared. Heath glanced at the ceiling. It was so dark out now, but he could see the grizzlies' paws pressed flat against the skylight. One of the bears rubbed its nose against the glass, and a thick strand of foamy saliva spilled from its mouth and pooled out toward the edges. The bear tilted its head and pressed one wild eye against the skylight, sliding its face along the surface until it met Heath's gaze and stopped. It rose up on its hind legs and thundered down fiercely. The glass cracked and fractures spread across the pane like tiny lightning bolts. Again and again the bear pounded away at it.

"It's a long drop," Dunbar said, considering the height from ceiling to floor. "Do you think they'll survive it?"

"Not without broken bones," Heath replied, "but *they* will." He pointed out the squirrels skirting the edges of the skylight, a brave few ducking between the legs of the two bears, waiting for their moment to strike. "They use their tails as parachutes and cushions when they fall from great heights. They'll hit the ground running."

"I don't think it's working," Miles groaned. He hovered over Cricket like a doting parent.

Heath checked Cricket's pulse, a trick he'd learned during swim team CPR. He searched hard and found the faintest beat. "Come on. Please work," he whispered.

Seconds ticked by. The protective bubble of hopeful energy projected by Cricket's friends enveloped the boy, filtering out the nightmare that surrounded them on all sides.

"Please . . ." Dunbar breathed.

Heath had never felt so helpless in his life, not even when he found out he had cancer again. At least there were several options for him if he wanted them. For Cricket there was only two: beat the virus or slip away. Fight or flight—the only options a person has when something's trying to kill them.

Fight, Cricket, fight. Heath repeated these words over in his head.

"Look . . ." Dunbar said. "Is it just me, or are those purple vines fading?"

Heath repositioned himself to allow more light to fall over Cricket's skin. "It's not just you," he said excitedly. "It's working!"

Cricket's mouth closed, and he started to take air through his nose in easier, calmer breaths. The drug was attacking the virus in his body and winning.

Glass splintered above them. *Crack!* The skylight shuddered. The hyena laughed nervously from the back of its cage.

"Where do we go?" Emma asked, looking to Heath for answers.

He didn't have any at first: the foyer belonged to Quilt

Face, while the squirrels had invaded the warehouse and would own the labs soon, too. He thought for a bit, then a spark of an idea came to him. They needed water to fight back. "Did anyone see a restroom? Or a sink in one of the labs?"

Dunbar's eyes lit up. "Yeah! There's a bathroom down the hall toward the warehouse! Good thinking! We can fill buckets with—"

"No can do," Miles said. "I tried the faucets on my way back to the foyer to get Heath. They don't work. Not a drop. The water has been cut off, probably at the main outside. I checked for Internet on the computers, too. Nothing. I'm surprised the power is still on."

"Maybe that's what Carl the Scientist was doing before he was shot—wrapping things up."

Dunbar said, "Looks like the guy in the Jeep wrapped him up first. This is crazy."

Emma crossed her arms. "Will would know what to do."

"Well, he's not here, is he?" Heath shot back. He hurled the empty bottle in his hand across the room, more out of frustration than anger. It shattered against the wall, stunning the group into terse silence. "We need to stop relying on Will for every little thing!" he scolded the group, himself included. He wanted to tell them how Will had probably been using them all, manipulating him . . . them . . . to save himself, but he just couldn't do it. Not when Will had stayed behind in the river to provide them with the chance to save Cricket.

"Then *you* think of something, genius!" Emma ripped back.

Heath started pacing in quick, stomping strides while the others watched him nervously. He'd scared them when he threw the bottle. He shouldn't have done it, but it had made him feel better. He was sick of their small victories being shoveled over by new, surmounting threats. They'd come so far, saved Cricket's life, and now, unless they thought of an escape plan, it would all be for nothing. Deep down he knew what they had to do, but it was practically unthinkable.

"Okay, fine." He came to an abrupt stop in the center of the group and addressed them all. "You want a plan. Here it is. We go back to the river."

His friends' facial expressions were illegible. No one said a word.

"If you want to vote, or throw down with rock, paper, scissors"—he bandied a look between the Ems—"we need to hurry it up, because we're almost out of time."

"We don't need to vote," Miles spoke up. He bent down and cradled Cricket's unconscious body in his arms. "Let's get out of here before the skylights break. If we're gonna die, let's do it fighting for our lives. Maybe a couple of us will make it at least."

"You guys sure?" Heath asked, looking for unanimous consensus.

They voted with nods.

"But how do we get out?" Emily asked. "We can't go through the foyer. And the warehouse . . ."

"The squirrels, I remember." Heath imagined a room swimming with diseased rodents.

"I think I know," Miles told them. "I saw it on the monitors."

"Lead the way," Heath said, then he and the others followed Miles out of the lab and down a long hallway connecting to the back of the building. They took a right, then a left, and then ducked into a large room with a couch, a Ping-Pong table, a card table, a coffeemaker, and a normal refrigerator.

"Looks like the teachers' lounge at my school," said Dunbar. "I guess even mad scientists need to relax once in awhile."

Miles pointed to a narrow rectangular window high up the wall, close to the ceiling. "There it is."

Heath's heart sank. It was so small. Maybe even *too* small for Miles to squeeze his broad body through. "It's no good," Heath said. "Let's find another way."

Miles ignored him. "You take Cricket for a sec," he ordered, handing his fragile burden off to Dunbar, who hadn't lifted a weight in his whole life and struggled to keep from toppling over. Miles briefed them on his plan. "Heath, I'll boost you up first. You open the window and crawl out. Then I'll pass Cricket through. Then the rest of you."

"How are you gonna fit through that?" Emily sized Miles up.

"I'm limber," he reassured her. "Trust me. I'll get through if I have to leave my butt behind to do it. Now c'mon, less talk, more action."

Standing directly under the window, Miles quickly hoisted Heath up onto his shoulders. Heath still had to reach high and crane his neck to see the latch and unlock it. He grabbed the edge of the sill and pulled himself up, with Miles pushing vertically against the soles of his feet. Heath stuck his head out the window and looked side to side then straight ahead into the inky blackness of night. It was so dark out. He couldn't see the river, but he could hear it gurgling away, calling out to him. He tried to stretch his range of hearing, listening for any rustle, scratch, or breath. He could hear the bears still pounding away at the skylights and the wolves baying at the building's entrance, but as far as he could tell there was nothing directly between him and the river.

"The coast is clear. I'm going out," he whispered, then shimmied his way through the window. He dropped down headfirst into the grass. Luckily the landscaping around this section of the building sloped up along the wall so that Heath, on his toes, could look inside the window. He stuck his head and arms back inside. "Give me Cricket."

Miles took Cricket from Dunbar and pressed him up like a barbell, high enough for Heath to grab on to. Heath dragged the boy's limp body outside, then spent a few seconds making sure he was positioned comfortably on the ground. When he returned to the window he found Emily there reaching out to him. Next up was Emma, who was considerably easier to lift now that Emily was beside him helping. Even with Heath and the twins tugging from above and Miles hefting below, getting Dunbar through the window left everyone winded. "Okay, okay! I'll start my diet tomorrow," he promised.

They heard the obnoxious squeal of a chair sliding across waxed flooring. Heath and Dunbar ducked their heads back inside as Miles climbed on top of it.

"You're next, big guy," Heath said, and he and Dunbar each extended one arm toward him. Miles took their wrists and hopped upward. Immediately Heath felt himself falling forward; Miles's weight was too much. Emily grabbed the waistband of Heath's swim trunks to steady him, and he was grateful that it was too dark out for her to see his plumber's crack. Dunbar propped one foot up against the wall for leverage and pulled as hard as he could.

"Don't let go of me!" Miles said. "I'm almost there."

When enough of Miles's arm was outside for Emma to latch on to, she jumped in to help.

BOOM!

A loud crash followed by the painful roar of a bear. The skylight had finally caved in. A grizzly was inside the building, and from the sound of it, badly hurt in the fall. Miles eyes widened into disks of pure terror.

"Let's go! Let's go! Let's go!" Heath felt renewed strength, fueled by adrenaline coursing through his body.

"Pull!" Emily spurred them on.

Miles got his head and one shoulder free, and then he stopped coming. "Wait!" he hissed, grimacing in pain. "You're gonna rip my arm off."

"What's wrong?" Heath asked.

"I'm stuck!"

"I knew this wasn't going to work!" Heath was furious with himself for listening to Miles in the first place. Dunbar squeezed through because he was fat. Miles was solid muscle, and muscle doesn't give. It was the difference between squeezing soft and hardened toothpaste out of a tube.

"Give me a second," Miles said. "Maybe I can turn my body a bit and come through at more of an angle."

He tried to twist around so that his torso would fit diagonally in the window frame. He used his free arm to push against the outer wall. He groaned through clenched teeth as he worked to corkscrew himself free.

A twig cracked in the woods behind them. It was too dark to catch a glimpse of the source.

"Almost there," Miles huffed. His other shoulder popped free of the window. Miles flailed both arms at his friends. "Okay! I'm free! Pull me through!"

Heath clutched both of Miles's wrists. "Here we go," he said, but just as he was about to pull, he saw something creeping along the surface of the skin on Miles's arms. "Miles?"

Miles didn't answer. His mouth was open, but no words came out. He blinked once and tears spilled out. His face was a frozen mask. Purple vines weaved across it as if drawn by an invisible hand.

"He's got the Flash!" Dunbar cried.

"Oh no, no, no, no!" Heath tugged hard, and Miles shifted a few inches forward. "Help me, you guys!"

The Ems clutched each other tightly. Emily let out a little bleat of grief and Emma gently shushed her.

Dunbar didn't know what to do. "Dude . . . Heath . . . he's—"

"Shut up and pull!" Heath hollered. He didn't care if every animal in the forest heard him. He would drag Miles free if it killed him. It would.

A squirrel stabbed its head out the window, hissed, and showed them its teeth. Heath saw blood dripping from its tiny jaws and knew immediately that it had bitten Miles. Their friend was dead and there was nothing he could do to change that. He let go.

The squirrel was trapped between Miles's rib cage and the upper part of the window frame. Its black eyes were bulging from their sockets as it struggled to squeeze itself through the tiny gap. Heath heard chattering inside the lounge. Squirrels were rushing into the room, and Miles's body was the only thing plugging their way out. Moving Miles farther meant unstopping the swarm.

"I'm sorry, Miles." Heath broke down into tears. "I'm sorry, man." Dunbar led him away from the window. Emma and Emily worked together to gather up Cricket until Heath had regained some measure of composure. He was the only one strong enough to carry Cricket to the river. "I've got him," he said between choking sobs. He felt the strain of the added weight burning in all parts of his sore body and was overcome with gratitude to Miles, whose steadfast strength had carried Cricket this far. "I'm so sorry, Miles. Thank you, man. Thank you."

"Ready?" asked Dunbar.

More squirrel parts poked out all around Miles's corpse. It was time to go.

As they trotted in the direction of the river, Dunbar and the Ems huddled like a force field around Heath and Cricket. They held on to each other tightly, moving as one, afraid to be separated in the dark. They could barely see the trees, often shifting at the last second to avoid colliding with one. The river was much closer than it had been in the livery, but because they could barely see a foot in front of their faces, it was slow going. They honed in on the sound of flowing water and let that be their guide.

They were fifteen yards from the Dray when they heard hooves clopping across the rocky shore. Heath strained his eyes and with only the slim evidence of a bolt of white underbelly, he knew that the thing between them and salvation was a deer. The kids froze, melding together, hoping it would clear out of their way.

More clopping. Flashes of white at differing angles. Two deer had joined the first. Heath knew deer had a keen sense of smell, so he guessed the breeze was blowing in the group's favor. And the animals' sense of hearing was exceptional. Their ears were basically satellite dishes connected to the head by a root of muscles that could turn them in every direction. If they moved, the deer would hear them. But if they stayed, the squirrels would wriggle free and come after them. Deer were faster than squirrels, so for now, the best course of action seemed clear. Heath whispered his plan as quietly as he could, risking only one word. "Wait."

The seconds ticked by. Heath listened for any sound that would force a decision. He could tell that the virus was killing the deer; their raspy, shallow breathing was proof of that. They were so sick he might be able to fend them off long enough for the others to reach the river, but he couldn't fight and still carry Cricket. Then Heath realized a disquieting truth—he wanted to make it to the river, too. Not just for the sake of the boy in his arms, although Cricket's survival was important. Heath didn't want to die, either. Not there in the forest or on the shore. Not in a hospital bed in Seattle. Not home. Not anywhere. Maybe he'd feel differently once they'd made it safely to the river, but at that moment, the only thing Heath could say with any certainty was this: *he wanted to live.*

"Where are we?" muttered a groggy voice below Heath's chin. Cricket waking up was something Heath hadn't calculated for. Maybe Will would have, but not him. And Cricket was one noisemaker that Heath couldn't toss away.

Dunbar lunged forward and clamped his hand over Cricket's mouth, but it just made matters worse when a stick cracked under his foot. This set everything into motion.

Angry grunts on the shore.

Clacking of cloven hooves scraping across rock.

The whoosh of big animals bounding into the air.

"Go!" Heath ordered. The group took off through the forest, dashing parallel to the shore and the building. Dunbar took the lead, arms extended outward to find and guide them around trees, colliding with them now and then. He was getting banged up badly, but he never stopped moving. Courageous Dunbar. Fortunately the deer were slow, no longer graceful or fleet-footed. They were badly disoriented by the virus. Heath heard them crashing into the trees and into themselves. He looked back at the building. In the faint light emanating from the lounge, he saw bushy-tailed shadows pouring out from the window. Miles's body had slipped back inside the building, allowing the squirrels to escape. Heath could see dozens of them bounding in diagonal hops across the ground, heading in their direction.

"Where can we go?" Emma asked. "We can't outrun them forever!"

"Dad . . ." Cricket moaned.

"Quiet, buddy," Heath said. "Go back to sleep, okay?"

Cricket obliged.

"We're heading away from the river," said Dunbar. "I can barely hear it anymore."

Heath had intended to say something, but in the next instant the ground beneath his feet disappeared and gravity yanked him down the side of a steep gully. He instinctively maneuvered his body to safeguard Cricket from the brunt of the fall. The others were rocketing down the bank beside him, carried to the bottom on a carpet of pine needles that folded like blinds under their weight. They landed in soft soil and rolled to a stop. There was no time to shake it off. Heath made out the lithe shapes of deer at the top of the gully. They seemed confused, sniffing the air, trotting along the edge. After ten Mississippis, the deer bounded away. The kids were safe for the moment.

"Everyone okay?" Heath rose to his feet, which was no easy task since he was dizzy and miraculously still had Cricket securely in his arms.

"Yeah, we're okay," Dunbar replied. "Scraped up, but alive."

"The Dray must have carved this gully, then dried up here," Heath told them. "We should be able to follow it to the river."

"I can hear it again," Emily said.

"I hear something, too," Dunbar confirmed, but he was peering down the gully, facing away from the river. "Something's coming."

Dunbar was right, Heath thought; there *was* something in the gully with them, maybe fifty yards off. It was hard to see, the night sky was only slightly lighter than the gully's beveled silhouette, but the shape moving toward them contrasted against it just enough to see there was definitely something there. He couldn't tell if it was walking in a crouch or crawling, yet he was sure it was heading their way. It looked human-shaped one second, and then the next it seemed to break apart at the edges, morphing into an indefinable blob. With barely any light, Heath knew that could be a trick of the eye.

"It's Will! It has to be!" Emma said.

"Stringer?" Heath whispered. "Is that you?"

The shape didn't answer. It just kept coming. Heath

strained his eyes to take in whatever scraps of light were available, but he could still barely make it out.

"Will!" Emma called out.

"Shush!" Heath ordered. "Maybe the deer are too afraid to climb down here, but the squirrels won't be. They don't know we're here, but they will if you keep yelling."

"Fine," she said. "Why won't he answer us?"

They watched the inky shape approach. Instead of becoming more humanoid it grew larger and erratic, crumbling then rebuilding, as if held together by weak magnets.

"That's *not* Will." Emily caged Emma loosely with her arms to restrain her sister from wandering toward whatever the thing was. It certainly wasn't the blue-eyed object of Emma's former crush.

In the darkness they'd misjudged the distance between them and the baffling figure. It was actually much farther away. Now, as it drew closer, they began to hear a cacophony of overlapping sounds. Heath saw that, although it was alive, it was a lot larger than a person and consisted of many disconnected parts. The pungent smell of a zoo on a hot day rolled in ahead of it.

"Those are animals!" Emily gasped.

The thing headed their way was a super-herd of mammals, a hundred maybe, all kinds: deer, foxes, rats, minks, raccoons, squirrels, and more. The gully was funneling the stampede directly at them. Heath knew they couldn't outrun it, and the banks were too steep to climb in the dark. There was absolutely nothing to do but let the tidal wave of teeth, claws, and fur wash over them, carrying them away into oblivion. Still, he wouldn't steal their hope.

"You three try to get to the river," Heath ordered.

"But Cricket—" Dunbar started.

"If you carry Cricket, you won't make it," Heath said. "It's harsh, but that's the truth. Maybe the animals will focus on me. Get out of here."

Heath laid Cricket on the ground. With his back to the herd he leaned over his friend, hoping that his own dead body would become a shell against the onslaught, but he knew that was foolish thinking. They were going to be mauled to shreds, meat in a blender. If that was the way he would go, then so be it.

The Ems and Dunbar disobeyed him. Instead of fleeing, they knelt across from Heath, wove their arms together, and huddled close, cocooning Cricket entirely.

Heath didn't know what to say, so he gave them the first thing that popped into his head. "Thanks, guys."

"We tried," said Dunbar. "That's all we could do."

"Yeah," said Emily. "We got pretty far. We did good. *You* did good, Heath."

"Not bad," Emma agreed.

The ground quaked under the thudding hooves and paws. The growling, grunting, squeaking, chattering, and snorting—all of the terrifying beastly calls—swelled to a thundering peal. Heath braced himself for the end.

The herd hit them hard. Heath felt himself ripped away from Cricket and the others and tossed through the air like a feather. He landed on his side in a bed of moss, was picked up again and slammed hard into the bank. A hoof stomped down on his leg. His whole limb went numb for a few seconds. Something fat and furry leapt on his chest, breathed hotly into his face. A blink later, it was gone.

The animals weren't attacking them. They were barreling *through* them, fleeing in fear from whatever terrifying thing was hunting them. Something off in the distance.

When the last animal had passed by, Heath surveyed the damage. The group was worse for wear, but everyone seemed to be moving okay. Even Cricket, who was exactly where they'd placed him, was awake, struggling to sit up. Heath crawled over to him. "You okay, buddy?"

"My arm hurts," he whimpered, twisting it slightly to get a good look at the needle mark. "Did I get bit by a bullet ant?"

Emma held up her hand and inspected her fingers. She winced when she tried to bend the little one. "Broken pinkie."

"I'll live," said Emily.

"I think I got a little skunk on me, but I'm okay, too. What happened?" asked Dunbar.

The answer came roaring through the gully in hot pursuit of the herd.

Rain. A torrential sheet of rain. The downpour washed over everything, turning dirt to mud in a flash, drenching the kids and filling the gully with one long, ankle-deep puddle. The rain had arrived earlier than Heath predicted on the bridge and intensified quickly, pelting their skin in wonderful, blossoming splatters. They giggled. Then laughed. Then they whooped and hollered and hopped about in the mud like nuts, dancing their hearts out in the rain until finally Dunbar sneezed, a signal it was time to get to shelter.

"C'mon." Heath grinned. "We should get back inside. We didn't survive all this just to die of pneumonia."

Not far off in the distance the mournful singing of wolves ended before the last verse was sung.

(Typically sung at the last bonfire)

Every good thing eventually ends.
We leave Camp Harmony richer, my friends.
If I have wronged you at all, if my words did offend,
Let's bury the hatchet, let's make amends.

I promise this, I'll remember you all.
Each one I will miss, as we head into fall.
I'll never forget the memories we've made.
I'm so glad that you came, and so glad that I stayed.

Out here in nature, where the deer raise their young,
Beneath the Cascades where the clouds are all hung,
Let's not be sad, though the last of us parts.
I'll see you all soon, when next summer starts.

The time will fly by, it won't be too long,
But for now, my dear friends, I leave you this song.
Remember good times, God bless you and me.
Remember this place, God bless Camp Harmony.

Epilogue

IT RAINED NONSTOP through the night. For once Heath was thrilled that he lived in the Pacific Northwest, where rain was unpredictable and could blindside a picnic faster than Cricket's precious ants. In an area that could receive as much as fifty inches of rain a year, it was nice that fate saw fit to deliver two or three before dawn.

When the group left the facility early in the morning, a slip of light fog and the clean fragrance of pine met them at the door. They stepped out into the parking lot; the soles of their shoes crunched broken glass.

"The map I found says we're still three miles from Granite Falls," Heath said, then he folded it up and tucked it into his bathing suit pocket. "But at least the trip will be easier today. This service road connects to the Mountain Loop Highway not far from here. That'll take us straight into town."

Heath agreed to pass Cricket off to Dunbar when he

needed a break from carrying him, but now that Cricket had the strength to wrap his arms around Heath's neck he could ride piggyback, and that made it a lot easier. Cricket was still very sick but improving by the hour. "Giddyup," he murmured, his voice weak, but returning.

"It's so quiet," Emily said, adjusting the new shoes she'd fashioned from several layers of paper laboratory slippers. Once she'd removed her leather riding boots she couldn't get them back on again.

Emma disagreed. "It's not quiet. It's so *normal.*"

The group exchanged smiles.

They headed toward town, stepping over a dead animal every few yards or so. The ground was littered with them. The only one they stopped for was Quilt Face, who was lying in the parking lot, curled inward so that her front and back paws were touching. She looked smaller. Pitiable. Not at all the big, bad wolf that Heath had come to know her as. He wanted to stroke her soft coat, but she was still a dead and diseased animal, and he decided against it.

The walk was uneventful. Even pleasurable once the fog lifted and the sun came out and warmed their skin. As they neared Granite Falls and heard the assuaging sound of small-town traffic, they spotted a group of six or seven rufous hummingbirds stealing nectar from a roadside patch of wildflowers. The tiny birds' orange heads caught the sun like shiny new pennies.

Heath and his friends stopped for a moment to watch them flit between petals and hover as if on wires in the air. When he saw the four relaxed, happy faces surrounding him he knew their ordeal was finally over. They were survivors. The lucky ones.

"They're called a charm," Heath said with a thoughtful smile. "A group of hummingbirds is called a charm."

Just like all kids do at the end of summer camp, they promised to keep in touch once they got home, except, after what they'd been through, they actually would. Heath lost interest in Emily. There'd be no pining for her love or stalking her on Facebook. He didn't know her well enough to have lasting feelings, so he left his crush behind in the river. She ended up breaking things off with Josh because of the distance. After her ordeal in the Dray she was diagnosed with severe sciurophobia, a phobia of squirrels. Her parents decided she should live with her father in Hawaii, as it's the only state in the country where there are no squirrels outside captivity. Heath suspected her fear wasn't as bad as she'd let people think.

Heath visited Cricket in the hospital during his long recovery from the virus, and occasionally Skyped with Dunbar, who was true to his word and started a diet the minute they'd uncorked him from the window. He'd lost five pounds in quarantine and kept at it until he was looking pretty fit.

Heath was relieved to hear that Theo and Molly were alive, although they were taken to Seattle soon after they paddled into town and placed into quarantine for a few days (Heath's group was sent to Spokane). Theo made good on his promise and convinced the sheriff to organize a rescue party to search the Dray River, but Heath's group had gone the wrong way at the fork and the few locals who knew about the lab never thought to look for them there.

A few months after their ordeal, Sylvester's dad invited Heath and the others to speak at a big fund-raiser/memorial service for his son. Their testimonies helped to raise a lot of money for rabies research, so it was worth the public tears. Heath was glad to see his friends again, with the exception of Theo, who declined the offer to attend. No surprise there. When Heath got home from quarantine, he e-mailed Theo to let him know that Miles had regretted the way he'd treated him and had hoped to apologize before he died. Theo's reply was brief, clear, and written in the subject line of a blank e-mail: *Leave me alone!* Whoever said "Time heals all wounds" never met Theo Seung.

At the reunion Heath especially enjoyed spending time with Emma, who turned out to be pretty cool on dry land. In fact, he liked her a lot. And she liked him back. She admitted it wasn't just Will she'd had a crush on in the river, but she had rightly sensed that Heath had a thing for Emily. As a twin she'd learned to pick up on stuff like that.

"Don't you prefer bad boys?" he reminded her, expecting her to change her mind.

Instead she replied, "I have a thing for brave boys, and you're the bravest boy I know." She turned out to be a good match for Heath. He would come to draw strength from both her tough, scrappy spirit and the sweet, nurturing side she'd hid so well in the river. Heath leaned on Emma for support as he did literally when he first entered the Dray.

Heath decided to accept treatment for his cancer. This

was based on a combination of two things (although the promise of a first real date with Emma outside a hospital room was pretty sweet, too): first, he felt he owed it to Miles, Sylvester, Marshall, and the rest of the hundred and fourteen kids and twelve adults who died during the attack at Camp Harmony. Heath was one of only thirteen people to have survived the event that the national news dubbed the Skagit County Massacre, even though technically the camp was just over county lines. He learned that six kids had snuck away from camp to spend the day at Lake Tupso and survived by staying crouched down in the water for fifteen hours straight. Both the laboratory and the murder of the microbiologist Carl Schroeder were eventually "looked into." The man in the Jeep showed up on the news a few months later, but all they would say about him was that he was a part of some extreme anarchist group. And that he was still at large.

It took two days to find the body of Will Stringer. A search party discovered him half submerged in an offshoot stream, a quarter mile from Granite Falls. He was bloated and covered with bat bites on his face, hands, and neck. The water had been too shallow to hide in. The sheriff of Granite Falls determined that Will had gone off on his own to try to find help for their group and had died a hero's death. Heath decided to let this rose-colored version of the story stand, but he knew Will was probably just trying to save his own neck again. Because Will didn't owe anyone. He didn't need anyone but himself to survive. He sure showed them.

Although he never discussed it with anyone, Heath often thought about the last conversation he'd shared with

Will. For weeks after, he replayed it in his mind, unable to commit to the idea that Will was a bad person. That he'd know that the animals would be attracted to the noise-makers. After all, Will had never outright admitted it. He'd asked Heath to make up his own mind about that. And then one day it hit Heath like a kick in the gut: during that last conversation in the river, Will mentioned Heath's broken noisemaker. But Heath realized he'd never *told* Will that his noisemaker was broken. There was no way he could have known that, unless . . .

It didn't matter. The boy was dead, and that was that. Heath would be a hypocrite if he didn't take his own advice, the advice he gave Theo about Miles. He forgave Will, because it was the right thing to do.

There was something else that Will Stringer had said during their last conversation—the second reason Heath decided to accept treatment. To be precise, it was the last few words Will ever spoke that ultimately swayed his decision.

Watch out for squirrels, okay? Try to stay alive, Heath.

At the river, Heath had taken this advice and applied it to the moment, but he came to understand that Will hadn't meant it that way. Will, the master chess player who won books and compasses. Will, who sacrificed pawns when necessary. Will, who predicted checkmates and bats. Will, who fought to survive, no matter what it took.

Try to stay alive, he'd said.

That's *exactly* what Heath would do.

Acknowledgments

THIS BOOK would not exist without the support of:

My friend Chris L. Cannon, whose kindness and generosity continue to inspire all who know him; Funmi Oke, the world's greatest teacher, a shining example of integrity, and beloved friend; my agent Lauren MacLeod for her guidance and for the Tweet that sparked a *Frenzy*; my editor Ricardo Mejías, whose keen insight was a laser pointer trained on the deeper emotional core of the story.

I'd also like to thank: Christian Trimmer for seeing the potential in this book; all of the fine people at Disney-Hyperion who had a hand in the production process; Mara Purnhagen for teaching by example that persistence and hard work pay off in the publishing world; my ambitious siblings who pursued their dream careers, too. I'm proud of you; my agency sisters, a boundless source of support and camaraderie; my family and friends for keeping my head above water and the wolves at bay; and I can't overlook the contribution of the brazen squirrel that stared me down through the kitchen window, putting ideas into my head. I blinked; you won.